the
strays

emily bitto

Legend Press Ltd, 175-185 Gray's Inn Road, London, WC1X 8UE
info@legend-paperbooks.co.uk | www.legendpress.co.uk

Contents © Emily Bitto 2014

First published in 2014 by Affirm Press, 28 Thistlethwaite Street, South
Melbourne VIC 3205, Australia
www.affirmpress.com.au

Print ISBN 978-1-7850795-1-1
Ebook ISBN 978-1-7850795-2-8
Set in Times. Printed in the United Kingdom by Clays Ltd.
Cover design by Josh Durham/Design by Committee

Emily Bitto co-owns a wine bar in Carlton, Melbourne, called Heartattack and Vine, which she opened with her partner and two other friends in October 2014.

She was previously employed for several years as a sessional lecturer and supervisor in the Creative Writing Programs at both the University of Melbourne and Victoria University.

The Strays is her debut novel. It garnered huge praise in Australia, winning several national prizes, including the Stella Prize, the Kibble and Dobbie Literary Award, the Davitt Award and the Barbara Jefferis Award. It was also longlisted for the Dublin Literary Award 2016.

Follow Emily on Twitter
@emilybitto

'To burn always with this hard, gem-like flame,
to maintain this ecstasy, is success in life'

– Walter Pater

Prologue

I once read that the heart's magnetic field radiates up to five metres from the body, so that whenever we are within this range of another person our hearts are interacting. The body's silent communications with other bodies are unmapped and mysterious, a linguistics of scent, colour, flushes of heat, the dilating of a pupil. Who knows, what we call instant attraction may be as random as the momentary synchrony of two hearts' magnetic pulses.

Eva's mother believed in past life connections, that two souls can be twinned over and over, playing out different roles so that in one life they may be mother and daughter, in another husband and wife, in a third dear friends. I only know that throughout my life I have felt an instinctive attraction to particular people, male and female, romantic and platonic; attraction inexplicable at the time but for a certain mutual recognition. It was this way with Eva, although we were only eight years old.

I remember that day, after it all fell apart, when Eva came to me through the misty garden so that her red coat bled into view from white to pale rose to scarlet, the pride I felt. That I was the one she turned to. That I could give her what her own family could not. All those years as part of the Trenthams' lives. Feeling loved, but never needed, never family. I am an only child; it is my lot to be envious, even grasping, to long for the bonds that tie sisters together, the fearless, unthinking acceptance that we are social creatures, pack animals, that there is never, truly, the threat of being alone.

I am sitting outside at the wooden table marking student essays when I hear the tidy creak and clap as the letter slot opens and shuts its mouth. I shuffle the papers into a pile, set them on a chair and walk through the open French doors, across the lounge room and down the hallway, lit cobalt by the panels of glass that flank the front door. The envelope is narrow and rust-coloured, shot through with metallic strands. Inside is an invitation that I recognise immediately, to the opening of Evan Trentham's retrospective at the National Gallery of Victoria. Tucked behind it is a sheet of notepaper folded into three. I open it and see Eva's loose sloping handwriting, unchanged, so that some part of my mind slips, unsure if I am a middle-aged woman standing in her hallway in blue light, or if I am a girl again.

Beyond the front door I hear a man and a child walk past the gate, the man's head swimming, rippled, across the panel of glass, the child's voice falling indistinct from a high note like the carol of a magpie. I turn and walk back through the blue tunnel of the past towards the clear kitchen, reading as I go.

Dear Lily,

It has been so long. Far too long. I know it's difficult to keep people in our lives, and I know that what happened in the past has made it hard for us to be in contact, although I've thought about you often over the years and have started letters to you several times. I've thought of you more since Heloise's death, and now that the grief has eased a little bit, I'm determined not to let it go any longer. Being back in the country for Dad's retrospective seems a good opportunity to reconnect, although I'll understand if you don't want to after all this time. Mum and Dad

10

would of course love to have you at the opening, and for me it would be wonderful to see you again, dear friend of my childhood.

I know you are in contact with Bea, and she has my dates and details.

Please do come.

Love always,
 Eva

I brace my body against the edge of the sink and pull my eyes up from the page. It is so many years since the last time I saw her. Three full decades at least. And now, Eva has come back to me like a good deed returned. Already I am imagining how it would be to see her again, and I become aware of that old compulsive pain I have pressed like a bruise again and again throughout the years.

Who else will be there, which members of the circle willing to be brought together once more, alongside art historians and critics who are aware of how it all went and who will no doubt be nudging one another and staring blatantly as greetings are exchanged and the past flashes between Evan and Helena Trentham and the artists, now old, whom they once took into their home?

And Eva.

I stop myself, tuck my grey hair behind my ears. I gaze out at the garden. The silver birches at the fence ease my mind along their straight, kind trunks. I notice that the mulberry needs pruning. I take the letter and invitation to my study and sit down, lining up the invitation along the edge of the desk, running my thumb along the card as though absorbing it gently through the skin. I have already received a copy of the invitation from a colleague in the art history department who works in Australian modernism and who has some involvement in the exhibition. As far as I know she is not aware of my past connection with the Trenthams. But I had no intention of going until now.

I examine the invitation again, reading the text on the back. *You are invited to the opening of the retrospective exhibition of Evan Trentham's work at the National Gallery of Victoria. 6 to 8 pm, Friday the 10th of May, 1985.* I turn it over and look closely at the image for the first time. I had thought it was simply an early self-portrait, Evan's face aligned with the narrow card, his shaggy red beard and blue-pale skin. But now I see that there is a thin green line protruding from the corner of his mouth and curving over the paler green background behind his head. Above his right ear I notice a small house, a replica of the Trentham home with its gabled roofs and the portico over the door. Smoke is swelling out of a downstairs window and the green line has become a hose in the pink dot hands of a tiny man who must be Ugo.

I feel a tenderness in my chest, and the past rushes in as a deluge I can no longer hold back: the house and garden, the smell of smoke that will always be the scent of things gone wrong. Those twilight days in the hotel room with my dear, sad Eva.

I flip the invitation over again and search for the title. It is there, in small letters along one edge: *Self-portrait with Miniature Disaster 4*.

After a time, I haul myself back to the present, to the daylight and the fact that I am cold. I search for the cordless phone and find it stashed behind the empty bowl from the muesli I ate at my desk this morning, the residue in the bottom like a fortune waiting to be read.

It is a reflex, by now, to go to Bea when the old scars begin to itch.

'Bea, it's Lily.'

'Hi, Lily.' Her voice is an instant salve. 'How are you?'

'I'm okay. You?'

'I'm well. How's Tim?'

'He's good. Busy, as usual. Can you chat for a minute?'

'Sure. I've just got my little Mardi here. You know I'm minding her one day a week now.'

I picture Bea with her adored grandchild, the way she explains everything so patiently. 'I'll call back later,' I say.

'No, no. We're just sitting here with some playdough, aren't we, Mardi? As long as you don't mind my divided attention.'

'Not at all.'

'What are we making, Mardi?'

'Snakes!' Mardi says in the background.

'I'm so glad you rang actually,' says Bea. 'I've been meaning to call and ask you and Tim over for dinner this week. Is it too late?'

'Lucinda's moved back home for a bit, so I feel like I should probably be around for her. She and Eli are having problems.'

'Again? That's difficult, isn't it.'

I laugh. 'That's what I said when she told me – *Again?* – and she got angry with me.'

'You must just want to smack that boy.'

'I do. But Luce is very good at telling me when to back off.'

I hear Mardi's voice again.

'Yes it's very slithery-snaky,' Bea responds. 'Maybe now you could make a basket for them to live in … Sorry,' she says as she returns to me. 'Well, let me know when you're free and we'll organise something.'

There is a banging of playdough.

'Bea …' I begin and then hesitate.

'Hmm?'

'I just got a letter from Eva.'

'Oh, you did. She said she was thinking of making contact while she's back.'

'Why didn't you warn me?'

Bea pauses for a moment.

'I'm sorry, Lily. I didn't think. I forget it's been so long since you two have seen each other.'

'I feel like I'm slightly in shock,' I say, thinking how much of an understatement this is.

'Careful, bubby,' says Bea.

There is a crash, and Mardi begins to wail.

'Oh no, upsadaisy. Lily, I'm so sorry. I'll have to go. We've had an accident.'

'No, no, of course, go.'

'I'll call you back later, but you know you don't have to see her just because she's decided to make contact now. Although I think it'd be great for both of you if you did. But I know she's left it far too long.'

Mardi's shrieks grow louder as Bea bends close to her.

'I know, I know. You go, Bea. We'll talk later.'

I hang up and walk back to the garden, but the table has fallen into shade and the essays have blown onto the pavers. I gather them up and come back inside, shutting the French doors behind me. I set the essays on a shelf in my study, watch a pigeon curtseying to its mate outside the window, allow myself to fret about my daughter and her heartbreak, to take my mind off Eva's letter. Eventually I give in. I open the deep bottom drawer of my desk and pull out a pile of journals. I place them on the desk in front of me and rest my hands on top of the solid stack. I let my mind turn back once more, to recreate again that distant, still wracked past.

1
The Switchgate

I

This is how I recall it.

1930: My mother and I paused on the brick path and she straightened my uniform – a navy blue tunic dress with a starched white collar, a blue felt hat and white gloves. I clutched my toy dog, the one upon whom I had heaped all my guilty love since my mother told me I didn't appreciate the things she bought for me. She took my hand, and we continued up the path to the third-grade classroom. It was still early, and the summer sun had not risen beyond the roof of the school building. The path and garden were in shade, the leaves of camellia bushes freshly varnished by the morning, and blackbirds turned the soil, pausing, listening, scratching again in darts. They froze as we passed and flicked their yellow eyes towards us.

And then we entered the classroom, and there was Eva, the smallest child in the room, with her dark bob and brown eyes beneath a heavy fringe. She was kneeling with several other children on the carpet beside a wooden doll's house. On one hand she had a threadbare velveteen hand puppet in the shape of a dog. She smiled at me, and the teacher, Miss Butterworth, pushed me forward.

'Lily, this is Eva, and Christopher, and Phyllis. Children, this is Lily. She's going to be joining our class this year, so make her welcome.'

'Hello, Lily,' said Eva.

'Make room for Lily,' Miss Butterworth said. 'What are you playing? Doll's houses?'

Eva shuffled over and patted the carpet beside her.

'We're playing Deadybones the Wolf,' she said.

'Oh. I see,' said Miss Butterworth, raising her eyebrows.

I glanced back at my mother. She was taking a seat awkwardly on a child-sized wooden chair along with the other mothers. She nodded to me and turned to the woman next to her.

'Which one is your mother?' I asked Eva as I sat down beside her.

'None of them. She's gone home. But you can see my sisters at recess. Have you got any sisters?'

I had to admit that I did not.

After a while, I was drawn back to the comfort of my mother, and retreated for a moment to her familiarity in the midst of all this newness. She lifted me onto her lap, still talking. I listened to the whispers of the women while I sat, pinching the skin on the back of her hand as I had done since I was a baby. They were talking about Eva, saying that she was the daughter of Evan Trentham, the artist, that her mother was 'old money'. I pictured a woman made out of dirty pound notes and tarnished pennies.

Miss Butterworth approached the seated women and told them that it was time for them to leave. My mother stood, and I slid from her lap. I began to cry, and she hushed me and then squeezed me tightly for a second. Eva got up and came over to me, holding out her hand, and I put my hand in hers, still sniffling, and went back with her to the game.

At recess I met Eva's two sisters, who came to find her on the quadrangle, where children were jumping rope, playing hopscotch or marbles, and the older ones were starting a game of British Bulldogs. Her older sister was called Beatrice, or Bea for short, her younger, Heloise. It was obvious that Beatrice and Eva were sisters. Their faces were free of the roundness that conceals the future shape of most children's faces. They were fine-boned, but did not seem delicate or cosseted. Their arms and legs were brown from the sun, and their hair was dark and, in Bea's case, tangled. There were scratches on their shins, and Bea had a scab on her knee as big as a tombola. Heloise was different. She was a serious little girl with milky skin, copper hair, and an uncertain, freckled face. It was her very first day of school, not just at a new school as I was, and she would not join in the game of British Bulldogs.

'You've got big teeth,' she said to me.

She sat down cross-legged on the asphalt and ran her hands over its gritty surface. Bea took Eva and me by a hand each and ran with us across the quadrangle at the call of 'bullrush' so that we would not be scared of the boys who were the bulldogs. When I looked back at Heloise, she was absorbed in a secret game of her own. Her lips were moving, and she was pecking at the loose gravel with the beak of her thumb and fingers.

At the end of the day my mother returned to collect me, and I clasped myself to the front of her dress, burrowing into the laundry soap and porridge smell of her. I glanced around to see whether Eva's mother had arrived, but Eva was standing beside a tall man who was speaking to Miss Butterworth. Eva waved to me, and I ran over.

'Is that your dad?' I whispered.

'No. It's Patrick,' she replied without further explanation.

'I'm sorry, but her parents are busy,' the man was saying.

As we left the classroom, Eva waved and called out, 'See you tomorrow.' I waved back, the next school day suddenly a gift held out to me, then turned to my mother's hand around my own, pulling me homewards.

Eva's mother collected her the next afternoon and spoke briefly to my mother. I remember Helena as pale and long and light, like a taper, swathed in floaty cream fabric and with her dark hair set like ladies in magazines. She smelled of cigarettes and a heavy floral perfume, not the kitchen and laundry scents exuded by my mother.

A few days later I was sitting with Eva and Heloise on the slippery leather seat in the back of their Morris while Bea sat in the front and Helena drove, her face in profile with its flawless skin and rouged cheek, her bouncy hair visible over the seat. Her hand on the wheel was adorned with an emerald ring, and her perfume filled the cabin. We drove out of Box Hill and into the fields and orchards that lingered at the edge of the main streets in those days, until we reached a high gate. Helena sprang out to open it, leaving the motor running, and we crunched onto the gravel driveway and over the threshold. Bea was leaning into the back seat clapping hands with Eva – *Miss Mary Mack, Mack, Mack, all dressed in black, black, black, with silver buttons, buttons, buttons, all down her back, back, back* – while I gazed out the window at the garden and the house coming into view around the bend.

That garden. I still wander in dreams between the pale grey pillars of the lemon-scented gums, the eucalyptus citriodoras, towering out of mist, gigantic, as they appeared to me as a child in that magical place. Perhaps Eva showed me the house first, but in my memory we went straight to the garden, and she led me around its open spaces and secret nooks, trailed by a silent Heloise. The garden had a formal section in front of the house, but it had gone more or less to ruin. The hedges were twiggy, and the rose bushes stuck out their arms in all directions. The rest of the garden was wild, with banks of hydrangeas and scarlet geraniums and a huge tussock of sacred bamboo into which the girls had carved a warren of narrow paths like a crazed hedge maze with no centre. There was an old train carriage in the back corner of the garden, its walls and floor plumped and buckled by damp. It was called the seed train because it had been a seed and tool shed when Helena's uncle had lived in the house. It still contained the skeletons of rakes and picks, their once-bright blades blistered with rust. Mice and spiders lurked behind ancient bags of bulbs and garden fertiliser. The sisters had their headquarters in a disused chook shed, and a secret den in the hollowed-out bowl of earth beneath the boughs of a casuarina. At the rear of the garden there was a high gate that Eva called the switchgate. It led out to a dirt lane that backed on to orchards.

'We can't go out there because we'll be locked out,' Eva told me.

'Why?'

'You can go out but then you can't get back in. That's how it works.'

'How do you get back in then?'

'You have to walk all the way around to the front gate. It's a long way. Except I can't reach the handle so we need Bea to go with us, and she never wants to.'

I stood back as Eva opened the latch, for fear that the switchgate would somehow suck me out.

Eva took me up to her bedroom on the house's second storey, shutting the door against Heloise. She began to change out of her school uniform, flinging the discarded clothes onto the floor. When she was stripped to her singlet and knickers, she opened her wardrobe and roughed the hanging garments about, making the wooden hangers clack together and thunk against the back of the wardrobe.

'Do you want to change too?' she asked.

'I don't have any other clothes.'

'You can wear mine if you like. You can pick whatever you want.'

Glancing back at Eva, I chose a straight smock dress in apricot cotton. She chose a green gingham dress with puffed sleeves. I felt that we were now linked in some important way.

Eva opened the bedroom door.

'Good, she's gone.' She took my hand and led me to the top of the staircase. 'Watch this,' she said. She clambered onto the banister and when she was in position, facing backwards with one small leg over each side of the rail, holding on with both arms, she grinned at me and slid fast to the bottom of the stairs.

The Trenthams' house had been in Helena's family for three generations. Its charm was of the ramshackle kind, tacked together over years and across architectural periods so that it resembled those European churches with one Gothic wing and one Renaissance. The main building was of timber, but there was a bluestone former laundry and storehouse, now a vast kitchen; a cellar, cold and smelling of mildewed root vegetables; a sunroom and an attic that, through a dormer window, accessed a small platform between gables of the roof, fenced by a low wrought-iron railing, from where the surrounding paddocks and the roofs and gardens of neighbouring properties could be surveyed. Eva took me proudly to this crow's nest balcony, where we played ship's captains, peering through a brass telescope at the upper windows of distant houses. We clambered up the slate gables and peeled off the blooms of lichen that flattened themselves against the stone, collecting them within the pages of an atlas that the sisters consulted as their book of sea charts.

Part of the thrill of this perch above the ground-dwelling world of adults, this small fenced plot the sisters had requisitioned from the crows and pigeons and made their own, was its hint of danger. I knew my mother would never allow me to be up there if she knew, and each time we scrambled up the slope of the roof to sit astride the apex was, for me, a mild rebellion against her interminable loving scrutiny. At the Trenthams' we were left gloriously alone to ride the rooftops or circumnavigate the garden as we desired.

On that first afternoon, Eva took me to meet her father in his studio, a large room on the ground floor of the house. The door was ajar, and Eva pushed it open and walked in without knocking.

Evan Trentham resembled the pictures of fearsome bushrangers I had seen in books. He was tall and lanky with a red forest of a beard that parted in a grin when he saw his daughter.

'Chook, chook chookie!' he crowed horribly, setting down a long-handled brush and hoisting her into the air with his stringy arms, which were pale like Heloise's and covered in ginger hair.

Evan Trentham was put together from mismatched stuff. The sinews were too short for the long bones. The tendons behind his ankles and the bald stones of his knees stuck out, hard as the catgut on a tennis racquet. He was like a rubber band stretched tight and close to snapping. He wore blue work pants cut off at the knee and a white undershirt that was yellow beneath the armpits. He was paint-stained and sweat-smelling.

The room itself was cluttered with paint tins, brushes and books, and reeked of tobacco and turpentine. There was a green chaise longue behind the door, its horsehair stuffing erupting through a hole. A huge half-finished painting stood against the back wall.

Eva giggled as her father nuzzled her with his beard.

'Scratcheeeee,' she squealed.

Evan held out his hand to me, shifting Eva onto his hip. 'Who's this then?' he asked. 'Mrs Tiggywinkle?'

I was too scared to move, and did not hold out my hand.

'Don't be silly, Dadda,' said Eva. 'It's Lily.'

'Pleased to meet you, Lily Tiggywinkle,' he said a little more soberly. 'Any friend of Eva's is a friend of mine. Do you like barley sugar?'

I nodded, mute, and he offered me a tin of yellow barley sugars melted together around a teaspoon. I hesitated.

He passed the tin to Eva. 'Show her how it's done, chookabiddy.'

Eva dug around in the tin with the spoon and then prised the barley sugar off with her teeth, showing me how it stuck in the roof of her mouth.

Cautious of germs, I took the tin and dug out a small lump, pulling it off the spoon, wet with Eva's spit, with my fingers.

'Will you play Billygoat Gruff with us?' Eva asked her father.

'Not now, chook, still working.' Evan put her down and turned back to his canvas.

Eva stamped her foot and went and sat on the chaise longue. I followed her.

I remember staring up at the giant painting Evan was working on. It was one of his now-iconic desert scenes, filled with figures intertwined in an obscenity of postures against the scorching earth. My eyes darted between blues and ochres until I made out the terrible images of policemen in uniform bent over one another, some with mouths wide open. One policeman was tilting a barrel of liquid into the mouth of another. The barrel had a hose attached to it at the top, and it led across the canvas to the back of an outdoor dunny. My throat grew tight. I wanted to look away but I could not.

Eva nudged me and pushed a book towards me, open on a black-and-white reproduction of an artwork. I looked down at the tortured image and asked, 'Did he paint that too?'

Across the room, Evan laughed. 'A man called Hieronymus Bosch painted it. Isn't that a wonderful name? Don't you wish you were called Hieronymus Bosch? He painted it a very long time ago. I'm just pilfering from him. Bosch in the bush, I like to call it.'

'What's pilfering?' I asked.

'Stealing,' said Evan.

I didn't know what he meant, only that the book gave me the same rotten feeling in my stomach as Evan's painting.

'Are you hungry?' asked Eva. I nodded. She stood up and led me to the kitchen in the guts of the house, where two fireplaces sat side by side.

Down one end of the room was a great island bench with a wooden slab top. Copper pots hung above it from a metal frame. The sink was a deep marble trough, almost as big as a bath. The other end of the room was dominated by a vast kitchen table. Eva led me to the scullery, poking through the bread bin and the icebox. There was the nose of a loaf surrounded by crumbs, but little else. She spread the crust of bread with jam, and we took turns tearing off tough bites with our teeth.

When it was gone, Eva pushed open the screen door and I followed her to the rear of the house, where there was a flat area of grass backed by curved garden beds so that it formed a large half-moon. To one side of this clearing was an old enamel bathtub, up on stilts above a cast-iron brazier.

On clear evenings to come, Evan would fill the bathtub with water and heat it over a fire for himself or for us to bathe in. Sitting in that bath, breathing in the smells of the garden and the woodsmoke wafting from beneath the tub, still seems to me something close to heaven. After the bath, we would run around the garden, towels held out as wings, circling the fading coals of the bath-fire like huge pink moths.

It was a relief to be back in the bliss of the garden, to leave the feeling of Evan's studio behind. Helena was there in the clearing with the man who had collected Eva from school that first day – Patrick. She was propped up on one elbow on a wooden sun bed. He was sitting on the ground, leaning against the sun bed at the level of Helena's shins. There was something endearing about Patrick; his eyes were pale blue and kind, crinkling up when he smiled. He had broad shoulders and big hands. Though he didn't seem old, his hair was greying and stuck out around his face.

Eva wandered over to Patrick and her mother, who both picked up glasses from the grass and sipped from them – tall glasses covered in beads of moisture and filled with clear liquid, chunks of ice and slices of lemon.

'I'm hungry,' said Eva.

'Well, don't look at me,' Helena replied. 'Go and find some food.'

'There is none.'

'Oh, piffle. Ask Beatrice to boil you an egg.'

For the first time I glimpsed the underside of Eva's home life, and was glad to know that when I went home that night my tea would be ready, and the custard that my mother had made in the cool of the morning would be waiting under a muslin cloth.

II

What drew Eva and me together was our shared sense of imagination. Hers was formed from rich materials, mine from poor; hers developed over endless hours in the exotic garden kingdom she inhabited with her sisters, mine over hours alone. But the end result was the same, and each recognised it in the other.

Besotted as I already was with Eva, that first visit to the Trentham home threw my sense of my own life off balance. I felt as though my home, a semi-detached bungalow we had recently moved into, had shrunk since morning, and our yard was a shoebox sown with only those plants that refused the smallest taint of wildness, even in their names: sweet william, primrose, baby's breath.

That year, everything was new. New school, new house, overheard talk of my father's new job. I was too young to understand the Depression, but it was clear that this newness was not of the good kind, that our house was smaller than the one we had left behind. It was not the lustre of a new penny; it was a sharp, garish newness. But Eva was my penny. She had the soft light of recognition. She was warmed, as if by my own hand. I had been asking for a sister, but she was better. I wanted to be with her always and would have discarded my own parents, heartlessly, as only the securely cared-for can.

Thus began the hazy garden years of my childhood, when my life was marred by nothing but the *ache*. The ache became accustomed, but not mild with familiarity. I felt it whenever my mother arrived to collect me and I watched Eva and her sisters resume the game we had been playing even before I reached the gate. I realised then that the life I was part of one or two precious after-school or weekend days each week was Eva's life always, and continued when I left with little change. I tried not to think about the life that Eva led without me, but every time I saw the sadness of our parting slip from her face as she turned back to her sisters was like biting down on hard toffee and feeling a piece of tooth break away in my mouth.

It was not just Eva I was besotted with, but her whole family. It was a big, noisy, quicksilver family, even at first: Evan and Helena; Bea, Eva and Heloise; and Patrick. Patrick was the brother Evan had chosen even before he chose Helena, discarding his own brothers – both lawyers – who did not fit with his as-yet only imaginary career as an artist. Evan had met Patrick in the first year of a fine art course and convinced his new friend to drop out with him at the end of the year and enrol instead in night classes at the Gallery School under the less classical tutelage of the man who was to become their mentor, Victor Sorrensen. The two men had spent so much time together that they had taken on each other's mannerisms and expressions, so that it was impossible to tell in whom they had originated. They were always laughing, becoming boys again.

Patrick married Vera in the garden of the Trentham home during the year I met Eva, starting the expansion that would continue for the remainder of our childhoods. I remember the long tables with white tablecloths, silver cutlery and crystal glasses set out on the grass, as strange and wonderful as trees growing indoors. Vera was a singer with the Australian Opera, and a very fat man in a suit sang an aria, and later a woman, only slightly less fat, wailed out notes like balloons into the twilight trees. I remember thinking that the bride was not as pretty as a bride should be.

I learned early to mediate, a tiny diplomat between the foreign nations of the Trenthams and my own parents. Only once, during that first year, did my parents invite the Trenthams for dinner. They expected Evan and Helena alone, and I had been fed early and was about to brush my teeth. But, at seven o'clock, Evan and Helena arrived with their three daughters, and my mother had to whisper to my father to entertain them in the lounge while she set more places at the table and tried to make the food stretch. She called me into the kitchen and told me I must eat again.

'Don't let on you've had your tea already,' she said. 'And don't say we thought they were coming without the girls.'

'Why not?' I asked.

'Never mind. Just don't let on.' She brushed her hair away from her shiny forehead with the back of her hand as she tipped flour into a mixing bowl.

'But I'm full,' I said peevishly.

'Oh, nonsense, you're always hungry. Now get back to the girls while I see to this.'

In the lounge room I noticed that my father seemed awkward and uncomfortable. He was a large man but was sitting forward on the edge of his armchair, his knees too close to his body.

'I don't pretend to know about this new modern art myself,' he was saying to Evan. 'But I do enjoy a visit to the gallery.'

'Well, you're not likely to have to face any modern art there, whether you like it or not,' said Evan.

'I like the early paintings of the colony myself. You get a real sense of what things looked like back then and how the landscape's changed. History's a particular interest of mine.'

Evan had a strange smile on his face, and I felt suddenly ashamed for my father and protective of him.

'Would you fix the guests some drinks, Sam,' my mother called from the kitchen.

'Yes, righto,' my father said. He eased himself up from his chair and opened the fold-down bar in the sideboard.

'Joan will have a sherry, I know,' he said. 'Would you like a sherry too, Helena? It's a nice sweet one.'

'Gin and tonic if you've got it, please,' said Helena.

'Righto,' said my father again.

'Dinner's ready, everyone,' said my mother, coming into the room still wearing her apron.

'Shall we say grace?' my mother chirped after setting down the serving dishes.

'I'd prefer not,' said Evan. 'I don't like the girls saying grace.'

'Oh … of course,' my mother said. 'I didn't think.'

'It won't hurt them this once,' said Helena.

'Oh no, it's perfectly alright,' said my mother.

My father frowned but didn't say anything. He began serving mashed potato onto my mother's plate. Evan helped himself to the bottle of claret my father had set on the table.

'Got any more of that stuff, Sam?' Evan asked when the bottle was finished.

My father wordlessly fetched another bottle and opened it, pouring Evan a glass and then placing it back on the sideboard. My mother and Helena were chatting, but my father sat back, no longer making the effort to converse, and Evan became silent too, though his silence was of the drowsy kind. When he finished the glass he tilted back in his chair, straining the legs, and reached a long arm to the bottle. My father flinched and made a movement towards the sideboard as though to catch the bottle if it tipped. Evan refilled his own glass and my father's, and put the bottle on the table beside his plate. He pulled out a pouch of tobacco from his pocket and began rolling a cigarette, dropping curls of tobacco onto the white tablecloth. I observed all of this with anxiety, wanting my parents and Eva's to be friends.

'We tend not to smoke in here, Evan,' said my father.

'Oh, Sam, it doesn't matter,' said my mother.

Evan paused with cigarette in hand, looking from my mother to my father, amused.

'Really. Please,' said my mother.

My father made a small cough and got up from the table. I was afraid that something bad was happening, but he returned with a glass ashtray and set it in front of Evan.

Heloise became fractious during dessert, and we were sent to the lounge room to play snakes and ladders, where Heloise fell asleep on the carpet. I took Eva and Beatrice to the front sitting room and showed them a jigsaw puzzle I was working on with my father. There was much less to do at my house than there was at the Trenthams'. Our usual imaginary play was constrained by the smallness of the house and somehow, too, by the ordinariness of its rooms.

Evan and Helena left, Helena carrying Heloise in her arms to the car. I rested my head against my mother's waist as she waved the guests off from the doorway, my father standing back and raising his hand only briefly.

My mother sighed as she shut the door. 'That was lovely, wasn't it? It's very nice to get to know your friend's family.' I nodded. 'But it's well past your bedtime, so go and clean your teeth. You're very lucky to have been able to stay up so late. A special occasion.'

When I came to find my mother in the kitchen, I heard my father speaking in his angry voice.

'Well, I think he's a child.'

'It takes all kinds,' my mother soothed.

'I can't believe you just let him refuse to say grace like that.'

'I suppose artists can be temperamental,' said my mother in a pinched tone.

'And smoke at the dinner table too. I think I might take up painting myself if it'll give me licence to get away with whatever I like.'

'I wonder they haven't returned the invitation,' my mother lamented every so often. 'Perhaps we weren't interesting enough for them.'

'Oh, leave it, Joan,' said my father. 'I'd rather not spend another evening with Evan Trentham if it can be helped.'

'It's just common courtesy, that's all.'

'He was a bore as far as I'm concerned. Wasn't interested in talking about art or history or anything, just drinking himself into a stupor on my good claret.'

But my mother, impressed in her bourgeois way with fame and pedigree, could not quite let go of this simultaneous association with both.

'It's a good connection you've made,' she said to me, though I did not understand her meaning and loved Eva passionately for her own self.

'They're nice really, Dad,' I told my father.

'Alright, poppet, if you think so. You're probably a better judge of character than me anyway. I'm just a farm boy. I'd rather stay home and read a book than do all that socialising.' He tickled me under the chin and asked if I wanted to work on our jigsaw puzzle.

Whenever I saw Evan at his own table, loud and joking, tossing glasses in the air when they were empty and setting them back down again to be filled by his friends, I thought of that dinner at my parents' house.

Even on egg nights, the Trentham house at dinnertime was less austere than my own. On those evenings we would approach the table after dark, and Evan would lean out of his chair and clutch at his daughters' wrists. 'Egg night,' he would sing. 'It's an egg night, my pretties,' and Bea would lead the way to the other end of the kitchen to boil us eggs while the adults continued their noisy art talk.

Evan and Helena usually remained at the table long after we had left our egg cups or dirty dishes behind, talking over a bottle of wine.

'Buzz off now, girls,' Helena said, not infrequently. 'I want your father to myself.'

Evan and Helena were exotic in their desire to talk to one

another, to be in each other's company, so unlike my own parents, who split into their own domains as soon as the evening meal was finished: my mother to the kitchen to wash up, and my father to his armchair with a volume of military history or biography. Evan and Helena were romantic, a blurry form we glimpsed as we passed the kitchen doorway, haloed by a diminishing candle.

III

Instinctively, I knew not to tell my parents about Helena's absences. Even in those early years she was often away for weeks at a time, mainly in Sydney, visiting Evan's dealer there or seeing to matters to do with her uncle's estate. It had seemed strange at first that a mother would go away so frequently, leaving her children in the care of their father. But I grew accustomed to it. At some point a pattern had developed, and I slept over at Eva's on most Fridays, returning home on Saturday afternoon so that I did not miss church on Sunday. By then Eva and I were nine, Bea was eleven, and Heloise was seven, and we were allowed to catch the train from school to Box Hill station and walk the twenty minutes to the house, tired and dragging our satchels in the dusty road, Bea sometimes carrying Heloise on her back.

In the 1930s, the Trenthams' property was surrounded on three sides by paddocks and orchards, before they were subdivided into large blocks for new homes. The nearest house belonged to the owner of the orchards that backed onto the Trenthams' garden. He grew apples, and the picked fruit was stored in a huge barn. It was always cold in the barn, and the air smelled of tart apple flesh and pine crates as well as the not unpleasant trace of mildew and the yeasty cider scent of rotten fruit. We were allowed to take apples whenever we liked and, when we could convince Bea to go with us, we went out through the switchgate and walked across the orchards after school, entering the cool dark of the barn, bending over the crates and tumbling the apples until we found one we liked. What we wanted changed from day to day – golden delicious for the sweet, syrupy flavour and good crunch; granny smith for a hot day when the tart greenish-white flesh was the most cooling; the miniature, thick-skinned red apples for the blossomy perfume they gave off when bitten. We grabbed our apples and ate them as we climbed trees in the orchard or built houses with the empty wooden fruit crates. It was often nearly dark by the time we roamed back through the orchard and along three sides of the fence to the Trenthams' front gate. No one was ever waiting for us.

While Helena was gone we ran wilder than ever. Evan was always in his studio and did not emerge until late at night, leaving us to fend for ourselves. Bea became a determined little substitute mother, an eleven-year-old matriarch, scraping our tea together from whatever she could find in the scullery. Evan refused to have a housekeeper, saying they were all old busybodies. A woman from the neighbourhood, Mrs Mullins, helped with the cleaning and popped in each week with eggs from her chooks, but sometimes our afternoon apples were all we had to eat. Bea read to Heloise as we sat in the library, and we all fell asleep tucked into corners of the sofa or curled up on the rug. Evan emerged later and carried us to bed. Sometimes we woke on Saturday mornings still in our school uniforms.

One autumn afternoon, when the days were beginning to mellow, dusk starting to drift into the garden earlier, filling the air like smoke and making the green of the grass and the glossy, thick hydrangea leaves more intense, Heloise grew fretful in her mother's absence. We had been playing a game in which, as usual, Heloise played the minor role of baby, servant, pixie, rather than mother, doctor, or fairy queen. She had tired of this role and was beginning to sulk. Heloise cried often, but today she became inconsolable.

'I hate you,' she wailed. 'I hate all of you. I want Mamma.'

Her crying built until she began to breathe in shuddering gasps. Eva and Bea were unmoved.

'Stop right now, Heloise,' Bea commanded, and when Heloise couldn't stop, Bea threatened to tie her up in the chook shed. Heloise ran off towards the house, with an even more bereft tone to her sobs.

Eva, Bea and I continued playing, and when it began to get dark we went inside.

'Should we look for Heloise?' I ventured.

'No,' Bea said. 'She's got to stop being such a baby. She can't always get her own way. We should just ignore her and she'll come back when she's stopped sulking.' Eva and I nodded our assent, but I felt an anxious wish that there was an adult present.

Evan had friends over that evening, and they were drinking in his studio. The kitchen bench was strewn with breadcrumbs from a roughly broken loaf, and there was half a cold chicken on a too-small plate. Bea tore us off some meat, and we took it into the library, where a fire had been lit and empty wineglasses sat on side tables. 'Heloise! Teatime!' Bea called from the library door.

Bea, Eva and I ate our chicken and began a game of snap, taking turns to sit with our backs to the fire until we became too hot and had to switch places. There was an air of distraction to our game; Heloise frequently ran away from her sisters, upset by their teasing or by her inability to do things as well as the rest of us, but she always reappeared, tear-stained and supplicant, unable to follow through with her determination to do without our company for even an hour. Bea insisted, in a motherly tone, that she was concerned Heloise's sulking was getting worse, not admitting to any worry about where her sister was or why she had stayed away so long.

'You're too bossy,' said Eva. 'Come on, let's find her.' She took my hand and pulled me up. We walked from the warm firelight of the library and into the dark hallway. I was afraid of the dark without Eva's sense of familiarity in this old house, so full of the past compared with my own home, recently built and devoid of history. Eva didn't reach for a light switch until we were upstairs, and when I began to speak to her she shushed me, listening for sounds that might lead us to Heloise's hiding place.

We went through Heloise's room first, opening the cupboards and lifting the quilt off the bed. After searching Eva's and Bea's rooms next door, Eva led me to her parents' bedroom. I had never been in Evan and Helena's room before. It was startlingly messy, clothes strewn across the floor and the bed linen humped in a pile at the foot of the mattress. Above the bed hung the huge painting of Helena that I remember so well. It was done in thick oil paint, abstract but recognisably Helena. She was lying naked on her back, her body diagonally across the canvas and taking up most of the rectangular space. Her head was thrown back, her eyes closed, a smile on her lips. In the bottom corner, Evan's head protruded into the image, face down between Helena's spread thighs so that only his mass of curly red hair identified him. Helena's arms were also spread, Christ-like, and flowers sprouted from the tips of her fingers.

Eva didn't even glance at the painting in her search for Heloise, but I could not take my eyes from it. I knew it was of some ghastly private act between men and women that I did not understand. It made me feel the way I felt when I overheard a snippet of conversation between adults alluding to something I wasn't supposed to know about: something bodily, about women's 'time of the month', which I knew had to do with the blood stains on the pinkish-beige underpants my mother sometimes left soaking in the laundry trough; about the betrayals of our next-door-neighbour's husband that were frequently and tearfully discussed in our kitchen; or about the behaviour of one of the boys in my class, who had been caught bribing girls with lollies to pull their pants down.

'Dadda painted that,' said Eva, seeing that I was staring at the image. 'It's about the time when he and Mamma first met. Before we were born.' Her tone was matter-of-fact, and I could see that she didn't feel the same way I did about the painting.

Heloise was not in the house. We had been everywhere but the cellar – which Eva was sure was too scary for Heloise to descend into alone – even climbing to the attic to peer through the gabled window to the roof platform. Eva thought it was time to tell her father, but Bea, who was beginning to worry that she would be in trouble, still hesitated.

'She'll be here somewhere,' she said. 'You probably haven't looked properly.'

'We have,' said Eva.

Eventually, it was decided that we would wait until Evan came to put us to bed before saying anything, rather than breaching the adult domain of the studio, from where we could hear the scratchy music of a gramophone and deep male laughter.

Eva and I sat rigid on the couch, mute and fidgety, while Bea drew in a scrapbook with feigned nonchalance. At last, Evan came to check on us, still speaking over his shoulder to the adults in the other room.

'How are my little ones?' he asked. 'Where's Heloise?'

Eva burst into tears. I felt myself close to doing the same, as much from the lingering impression of the painting upstairs as from anxiety over Heloise going missing. I wanted to go home, to be watched over and freed of the awful adult feeling of responsibility.

'What's going on, chook?' Evan hoisted Eva onto his hip and kissed her cheek.

'Heloise is lost and she's been lost for ages and Bea wouldn't let me tell you,' Eva blurted out between sobs.

'I didn't,' said Bea in a panicked tone.

Evan was unconcerned. 'Let's look for her, shall we?' he said, as if it was a game.

We searched the house again, Beatrice and I trailing behind Evan as he carried Eva through the bedrooms, kitchen, laundry and sitting room. He didn't search as Eva and I had done, only peered into each room, flicking the light on and then off again, calling Heloise's name. A man and a woman emerged from the studio with glasses in their hands and questioning expressions.

'Sorry, my daughter's absconded,' Evan said, his eyes pink at the edges and moist with drunkenness.

'Oh goodness,' said the woman. 'Can we help?'

The night became worse. Evan concluded that Heloise was not in the house after two more searches, each more thorough and sober than the last, each with more participants, the woman joining in the second search and the man also in the third.

'She can't be outside still at this time of night,' Evan muttered, scrabbling for a torch in a kitchen cupboard. 'Blast,' he exclaimed as a jar of nails, drawing pins and elastic bands fell to the floor and scattered across the stone tiles. I drew in my breath. These adults were of no use in a crisis.

Once the search began in the garden, Heloise's hysterical sobs drew the adults up the driveway to where she was crouched outside the front gate, unable to reach the handle and let herself in. She had gone to the fruit barn by herself in defiance and had been locked out amongst the paddocks since before dark. Her small shrieks and beatings on the high wooden gate had not reached the house, and by the time she was found, she was inconsolable. Her body was shaking with cold and prolonged crying. Her face was red and swollen with tears. Evan carried her, screaming even louder now that she had been found. Her bare legs kicked against Evan's thighs, and it was all he could do to hold her in his arms.

He was at a loss to know what to do. The woman visitor ran a warm bath, and tried to take Heloise from Evan to undress her and put her in, but she stopped fighting and began to cling to him as violently as she had tried to escape until a moment before. Finally, she cried herself to sleep in Evan's arms on the sofa, wrapped in a blanket. Eva, Bea and I stood on the periphery of this scene, wide-eyed and horrified.

It is strange which events leave those deep scars we carry with us over a lifetime. When Heloise talked about that night, even years later, it was with a bitter seriousness, a complete inability to see the events other than as they occurred to her as a seven-year-old. It became a foundation myth, a lasting symbol of the troubled nature of Heloise's childhood, the real sufferings she endured, but also the way she experienced these sufferings, reliving them over and over until they wore away their own caged-animal paths within her.

IV

A new man began to appear at the dinner table. Guests were so frequent at Eva's house that it was not until he had been there three or four times that I began to notice him. He was younger than Evan and Helena, in his early twenties, and had an accent I later learned was Polish and an odd name: Ugo Ergom. He was a painter, and I overheard that he had just had his first solo show at Gallery First in Flinders Street, where Evan usually exhibited his work.

Ugo was tall and pale; not the bluish pale of Evan and Heloise, who looked as though they had grown up under a tarpaulin, but a fresh paleness that was more like an abundance of sunlight. His paint-stained hands were always moving, patting the packet of tobacco in his shirt pocket or rolling a cigarette, fast and thin, without even looking at it, and tucking it into his mouth or behind his ear, pushing back his hair from his eyes. He spoke to everyone alike.

Eva and I discussed him in her bedroom. We were thirteen by then, and thought him very handsome.

The next time I met Ugo, he arrived to dinner with Dora Fisk, the owner of Gallery First. I had seen her before, with her husband, who was much older. The sisters did not like Dora because she ignored them completely. She had a haggard glamour and a loud, raspy voice, yet when she accompanied Ugo to dinner she became almost shy as she put her arm

41

through his and walked with him from the library to the dining room.

'You're such a breath of fresh air, darling. So *European*.' She drew the word out, making it sound exotic. 'They hardly know what to make of you in these antipodean parts.'

'Don't forget, Dora, it was Evan who had to practically drag you away from the stuffy old art you've been showing for the last ten years,' said Helena with a smile at Ugo.

Dora glanced sideways at Helena.

'I'm sure you'll remind me if I forget.'

'Are you working exclusively on your painting?' Helena asked Ugo.

'No, not at all. I'm tarring roads all day and count myself lucky I'm not on the Sustenance.' He laughed and shrugged.

One Saturday Evan took me, Eva and Heloise with him when he went to visit Ugo at his studio in the city. We caught the train to Flinders Street station and then walked up Collins Street. It was windy, and men held their hats by the brim as if greeting everyone they passed. Women clasped their flapping coats around them, pulling children behind them like fallen kites.

'How far do we have to walk?' Heloise asked, dragging on the back of Evan's belt.

'Right to the top of this hill,' Evan said. He shook himself free and began to stride ahead of us. We lagged up the hill, Eva and I arm in arm and Heloise falling steadily behind. Eventually, almost at Spring Street, Evan stopped and waited for us in front of a shop, pacing. When we got close, he stepped up to a wooden door beside the shop and banged on it. There was a brass letter slot in the door, and he pushed it open and peered in, stooping, his beard pressed against the wood. Heloise stood on tiptoe and tried to look in too.

'Ugo,' she called into the opening.

There was a clumping descent from above, and then the door opened. There was Ugo, dressed in overalls and a red

42

wool jumper with frayed cuffs. He wore slippers on his feet, over thick socks.

'The whole clan,' he said.

'Except Bea,' said Heloise.

'Almost the whole clan. Welcome.' He held the door open, his arm outstretched to usher us past. Behind the door a steep, uncarpeted staircase led up through darkness to a square of light at the top. Heloise ran up, her tiredness vanished.

Ugo's studio and flat was a single room, about fifteen feet square. It smelled similar to Evan's studio, heavy with oil paints, linseed oil, the woody scent of graphite pencils and the tang of turpentine. But there were also food smells here: meat and fat and onions. And over everything the pungence of tobacco smoke.

Along the front wall of the room were two arched windows that faced onto Collins Street. We gazed out at the giraffe bark of the plane trees before turning to the room itself. The floor was of bare boards, except for a square of pink carpet in the back corner where Ugo's folding bed was set out. Along the back wall was a black pot-belly stove, a basin and a toilet, exposed to the room, with a cistern and a pull-chain hanging above it. By the window where we stood was a divan covered with drapery, some of which had evidently been curtains and still had the hooks attached, and an easel on a dirty sheet. On the other side of the staircase was a table covered by an incongruous tablecloth embroidered with an image of a peasant girl throwing grain to some chickens.

Ugo went over to the basin and washed his hands. We all followed him.

'Coffee?' he asked.

'Thanks,' said Evan.

'It's not fresh but it's hot.' Ugo picked up the pot from the stove, poured a small amount into a blue teacup.

'Fine,' said Evan. He took a sip and grimaced. 'Ugh. Quite a brew.' He inclined his head towards the toilet. 'Do you mind?'

'Of course not. Girls, let me show you this photo of my mother. She's very beautiful.'

Ugo gestured back to the windows, where a photograph was stuck to the wall between the two arches. Across the room I heard Evan unzip his trousers and begin to piss.

The woman in the picture was indeed beautiful. She had the same wide mouth as Ugo, but her lips were fuller. Her eyes were laughing and creased at their corners like his.

'What's her name?' Heloise asked.

'Her name is Bella,' said Ugo. 'Do you want to hear something funny? My father's name is also Bela, but not spelled the same. His is B-E-L-A.'

'That's silly,' said Heloise.

'I know. Bella and Bela.'

Evan came over, adjusting his belt.

Ugo pointed to another photo. 'This is a picture of my village.'

'It looks cold,' said Eva.

'Very cold. Sometimes in winter it would snow so much that we would be trapped in the house for days. Even weeks. Imagine that.'

'You could starve to death,' said Heloise.

'You could, but we never would. My mother was prepared. That's why I love pickles so much; because they saved my life so many times.' He smiled at us. Three girls standing close together, gazing at him, smiling back.

Evan was examining some paintings stacked against the wall.

'Show me what you've been working on.'

'Alright,' said Ugo. 'Would you like a drink?'

'Please.'

Ugo went over to the table with the embroidered cloth and reached beneath it, bringing out an unmarked bottle full of clear liquid.

'You know,' he said, reaching for glasses from the shelf above the sink, 'when I was a boy in the village it got so cold that your hands would stick to anything metal. My friend Thomasz's hand once got stuck to a railing and I had to wee on it to get it unstuck.'

We giggled, and Heloise put her hand to her mouth.

'True,' said Ugo, nodding, his eyes still a boy's.

'Why couldn't he just pull it off?' Eva asked.

'Because the skin on his hand would have ripped off and been left behind on the railing.'

I pictured the handprint of skin on the icy railing, the torn pink palm of Ugo's friend.

Visiting Ugo's studio had seemed an exciting prospect, but I soon grew as restless as Eva and Heloise, sitting uncomfortably while the two men talked and drank, shuffled through paintings on cheap boards, held one up to the light. This is how we spent the afternoon at Ugo's, waiting on the divan with nothing to do but listen.

'An artist is someone who sees the structures of order and recognises them as arbitrary,' Evan said to Ugo.

I didn't know what he meant, but tried to remember his words, to store them up until I grew into them, like the clothes of an older child packed away for a younger. I was interested already in what makes an artist, or perhaps just in Evan and Ugo.

Ugo disagreed. 'By that logic every madman raving in his cell is an artist. Surely there has to be an act of creation. The making of some object.'

'Maybe he is,' said Evan. 'Maybe the madman is an artist.'

'And what about the criminal who sees the system for what it is and exploits it for his own gain?'

'Does he really see through the system though? He *understands* the structures. But does he realise that they are arbitrary? Not enough to imagine an alternative order.'

V

'I have to leave my flat,' said Ugo at dinner a few weeks later.

'No. Why?' Helena asked.

'The shoe shop downstairs is closing and they're putting it up for sale.' He shrugged, his habitual gesture of acceptance.

'Where will you go?' asked Patrick.

'Not sure. Probably I'll stay with my parents in Coburg for a while until I find somewhere else. It's alright. Can't afford it anyway.'

'Ugo,' said Heloise, picking individual peas from her plate and popping them into her mouth. 'Tell us again about your mother.'

'Shhh, Heloise,' said Helena. 'Not now.'

Heloise pouted, staring down at her buttery fingers.

'Have you got room to paint there?' asked Patrick.

'Not really.' Ugo ruffled Heloise's hair as he replied, and she beamed up at him.

'Why don't you move in here?' said Helena. 'There's plenty of room.'

'Grand idea,' said Evan. 'You're part of the group show now, so you'll be here all the time anyway. Makes sense.'

Ugo shrugged again, leaving his shoulders hunched up by his chin.

'I couldn't,' he said. 'Ask you to take me in like a stray dog?'

46

'You didn't ask,' said Helena. 'We offered. Anyway, we love stray dogs, don't we, Evan? They're the most interesting kind.'

And so Ugo came to live at the Trentham house, the first member of the circle to take up official residence. He moved into one of the downstairs rooms that had served until then as a storeroom for Evan's work. Eva, Heloise and I sat on the bed as Ugo unpacked the last of his possessions. The photo of his mother was already tacked to the cupboard door beside the picture of his village. I imagined again the scene of Ugo pissing on his friend's hand against the cold railing.

'Look at this, girls,' said Ugo, pulling a picture from a large envelope. 'This is a print of a painting by Gauguin. *The Moon and the Earth*.'

In the black-and-white picture, a naked woman stood with her back to the viewer. Above her, a man's face floated in the sky. The woman's face was pointed towards the floating man, and she looked as though she was drinking from his head through a straw of leaves.

'Is that what it's called?' Eva asked.

Ugo nodded.

'Is the man meant to be the moon?'

'Actually the opposite,' said Ugo. 'The woman is the moon asking the earth to give humans eternal life. It is a Polynesian myth.'

'But the man is in the sky, like the moon,' said Heloise.

'Well, maybe we are standing on the moon with the woman,' said Ugo. 'From the moon, the earth is in the sky.'

'I've seen this before,' said Eva. 'At Gino's.'

'Yes, that's where I got it.'

'Who's Gino?' I asked.

'He has the Leonardo bookshop in the city. We go there lots. He makes us cocoa at the back. He's lovely.'

'He is,' said Ugo.

Again, I felt the ache at the mention of this Gino, who

was so familiar to Eva, a central figure, I imagined, in her life without me.

Ugo brought new smells to the house: pickled cucumbers, hot salami, the clean whiff of Slivovitz left in glasses and sticky rings on the kitchen table. Ugo and Evan were as fiery as each other, but their natures were different. Evan had the ruffian Irish blood that gave him an air of being hounded by restless spirits. He was moody and chaotic, working in bursts of energy that kept him shut up in his studio for days on end, and at other times listless and petulant, not working for weeks so that he began to pick fights with Helena and his friends, to drink too much, to complain that he had lost his inspiration.

Ugo had a routine, painting from sunrise until mid morning, when he cooked a hot breakfast for himself and Evan, sitting outside in the sunshine and eating with a fork only, holding the plate balanced on one hand, his legs crossed and his elbow rested on a knee, transferring the food to his mouth with quick movements and always finishing first. He painted again until three or four, and then worked in the garden, building a vegetable patch for Helena.

He helped the girls clean out the old chook shed and convert it into a workspace of their own. He laid some scraps of carpet over the dirt floor, patched the corrugated tin roof, and replaced the chicken wire that covered three sides of the structure with wooden planks. He constructed three small desks out of wooden crates, and the sisters began to pass the time after school in their 'studio'. Bea was really too old now to want to spend time with her younger sisters in the chook shed, so I largely took over her desk. If she did spend time with us there, it was because she wanted Ugo to know that she appreciated his transformative efforts.

Ugo was never tired, and after this outdoor labour he often cooked dinner. Evan, Patrick and Ugo were plotting the formation of what would become the Melbourne Modern

Art Group, and were now frequently discussing their plans for a group show, their ideas for the manifesto they planned to include in the programme and, as always, the cliques and controversies of the Melbourne art world.

I grew used to the conversations of men.

'Did you hear about Gino?' asked Patrick one night.

'Bastards,' said Evan.

'What?' said Ugo. 'What's happened?'

'The fucking vice squad came and confiscated a Renoir he had in the window of the shop. A *Renoir* for Christ's sake.' Evan turned to us. 'Are you listening, girls? This is the kind of country we live in.' He paused for a moment and then continued, his voice serious. 'I want you to understand that art is never wrong or immoral. Do you hear me?' We nodded. Then he smiled and said, 'Lesson over.'

We were all infatuated with Ugo. Heloise, the closest to childhood's sweet egocentrism and wide open arms, was the only one who freely displayed this infatuation. She was constantly in his wake.

'Can I sit next to you, Ugo?' she asked every night. 'Can I come and watch you paint, Ugo?'

'Certainly,' he replied.

One afternoon, soon after Ugo moved in, Helena gathered us into the library.

'Girls,' she said. 'I know you like Ugo very much, but he needs to be left alone to work. You can't go into his studio anymore.'

'Why not?' said Heloise.

'We don't,' said Eva. 'It's Heloise that never leaves him alone.'

'Well,' said Helena, frowning at Eva. 'It doesn't matter who. Just stop, that's all.'

'Why?' Heloise repeated, pulling at the sleeves of her jumper. 'He doesn't mind.'

'I think he might.'

'You don't know.'

'Heloise, I don't want you distracting him, do you hear me? He's here to paint. The show's coming up. You need to play with your sisters and Lily, not pester Ugo.'

'They hate me,' said Heloise, beginning to sniff. 'They never let me play with them.'

It was true. We were eleven and thirteen now, and the two years between us had cracked open and become a chasm. Eva and I no longer wanted Heloise around. She still wanted to play dolls and put on pantomimes in the attic, while we wanted to sit for hours with our backs against the seed train and smoke the cigarettes Eva stole from her mother's purse.

'Go away, Heloise,' Eva constantly told her, and Heloise would wander off disconsolate, her auburn hair and pale face glimpsed amongst the bushes deeper into the garden, like a solitary will-o'-the-wisp.

VI

There were frequent, spontaneous parties at the Trentham house. When we were younger, we were sent to bed to lie on our narrow mattresses, me in my accustomed place on the pull-out bed in Eva's room, listening to the sounds of voices floating up from the garden below. Firelight gave the windowpanes a burnt glow like homemade toffee. The air smelled of wood smoke. Some nights we climbed to our rooftop platform and peered down from the peaks. We tried to locate Evan by the sound of his voice, amplified by drunkenness and the presence of an audience. Sometimes we stayed awake at our elevated post until the party ended, or dragged quilts up through the gabled opening and fell asleep together, waking cold when Bea shook us to tell us that everyone had left. Or Bea would sneak down to the kitchen and reappear with a teapot full of hot cocoa. One night she brought back half a cake she had found in the kitchen, but we did not like its liqueur taste so instead of eating it we broke off pieces and rolled them into sticky projectiles that we launched from the roof at the adults below.

There was a sense of occasion to these nights that prevented us from sleeping. The laughter and raised voices; the imagined night-time world of adults. There was also an uncertainty that drew us closer together and away from sleep. One night, as Eva and I were lying in our beds, we saw a light go on across the hall and heard a scream from Heloise. Eva leaped from her bed to find a young man and woman stumbling from Heloise's room. The man's shirt was untucked, the woman's face flushed. Both had cigarettes in their hands, and they glowed red like the beady eyes of some broad-headed monster as the couple hurried back down the dark stairs laughing, their arms draped around each other's shoulders.

As we grew older, we were no longer commanded to go to bed when there were guests or a party, and sometimes Eva and I sat up together and watched, quiet amongst the laughter of adults like stones in midstream.

Ugo brought new guests to dinner. A man and a woman I had never seen before. He introduced them to Helena, Patrick and Vera, who were all seated at the table waiting for Evan. Then he introduced them to us.

'Girls, these are my best friends. Maria and Jerome.'

Maria was small, olive-skinned, with a round face. Her head was wild with dark curls. She smiled at us with her wide, friendly mouth and held out her hand to each of us.

'Very pleased to meet you,' she said. 'Ugo has told me so much about you.'

'How did you meet Ugo?' Heloise asked.

'We were in painting class together. At the Gallery School.'

Heloise nodded seriously. 'Like Dadda and Patrick.'

The man, Jerome, did not shake our hands. He smiled at us, but the smile slipped from his face, and he kept glancing around as Maria spoke, as if watching for something. The three young artists would have been roughly the same age, in their early twenties, but Jerome seemed different from the others in a way that I might have described at the time as posh. He was dressed in a shirt and tie, and when he spoke it was in a proper, English-sounding voice.

Evan came late to the table, his hair wet and his pants crumpled. Jerome stood up, dropping his napkin to the floor. Evan offered a hand to the newcomers.

'These are the friends I was telling you about, Evan,' said Ugo. 'Jerome Carroll and Maria Caballo. Both wonderful artists. Jerome, Maria, meet Evan Trentham.'

'Pleasure,' said Jerome.

'I'd love you to see their work. You too,' Ugo said, addressing Patrick, who was seated by Helena. Ugo was unusually formal, introducing his friends. Tonight, having cooked the dinner, he was the host in this house in which he was neither guest nor family.

Ugo had made a stew. The bone of a pork hock rested in an iron pot in the centre of the table. There were potato dumplings, bread, red wine. There were no vegetables, save the carrots and celery cooked down to pure flavour in the stew. Ugo left the room and returned with a bottle of clear spirits and six small glasses. He filled a glass for each of the adults. They raised them ceremonially, looking into each other's eyes, and tipped their heads back as they tossed the liquid into their throats. It was a fast gesture, yet somehow sensual. Maria's hair spilled over the back of the chair as she let her neck fall backwards.

Formality disappeared with that first shot of spirits. The table became rowdy with conversation. I studied the features of these new guests. Maria was loud, and her hands were always active, underlining her speech or twisting the stem of her wineglass. Jerome had a sharp, concentrated energy about him that made me glance at him often.

Other guests began arriving as Maria helped Ugo clear the table. Evan and Patrick went outside to light a fire in the half-moon clearing. Helena went to the cellar for more wine. Jerome was left alone at the table with the daughters of Evan Trentham. He chatted comfortably with us, but his eyes wandered now and then towards the garden, where Evan and Patrick had gone to stuff newspaper into the chinks between the logs that had already been piled up in the clearing.

'Now, tell me your names again. Eva I know. It's almost your father's name. And Beatrix?'

53

'Beatrice.'

'Beatrice, sorry. And Heloise, is that right? You're clearly your father's daughter. And you're the friend, aren't you?'

'Yes,' I said. 'I'm Lily.'

'Pleased to meet you all. I'm hoping to join this show that your father and Ugo and Patrick are putting on. But to be perfectly honest' – he dropped his voice to a mock-conspiratorial tone – 'I'm not sure if I'm at all good enough.'

The night that followed was a slip down the rabbit hole. Summer was taking up its place like a chestnut seller setting up his stall, lighting the coals and letting the scented smoke drift down the street before he begins to call out to passers-by. It was not too hot by the fire in the centre of the garden clearing, nor too cold away from it in the darker, leafy peripheries.

We girls took up a spot to the left and slightly back from where Evan was sitting with Ugo and the new guests. People were arriving with the sound of tyres crunching down the gravel driveway, and the beams of headlights painted the side of the house.

'Maria has recently come back from a trip home to Spain,' Ugo was telling Evan. Maria was removing a rectangular embroidered case from her bag. She glanced between Evan and Ugo, nodding her head. She seemed to me so bold.

'Yes,' she said. Her accent was thick and her English formal. 'I could not believe what is going on there since I left. It is truly modern. We are stunted here.'

'I know it all too well,' said Evan, watching Maria as she spoke.

'It made me want to move back to Spain. But then, as I said, I began painting in Australia. I feel I paint as an Australian. That may seem strange to you.'

'Not at all,' said Evan.

'I have admired your work for a long time. Very much. It seems to me that you were one of the first to work in the modern style here. But your aesthetic is still Australian.'

'Thank you,' said Evan. 'I appreciate that. I'm interested to see your work.'

Maria bent her head, showing her first hint of shyness. She twisted her hair into a knot and bent over the open case in her lap. She brought out cigarette papers and rolled two plump cigarettes, picking flecks of tobacco from her tongue and flicking them towards the fire. She put one of the cigarettes back in the case. 'For later,' she said, 'when I can no longer roll.'

Ugo pulled a glowing stick from the fire, and Maria bent in, the end of the cigarette pressed against the burning wood, inhaling until it lit.

Helena approached us from the other side of the fire.

'Beatrice, can you put Heloise to bed, please?'

'No,' Heloise wailed immediately.

'Why don't you?' Bea replied.

'Don't answer back to me. Do as you're told,' Helena said.

But Bea simply got up and began to walk off into the garden.

'Come back here this minute,' Helena said to Bea's departing back. 'Horrible child.' She turned to Evan. 'Why do you let her speak to me that way?'

Evan shrugged and smiled, inhaling the cigarette that Maria passed to him and reclining onto the rug. The smell that reached us was soft and pungent, not like the smell of normal cigarettes.

When there was a pause in the talk, Jerome rose and asked who wanted another drink.

'You should see Jerome's work also,' said Ugo, when Jerome was out of earshot. 'He's a natural modernist. He's spent time in Europe, but not long periods. Until recently he was studying law and only painting in his spare time.'

Evan nodded.

'He's very good,' said Maria in agreement.

'Oh, I'm interested to see his work,' said Evan. 'If he brings me back a drink soon I'll like him even more.'

Ugo laughed. 'Alright, enough business for tonight.'

Evan reached out again for the cigarette. He inhaled deeply, holding the smoke in his lungs for a long time before he let it out in a ball of white, his mouth wide.

'You know they're smoking reefer, don't you?' Eva whispered to me.

'No,' I whispered back. 'How do you know?'

'Because I know. Dad smokes it sometimes. He takes cocaine too.'

There was a tone in her voice I did not like, that seemed to take pleasure in my naiveté.

'Guess what?' Eva leaned away from Heloise, who was sitting silent but attentive on her other side, and whispered into my hair. 'I've tried it. Reefer.'

'What's it like?' I replied with careful nonchalance.

'It's nice. Sort of floaty. Maybe we can smoke some tonight. Do you want to try it?'

'How?'

'I know where Dad keeps his. Go and wait for me by the seed train and I'll get some.' Eva rose and pulled me up.

'What are you doing?' asked Heloise.

'Nothing. You can't come with us.' Eva ran off, leaving me standing beside Heloise.

I hesitated for a moment, and then left her alone on the rug.

It was dark behind the seed train. I did not want to try the reefer. I waited a long time for Eva, squinting around the side of the carriage towards the fire, where people were clustered in groups, sitting or standing. At last, she came back.

'I couldn't find Dad's stuff.'

'Oh well.'

'But I took the joint from Maria's purse. She left it on the rug. No one noticed.' Eva held it up between her thumb and fingers like a stick of chalk. 'It's different from normal cigarettes. You have to hold the smoke in for a long time. Did you see how Dad did it?'

I nodded. The smoke was hot as it sucked down into my lungs. I held it, feeling its thickness, until I began to cough. I felt the particles of my body rise towards my head. By the time we had finished, I felt as if I were located entirely in a single spot at the crown of my skull. I floated after Eva, back to the fireside, holding on to her fingertips. Heloise was still there. She did not ask where we had been. I watched the fire, the adults moving in its glow as if bronzed. Their voices came to me from underwater. I could not feel my arms. I was mesmerised, watching an aquarium full of languid, colourful fish.

Late in the night three young women began a drunken balancing act. They were clumsy, giggling, but determined. One lay on her back with her arms and legs held up in the air. A second woman lay across her, stiff. The first woman's bare feet pressed into her thighs and their hands clasped together. With the help of two men, a third woman, a tiny blonde, clambered up and knelt on all fours atop the second woman's back. Heloise was standing close by, watching. One of the men picked her up and tried to lift her onto the back of the third woman. She screamed and her body went rigid. The three women toppled over, laughing, tangled together, and the man put Heloise roughly back down. At some point Maria began yelling about the stolen reefer.

'Bastard,' she shouted at the general gathering. 'I would have shared it if you had asked.'

I must have fallen asleep because I was woken by a shout from Patrick.

'Not that again, you dirty bugger,' he called out, his voice husky.

I opened my eyes. My mouth was thick and dry. Most of the party had left. Eva was asleep beside me, curled up. The fire had burned down to glowing logs. Only Patrick and Vera, Helena, Jerome, Ugo and Maria were left, along with a couple of others I did not know.

'Evan,' Helena drawled, staggering to her feet.

I peered across the coals to see what they were shouting about. Evan was squatting in the garden bed beyond the half-moon clearing, his pants down, his backside very white, shitting into the bushes. He grinned sheepishly at his audience and said something about his anal fixation.

'Years of analysis,' he said. 'Failed.'

Patrick covered Vera's eyes with his hands. 'Party's over, everyone.'

'Revolting,' Vera said.

Maria laughed. She was hunched up with her arms around her knees. Ugo was behind her, his head against her back. 'Let's sleep by the fire,' she murmured.

VII

The next time I saw Maria, she was lying naked on the green chaise longue in Evan's studio. It was the school holidays, and Eva and I had met for malted milks and then walked back to her house in the hot late afternoon. We drank a glass of water in the kitchen, and I followed Eva to her father's studio. Evan glanced up as Eva pushed the squeaking door open, then back down at the easel in front of him.

'Hello, Eva,' said Maria from her spread, sumptuous pose. She gave a tiny wave and then replaced her hand in its position along her sunlit thigh. The room smelled sweaty in the syrupy afternoon light and, as always, of tobacco and turpentine.

'Hello, Maria,' Eva replied.

Maria's other hand was propped under her cheek, and she raised her head and clenched and unclenched her fist. 'Evan, may I move?' she asked.

'No,' he said, his eyes on her breasts, brush moving. 'Another couple of minutes. I want to capture this light.'

Eva went around to examine Evan's painting, but I stood in the doorway, embarrassed.

'Where's Mamma?' Eva asked.

'I don't know. She's about. Look, Eva, do you mind?'

'What?' she replied, refusing to understand.

'Go away. You're distracting my sitter and casting shadows.'

'Eva,' said Maria, 'if you find Helena, tell her that I will be released soon and will find her.'

'Alright,' said Eva, flouncing away from her father and back to the door.

We found Helena in gardening gloves and a work shirt of Evan's, the sleeves rolled up, digging one of the vegetable beds. Her hair was tied back in a scarf, and her usual glamour disguised. She straightened as we approached, one foot on her spade, and wiped the back of her arm across her forehead.

'Hello, girls.'

'Maria said to tell you she'll be released soon.'

'Oh good,' said Helena. 'I'm just about ready for a G&T. Perhaps I'll go and clean up and make drinks.'

I wondered what she thought of the scene in the studio.

Helena's eyes swept the garden bed. It was three-quarters dug but still had a crust over one corner. 'You can take over here, Eva,' she said.

'No,' Eva said.

Helena removed her gloves and set them on the edge of the bed where they held the shape of her hands. 'Go on. Be agreeable, just once.'

Eva was standing by the crusted corner of the bed and she bent and poked a finger through the dry, lighter-coloured dirt, leaving a clean hole. 'Alright,' she said. 'Maybe I will.'

Helena turned to me with an expression of exaggerated disbelief. Eva always had her own reasons for compliance, but she had obviously decided that there would be satisfaction in this task, revealing the wormy-smelling, darker soil beneath the crust. I could see this pleasure too.

'I'll help,' I said.

Eva picked up the spade and stabbed it into the earth. She stepped up and balanced, one foot on each side of the handle. She stood there, swaying, and then jumped off and heaved out a thick wedge.

Helena was untying the scarf from the back of her head and shaking out her hair as she walked back to the house. 'Thank you, girls,' she called behind her.

We had finished the digging and were sitting on the edge of the garden bed, shaking the dirt out of our shoes, when Helena and Maria came around the side of the house, laughing, holding drinks in their hands.

'Well,' said Helena, surveying our work, 'you seem to have managed to spread as much dirt outside the bed as inside, but thank you.'

She had changed into her usual pale, floppy linens, and her hair was shiny as though just brushed. Maria was clothed, now, in a floral dress.

'We're going for a wander,' said Helena, linking her arm through Maria's.

Although it had only been a few weeks since the party, when we had met Maria for the first time, she and Helena seemed to have become best friends. I had not seen this girlish side of Helena before. She actually giggled as Maria said something close to her ear.

Going for a wander was something Helena often did in the evening with her first drink. These were the times when I saw her most, when she was not away or deep in adult conversation with her husband or Patrick or Ugo, not tucked into one of her unapproachable realms of bedroom or office or sunroom, where she liked to sit and smoke. In the garden, holding her clinking glass, she allowed her daughters to follow her when they wanted to. At these times, she grew nostalgic for her uncle, who had planted most of the garden, and with whom she had begun these botanical perambulations. She even became avuncular herself, losing the slight peevishness with which she often seemed to address her daughters, perhaps summoning up in them her own child self. They sensed the ritual nature of these occasions and assented to put on the spirit clothes of the child Helena, asking their uncle-mother the names of everything she had nurtured in this scented evening séance-garden. In this way I learned from Helena to tell the difference between elm and yew; salvia and lavender; acanthus and agapanthus.

That day, Helena was more niece and less spirit-uncle as she guided her new friend through her garden. It was a warm December evening, but as Eva and I walked behind them we entered glades of cool air as if we were swimming across a lake.

'I had a dear, dear uncle too,' said Maria. 'Yours taught you about plants, and mine taught me about art.'

The women smiled at one another, their dark heads in profile with the unctuous light filling the space between them.

'I'm so glad you came to us, Maria,' said Helena, resting her cheek briefly on Maria's floral shoulder. 'I feel like we've known each other before. In another lifetime. Don't you?'

'Perhaps,' Maria said, laughing. 'Who do you think we were?'

'I don't know,' said Helena, staring into the treetops. She plucked a leaf from a dark tree, crushed it and held it to her nose. 'Camphor laurel,' she said, and Maria bent her head to smell it. She passed it back to Eva, and we pressed our noses together into the leaf. It smelled like Vicks Vaporub. 'It's poisonous, so don't eat it, will you,' said Helena, laughing.

We wove around the sacred bamboo, Helena and Maria sipping from their perspiring glasses.

'I think maybe we were married,' said Helena.

Maria laughed again. 'Was it a happy marriage? Which of us was the husband?'

'I was the husband,' said Helena. 'I'm quite sure I was a man in my previous life. That much I haven't forgotten. I think we were very happy and lived until we were very old.'

'Ah,' said Maria. 'But you see, I think that I was a man also.'

'Oh?' said Helena. 'Then perhaps we were brothers who lived together in our old age.'

'Mmm,' said Maria. 'Yes. I think you could be right.'

VIII

Trying to describe my friendship with Eva is like showing the slides from a life-changing journey. The images can never break their borders and make their way into the body, into the nose, the ears, the entrails; they can never convey the feeling of profound change, brought about simply by altering one's place in the world.

From such a distance, I cannot even remember clearly the dailiness of our friendship. If I describe certain moments, rooms, or days in the garden with a crisp focus, it is because their newness or singularity imprinted itself on the blank, light-sensitive strip of memory. They are the flashes: the first day of school; my first visit to Eva's house; the first of Evan's exhibitions I attended. I see them still with a clarity, the way particular dreams from childhood are retained while the waking life around them slips unnoticed into the darkness. They are the clues, the forensics with which I reconstruct the past.

It is the ordinary days that are lost to me. Yet it was the ordinariness itself that made my days with Eva beautiful. The way we grew together; the way our hearts were known to each other, and our lives, I believed, joined forever in a lazy flow of days.

There is no intimacy as great as that between young girls. Even between lovers, who cross boundaries we are accustomed to thinking of as at the furthest territories of closeness, there is a constant awareness of separateness, the wonder at the fact that the loved one is distinct, whole, with a past and a mind housed behind the eyes we gaze into that exist, inviolate, without us. It is the lack of such wonder that reveals the depth of intimacy in that first chaste trial marriage between girls.

Chaste, and yet fiercely physical. Eva and I were draped constantly about each other's bodies. We brushed one another's hair. We sniffed each other's armpits and open mouths and nodded if they were free from staleness and sweat. We lay about the garden, one head on the other's stomach. We became blood sisters, pricking our fingers solemnly with a pearl-ended hat pin and pressing the red seed pearls of blood that sprang out of the dainty wounds against each other, grinding them together so that the mingled blood would squeeze back in to the tight-walled body and we would be part, each, of the other. We lay on the sun bed after school and took turns at tickling one another's arms, running our fingertips as lightly as possible over the skin so that goosebumps rose up and a delicious shiver ran down the arm and along the spine.

'You will all be turning fourteen this year, girls,' Mrs Hazlitt, our teacher, cautioned us at the start of the next school year. 'And a privilege of turning fourteen is that you will be permitted to swim at the Surrey Dive. However,' she continued, in her Scots accent, folding her glasses into her palm, 'if you take my advice, you may, on further consideration, forego that privilege. The Dive is a dangerous place, in more ways than one. A lower class of people congregate there; hoodlums and ne'er-do-wells.'

'I'm going,' Eva whispered. 'On my birthday.'

The Surrey Dive was a flooded clay quarry next to the old Box Hill Brickworks at the corner of Elgar and Canterbury roads. It had been bought by the council thirty years earlier and made into a swimming hole. There were few concessions to turning fourteen as a girl in 1936, but the Dive was one, and Eva fixed her eye on it like a gunman on a target.

I had already turned fourteen in January, but I waited to swim there, out of loyalty, until Eva's birthday in March. Eva had been born on her father's birthday and she had always been happy about this fact. It was a special bond between father and daughter, the reason she had been named after him. This year, though, she became petulant as their shared birthday approached.

'What shall we do for your birthdays this year, my dears?' Helena asked them both.

'I want to go to the Dive,' said Eva.

'Oh, really?' said Helena. 'I thought a party.'

'No, I'm not sharing another party with Dad.'

'Don't be horrible, Eva. It's both your birthdays. Why should you be the only one to get a party?'

'Well, that's the thing, I never do get a party, really. They're always Dad's parties that you pretend are mine too.'

'That's not true. You can invite as many friends as you like.'

'Thank you, Mother. I'm sure they'll love seeing Dad pooing in the garden and you falling over drunk.'

'Don't be such a little prude,' said Helena.

'Dad had a million years to have his own parties before I was born.'

'A *million*? Steady on,' said Evan.

'I didn't even get my own name. Just half of his.'

'Three-quarters, actually,' said Evan, pulling his daughter, fighting, into his long arms.

'Your birthday is on a Friday if I'm not mistaken,' said Helena. 'What if we have a party on Friday night, and then we all go to the Dive on Saturday?'

But on her birthday, after school, Eva decided that we were going to the Dive.

'It's hot,' she said, as we changed out of our uniforms. 'Let's just go.'

Helena was in the kitchen making punch. Maria was there too, her elbows up, pushing a metal corer into peeled apples.

'No, I won't drive you to the Dive,' said Helena. 'I'm getting ready for *your* party. And I could do with your help. We're going to the Dive tomorrow, remember?'

'It's *your* party. It's not even Dad's. I want to go to the Dive. That's all I want to do for my birthday.'

'My goodness, what a brat you're becoming,' said Helena. 'Go and help your father set up in the garden.'

Eva stomped out of the kitchen, and I slunk after her.

'God help us,' Helena said to Maria as we banged out the screen door.

I followed Eva to the chook shed, where she was pulling her bike out through the low door.

'What are you doing?' I asked.

'We'll have to ride,' she said, throwing her bike onto the grass with a clatter and ducking back into the shed.

We rode slowly in the heat. The air was apricot, as though there were fires somewhere. Clouds were sucked together over one half of the sky while the other was a deep blue. I rode Eva's bike, and she rode Bea's because it was too big for me. I was still much shorter than Eva, who was tall but not womanly, with barely a trace of breasts or hips. I now had stretch marks across my hips and pointy breasts that I loathed, but was still not much taller than I had been a year ago. It was a long ride, and it was after five o'clock when we got to the Dive. The light was even more intense here, distilled in the pale walls of the quarry.

At the opening of the Dive there was a weatherboard bathing pavilion surrounded by a wooden boardwalk that dropped off to deep water. There was a set of steps leading from the pavilion into the water, so that ladies and the elderly could ease themselves in, and long wooden diving boards were set at various heights along the boardwalk. A couple of families were picnicking by the trees that fringed the great rough crater of the pool, and a green rowboat bobbed on the surface.

Boys dove from the pale tree-lined cliffs more than fifty feet above us. They bulleted into the water and burst back to air and the sound of cheers and whistles. I had a new sense of scale now that I would actually be swimming here, perhaps even diving. The cliffs were higher than Eva's roof.

We changed into our bathers and left our clothes and shoes in the baskets of our bikes. By the changing sheds we found Robert, a boy who had been in our class in primary school, and who now went to our brother school.

'Sixty foot at the crow's nest,' said Robert, lighting a cigarette. 'I dived it just before.' He swept his hand through his wet hair and flung the water onto the warm planks of the decking. 'I've dived it twenty-nine times.'

Eva gazed over at the cliffs. 'Can I have a cigarette?'

Robert grinned and glanced around. 'Alright, but follow me up there and I'll give you one behind the trees. Your folks here?'

Eva shook her head. Robert stubbed out his cigarette and walked off towards the cliff.

We followed at a slight distance. The air there smelled of dry bush, gumleaves and wet clay, like the heavy blocks we used in pottery class, our teacher slicing them into pieces with a string tied between two clothes pegs. I remembered Robert and the other boys taking the string and pretending to garrotte each other, leaving a clay line the colour of rust around their necks as if they had actually drawn blood.

As we walked along the edge of the Dive, it got steeper, and the sounds of voices and splashing, the thunk of the oars against the side of the rowboat, grew quieter, echoey.

Robert stopped under a towering ironbark and gave Eva a cigarette. 'Want one?' he asked me. I nodded. 'Only got two left now.' He looked into the packet, disappointed, but held it out to me anyway. We sat down against the furrowed bark, which caught in our hair. Robert picked a fat lump of sap from the trunk and crumbled it into sugar.

'This is suicide point just here,' he said. 'It's not as high as the crow's nest, but there's rocks and things in the water.'

'But not at the crow's nest?' I asked.

'Nah, it's safe as houses. I've dived it twenty-nine times.'

Eva laughed. 'You said.'

I studied Robert surreptitiously as we smoked. He had a small face with suntanned skin and freckles beneath his eyes. He was burned pink across the top of his forehead where he had pushed his wet hair back. His nose was flat, almost like a baby's, and his chest was still narrow and hairless in the dip at the neck of his bathing costume. There was something about him that seemed both young and old at the same time, like a jockey.

Robert was more at ease with us than most boys were, and when he told us that he had three younger sisters, I placed the way he spoke to us: storyteller-like; almost conspiratorial but also slightly patronising.

'You can't touch the bottom,' he said. 'No one I know has. They reckon it could be eighty foot deep.'

'Do you like having sisters?' I asked.

'They're a pain in the bum sometimes. But they're alright.'

Eva sucked hard on her cigarette, then stabbed it out in the dirt beside her leg.

'Come on,' she said.

We got up, brushing twigs and grit from our bare legs, and bark from our backs and hair. Eva led the way to where a cluster of boys were gathered at the highest point of the cliff.

We reached the boys just as one was taking a short run-up. He made three quick hops and then leaped into blank air. From where we stood we could not see the water below, and my stomach rose. The other boys ran to the edge. The splash seemed to take ages, then there was another pause and then a long whoop from below, answered by the boys, who cheered and whistled with their fingers in their mouths. They faced us.

'You girls gonna jump?' asked one, his voice hostile.

Eva stared them down.

'I bet you won't,' said another.

'I bet she might,' said Robert. 'I saw her get caned at school once, and she didn't even cry.'

'Go on then.'

We dropped our towels and walked to the edge. The cliff was solid clay, and the point where we stood formed a lip that jutted out over a scooped-out section so there was no chance of landing anywhere except the water. But the water was sickeningly far below. The head of the boy who had just jumped was tiny as it bobbed towards the pavilion. I retreated, unable to trust myself even to stand at the edge. Eva stepped forwards even further. Her toes gripped the ground, and her legs trembled.

'What are you doing?' I whispered.

She didn't answer me, just sprang up and jumped, a sleek pin-drop through the air.

'She did it,' Robert shouted. He rushed up beside me, and we both peered down.

Eva's face appeared, a flat disk against the sun-chipped water, cut by a huge grin. 'Yippee,' she called.

The boys didn't cheer as they had for their friend, but Robert gave a proud whistle.

'Your go, Lily,' Eva called up to me.

I shook my head and moved back, losing sight of her.

'I knew it,' said one of the boys.

I felt angry with myself. I had taken Eva's triumph and diminished it in the eyes of the cliff-top boys, allowed them an escape from the reverence they owed her. But I could not jump.

'Go on. You can do it,' Robert encouraged.

'Get on with it or get out of the way,' said one of the other boys. I stared down at my feet and backed away from the edge, and they resumed their leaping and crowing.

When it was just me and Robert left, he smiled at me.

'It's alright. Most girls would never do that. Most girls wouldn't even come up here.' His eyes flicked back to the edge. 'Do you want me to walk back down with you?'

'No, that's alright.'

'I might dive then,' he said. 'It'll be my thirtieth.'

'When did you turn fourteen?'

'Three weeks ago.'

'And you've dived thirty times since then?'

He looked pleased. 'I will have in a sec.'

Instead of taking a run-up like the other boys, Robert stilled himself at the cliff edge. He held his arms out in a T then pointed them above his head, rising up on his toes. He took a deep breath and sprang.

'Thirty,' he yelled as his stringy body arced out from the cliff.

I saw Eva picking her way back up the slope towards me, treading carefully over the spiky ground. I went and met her halfway, and she put her arm through mine and pressed my elbow against her wet side.

'Did you see Robert dive?' I asked.

She nodded. 'He's good.'

The mozzies were out by the time we slung our towels over our shoulders and got back on our bikes. I watched Eva's hunched back and pumping knees as she pedalled fast ahead of me along the track to the main road. I replayed her jump again in my mind, the terrible distance of the water and the eye-blink speed of her body dropping through the air like a stick off a bridge. There was a ravenousness to the way she lived lately; the heat of her desires became fuel for motion, instead of torpor as they did for me. Eva believed that she could make things happen just by wishing for them, and for things to happen was her main wish.

When we got to Whitehorse Road, Eva put a foot down on the gravel and twisted to face me, still holding the handlebars.

'I don't feel like going home yet, do you?'

'What about the party?'

'Let's go to the pictures instead.'

'Won't Helena be worried?'

'It's *my* birthday.'

We turned into Whitehorse Road and pedalled to the Rialto.

'You know, I had an awful dream last night,' said Eva as we sat waiting for the picture to start. 'I dreamed that Heloise killed Mamma and Dad.'

'That's horrible.'

'I wasn't even upset though, in the dream. It was sort of a relief. It only seemed horrible when I woke up.'

'How did she kill them?'

'I don't know. It happened on the landing. The house was all dark and I came upstairs and Heloise was just standing there with them, dead. And I just knew in the dream that she'd killed them and I felt like I'd been waiting for it to happen. And then I woke up.'

'Strange. But you wouldn't be relieved in real life.'

'No.' Eva hesitated.

The lights began to dim, and the long red curtain swished aside.

'I *almost* wish Mamma would die sometimes lately,' Eva continued in a whisper, her breath smelling of peppermints.

IX

By the time we got back to the house, the driveway and the lawn were packed with cars. Music was coming from the back, and we threw our bikes down on the white gravel and walked around the side of the building to the half-moon clearing. The scale of the party was almost as shocking as Eva's sudden leap from the cliff. People were packed so densely into the clearing that we would have to push to get from one side to the other. There was a jazz band beside the house, with a double-bass and trumpet, and a drummer standing behind two upright snares. Braziers ringed the clearing, lighting up foliage as though we were on the edge of a jungle.

Eva and I stared at each other.

'There's your mother,' I said.

Helena had just emerged from the side door with Jerome. She was wearing a slim dress of cream silk and an emerald necklace. She was impossibly glamorous, too glamorous to be somebody's mother.

Helena leaned against the wall as though she could not quite stand unaided. Jerome lit her cigarette, and she tilted her head back as she inhaled. Eva walked towards them. Helena only noticed her daughter when Eva was right next to her. She took a step forwards and slapped Eva across the face.

'Where have you been?' she said.

I gasped in the same breath as Eva and Jerome.

Helena looked at Jerome and then smiled as if to reveal a joke. She put out her arm and pulled Eva in to her, squashing their bodies close. 'Brat,' she said. 'You missed the cake. It had your name on it.'

Eva jerked away.

'Where have you been?' Helena called after her. 'You look like a drowned rat.'

I followed Eva with difficulty into the throng of people. I recognised Dora Fisk, Vera, but the rest were strangers. We pushed through to the back of the clearing where the braziers sat in the trench of earth along the garden beds.

'Dadda,' said Eva, relief passing over her like a hand.

'The birthday girl,' said Patrick, who was squatting with Evan beside a brazier. I smelled the now-familiar scent of reefer. Evan held out his arms, and Eva fell into them, knocking him over.

'Mamma slapped me,' she said into his armpit.

'She made me cut the cake without you,' he replied, his backside in the trench and his feet in the air, one arm around his daughter and the other holding out a joint. 'I felt like a jilted bride.'

'We hate her, don't we?' said Eva, sitting back and wiping at her face.

'You look like you've been in the drink,' said Evan.

'We went to the Dive. I jumped from the cliff. It's sixty feet high.'

Evan whistled.

'There's a present for you inside from Vera and me,' said Patrick.

Ugo and Maria wandered over to our little break-away group.

'Maria and Jerome are going to join our circle,' said Evan. Maria nodded and smiled at Eva. 'They'll be exhibiting in the group show. Isn't that terrific?'

'I've been meaning to ask you,' Ugo said to Evan. 'Could Maria come and paint with me here during the day? You wouldn't believe the space she's working in at the moment. She practically has to paint in bed.'

'I'm hungry,' said Eva.

'There's cake over there,' said Maria. 'It has your name on it.'

'I know,' said Eva.

We got up and pushed our way back to the house, the hunched forms of Evan and the others disappearing as soon as we entered the crowd. The cake sat on a board on a wheeled trolley, the kind that brought around ribbon sandwiches and sweets in the tearoom at George's.

Eva laughed. 'It does have my name on it.'

Only the bottom right-hand corner of the cake remained. It was covered in white icing with piped edges and was dotted with silver cachous. All that was left of the lettering, done in a thin jam cursive, were the words *& Eva*.

'Happy birthday, me,' she said.

We did not talk about the slap. It was not particularly remarkable. Instead, that night, Eva told me things about her family that I had never heard before, as well as some that I had. We had retreated to the roof platform with supplies. Cake, blankets, a candle, a bottle and a half of stolen wine, and some of Evan's reefer. We ate the whole hand-wide square of cake with Eva's name on it and swigged from the half-bottle of wine.

'Why don't your cousins ever visit for your birthday?' I asked. 'I've never even met them.'

'We don't see them,' said Eva, licking icing from her fingers.

'Why not?'

'I don't know. 'Cause of Dad. He says he adopted Patrick as his brother because his real brothers are petty criminals.'

'I thought they were lawyers.' I passed the bottle back to Eva.

'They are.' She laughed. 'Apparently they were all criminals for a while. Dad says they became very naughty boys after

74

his mother was killed. His dad was an alcoholic. Dad hates them all now.' She held up the almost-empty bottle and then set it on the deck with a hollow clunk. 'Oh no, we forgot a corkscrew.'

'Damn.'

Moths were singeing themselves on the candle flame, spinning and whirring on their backs on the boards. The light went on in the attic, and Heloise appeared, her hair an amber gloriole. She opened the window and moths rushed past her into the lit room. She started to clamber out to the roof.

'Helly, Helly, wait,' said Eva. 'Will you do us a favour?'

'What?' asked Heloise with suspicion.

'We need a corkscrew. Will you fetch one from the kitchen?'

Heloise made a sulky face and slackened her shoulders.

'We'll give you some wine,' Eva coaxed.

'Alright.' Heloise hoisted her leg back inside and disappeared.

'What kind of criminal was your dad?' I asked, after Heloise had returned and been banished once more with the inch of dregs from the first bottle of wine.

'Oh, I don't know,' said Eva, rolling a clumsy joint. 'He'll tell you. He loves to talk about it. I'm surprised you haven't heard it before. Will you open the wine?'

'I've heard him talking about his dad and how he used to let them put on plays and sword fight with real knives,' I said, clamping the cold bottle between my knees and trying to get the corkscrew in the middle.

'Mmm,' said Eva, smoke in her chest.

'Your mother's an only child, isn't she?'

'Yep,' said Eva. 'Probably why she's such a brat. I mean … You're not a brat, of course. But then, you've got us.'

I was drunk already as we lay back on the hard boards, and Eva flounced the blanket over us and passed the joint. The stars kept blinking away and back again when I tried to hold my gaze on them. Later, I vomited cake and wine onto the attic floor as I crawled inside to rush to the bathroom.

We slept heavily, curled up in Eva's bed, until wine dreams woke us. I could hear music from downstairs.

'They're still going,' said Eva.

'Have you been awake long?'

'Not long. Do you want a cup of tea?'

We were wearing our bathing suits under our clothes, hadn't washed our hair after the Dive. We got up and went downstairs. The light was already paling towards dawn.

'Birds,' said Eva. 'What a wretched sound.'

We slid our socked feet along the hallway. The gramophone was playing in the kitchen beside the open door. Outside, the fire was dead and the air was cold. The artists were still gathered around the black ring of ash as though they hadn't noticed the fire was out. Everyone else was gone.

'Australia doesn't have a bloody cultural identity to assert,' Patrick was slurring as we approached.

'Well, that's what we're doing, isn't it? Making one,' said Jerome.

'Hear, hear!' said Evan. He was holding a pipe, his head leaning against Maria's shoulder.

Maria sat forward, breathing out smoke. 'If you'd seen what I've seen in Europe, Jerome, you wouldn't be so sure,' she said.

'Oh, fuck off, Maria. I've been to Europe,' said Jerome.

The light was increasing as we stood there, observing the wreckage of the previous night.

'This is horrible,' said Eva. 'Let's get tea.'

We slung our arms around each other and went back inside without being noticed.

'Maria and Jerome are always around now,' said Eva at school a few weeks later. It was the lead-up to the exhibition, and whenever I visited the Trentham house, it seemed even more chaotic than before. 'So many egg nights,' Eva complained. 'All Ugo does is paint. He hasn't made dinner for ages. And they're always talking about the bloody exhibition. Dad fired Mrs Mullins, so no one's even cleaning anymore. She told Dad that we're neglected children.' It was true; now, more than ever, the girls were left to their own devices, allowed to create their own small democracy in which law would always be decided by age or the ability to make the loudest protest, in which Beatrice was inevitably the ruler, Heloise was the rowdy proletariat, uprising and changing the course of a decision with her sheer vociferousness, and Eva was the silent majority, usually happy to keep the peace. If the addition of Ugo, of even one extra member of the household, had its effects, throwing still more off balance the already rudderless boat that was the Trenthams' family life, imagine the extent of their freedom and neglect when another three individuals were added to the household. Two of these were Maria and Jerome, the new members of the Melbourne Modern Art Group. The other was myself.

2

The Circle

X

'Family,' Helena told us, when Heloise asked why so many people were moving into their home, 'should be the people you choose to surround yourself with, not the people you happen to be related to. Like Lily, she's almost another sister that you've chosen.'

Hearing this, I was filled with elation.

But Heloise was unsettled. 'Would you have chosen us?' she asked, her forehead lined.

'Of course I would, my love,' replied Helena breezily.

Heloise bit her lip, gazing at her mother's face. 'But how do you know if you met us and we weren't your children if you'd like us or not?'

'Oh, don't be silly,' said Helena, standing up from the couch and smoothing down the linen of her pants. 'Of course I'd like you. Anyway, children are different. You make them with the person you've chosen to spend your life with, so you almost get to choose them.'

Yet the truth is, despite Evan and Helena's experiment in the redefinition of family, you cannot choose those people you are born to. I wonder if Evan and Helena ever thought of themselves as the source from which their own children would run in time, the blood whose welling-up their daughters would try to staunch with the tourniquet of friends, lovers and children.

The flooding of the Trentham household did not occur all at once. But I was witness to the turning on of the tap; the statement of intent that began it all. In a sense, Ugo moving into the Trentham house was more accidental than deliberate. He had been homeless, newly part of things, and he had been offered a place to stay. Now, things were being formalised on different terms.

One Friday night at dinner, Evan clinked his knife against his wineglass. He was at the head of the table, and had been sitting in a tipsy silence for some time. He had crumbs of bread in his beard. The other artists were all there, as was Vera. The long kitchen was filled with the sounds of simultaneous conversations, several of them heated and polemical, others merely drunken. Helena was on Evan's left, and next to her, Maria. Maria and Helena were arguing in a good-natured manner about some art-world controversy. Maria was waving her hands, and Helena was shaking her head and smiling sceptically. Maria was the only person from whom Helena tolerated disagreement. Not even her children were allowed to disagree with Helena, but perhaps she recognised Maria's insubordination as part of her nature. Maria criticised anyone whose actions she perceived as falling short of her own brash idealism, but her arguments with Helena seemed to intensify rather than diminish their sisterly intimacy.

Next to Maria was Ugo, and opposite him Patrick. Patrick and Ugo were talking intently, leaving Vera, beside Patrick, to converse with 'the children' at the end of the table. Vera was interminably the odd one out in the gatherings at the Trentham house. She was a reserved, private woman, and was, it seemed to me, actively shunned by Helena and Maria. Though Helena, the only other non-artist, should have been her natural ally, there was a coldness between the two women, as if the presence of the other reminded each of her status within the group as a wife rather than a member in her own right.

Jerome was opposite Helena, to Evan's right. Down our end, Eva and I were talking together, while Vera attempted to engage Bea in conversation, and Heloise announced her boredom by making patterns in her uneaten food.

'What do you think you might do when you complete your studies, Beatrice?' asked Vera.

'Oh, I'm really not sure yet,' Bea replied in a polite but weary tone.

When Evan clanged on his glass, conversation stopped, and everyone turned towards him. He had a habit of drifting in and out of discussions, but always demanded to be heard when he had something to say. He liked to hold forth in the mock-grand, sermonising mode of a painter-preacher. He raised his glass, and then noticed that it was empty.

'An announcement,' he said. 'I'm out of wine.'

The others laughed and began to resume their interrupted conversations. Patrick refilled Evan's glass.

'No, but in all seriousness,' Evan continued. 'Helena and I have been scheming.'

Even Eva began to pay attention at this. 'What now?' she whispered.

'I've always thought that I was a loner at heart. I've always worked alone. Work alone, drink in company, that's my motto.'

'Or alone,' Patrick added.

'Yes, I'm more flexible on the drinking I must admit. Anyway, since Ugo moved in I think I'm changing my mind.' Maria and Jerome looked at Ugo, who seemed pleased.

'Having you all around,' Evan gestured to Ugo, Jerome and Maria, 'has filled me with a very uncharacteristic sense of community.'

'I'm glad,' said Maria.

'Helena's noticed a change in me, haven't you, my love?'

Helena nodded. 'Much less grumpy.'

'Can't say *I've* noticed that,' said Bea. Helena shot her a look.

'Hush, progeny,' said Evan. He clinked his glass again. 'Order, order.'

'Just get to the point, Evan,' said Helena.

Patrick and Vera were exchanging perplexed glances.

'Yes, alright.' Evan gulped his wine. 'Helena and I see an opportunity. To squander her family fortune. To take advantage of what we have here. This house. This refuge from the tyrannies of the world. Nothing would please me more than to share this refuge with like-minded compatriots. Why should I be the only old bugger to be allowed the luxury to absent myself from my civic duty, from interaction with the frankly asinine majority, to closet myself away and not give a bandicoot's arse about what anyone else thinks or does or claims I should be thinking or doing. I've been living blessedly free, especially of the petty ... fucking petty concerns of the art market. As you know, I'm far from a capitalist, but I have to admit I've enjoyed reaping the benefits of capitalism. And one of them, and I'm not unaware of the irony of the situation, is getting away from the capitalists. The bastards who try to tell me my labour's not worth anything in the exchange market unless I'm producing something like cars or shoes or cheese –'

'Oh god, Evan,' Helena cut in. 'You're ranting.'

Evan eyed her with irritation. 'In short, then, my darling ...' He sat up straighter in his chair and cleared his throat. 'Helena and I would like to invite you all to come and live with us here. We'd love to take in a few more strays, and we invite you all to quit your jobs and join our commune. Work and live side by side. So we can *all* thumb our noses at the rest of the world.'

Helena smiled magnanimously around the table. 'My uncle Bertrand, despite being deeply and unapologetically a capitalist bastard, in Evan's definition, would have been thrilled. He was a cultured and generous and actually quite an irreverent man. He would have relished the idea of his home becoming an artists' colony. Would have dreamed up all kinds of debauches for us.'

Evan laughed and nodded.

Helena's eyes grew moist as she recalled her uncle. 'I would feel privileged to share his legacy with you all. Mainly because I believe so strongly in the work you are all doing. I think that the talent in this room is astounding.'

A hush fell over the other artists. Their faces held expressions more of uncertainty than excitement.

Patrick dabbed at the edge of his mouth with his napkin. 'Goodness,' he said. 'I had no idea you two were planning this.'

The silence continued for another couple of seconds, teetering towards awkwardness.

Then Ugo raised his glass. '*Na zdrowie!* Cheers!'

'Cheers! Cheers!' the others chorused.

The room became noisy again. Jerome stood and shook Evan's hand and kissed Helena formally on the cheek. At this gesture, the others also began to rise from their seats, and soon everyone was standing, their plates abandoned, hugging and kissing one another with an air of celebration that was still somehow subdued by a lack of reality.

Things moved rapidly after that night. Jerome and Maria were pleased to be joining the household. They and Ugo were inseparable, and the two of them moved in after a matter of weeks. For Ugo and Maria, there were very real benefits of patronage from Evan and Helena. Most importantly, it allowed them to work on their art full-time rather than around the low-paying jobs they would otherwise have had to continue. Ugo had come to the Trentham home with hands scalded and blackened from the bitumen he worked with in his road-building job. Maria had been working in a clothing factory, which she said was ruining her eyes, and sometimes as a life-drawing model.

Jerome was different. He was the only son of a wealthy grazing family from Ballarat. He had been educated in the most prestigious boarding schools, and had only recently decided to pursue his art full-time, after dropping out of a law degree at the University of Melbourne. Although his father had cut off his allowance when he abandoned his studies, he was currently living with an aunt in Toorak, and his mother secretly ensured that he did not need to work.

Helena and Maria were close, though their backgrounds could hardly have been more different. But a wordless communication between Jerome and Helena was apparent from the start. They understood one another. They were from the same world, and both knew the shame and the advantages of privilege. Where Helena's relationship with Maria was intimate and sisterly, and with Ugo it was playful and uneven – characterised by reverence on his side and affectionate indulgence on hers – her friendship with Jerome was that of complicit recognition between equals. When they spoke to one another, Helena dropped the slight air of tolerance that she failed to disguise in her conversation with others. They spoke the same language: articulate, self-assured, imbued with significance.

The initial uncertainty of the group gave way to elation, and the circle was never closer than in the following months, when their sense of community, their belief in the freedom and opportunity that had been offered to them all, was new. There was more planning and rule-making than Evan's speech would have implied, and this seemed to come mostly from Helena. She insisted that the point of everything was that the artists were to work together, and it was decided that the former stables, located not far from the kitchen, would be repaired and converted into an enormous shared studio. At first, Maria was resistant to the idea of working communally, claiming that she could not paint alongside the others, but at some point her resistance was toppled. Evan had been filling the downstairs rooms of the house with his work and supplies – stores of canvas, large glass bottles of turpentine and linseed oil, rolls of thick paper and stacks of masonite boards, and an old wooden dresser brimming with brushes of all sizes, notebooks, paint-stained palettes, knives and glass jars, pencils and charcoal. These rooms were all to be requisitioned as bedrooms now.

While the stables were being renovated, work on the exhibition paused. Everyone helped out with the building. The stalls had to be demolished, a job that took place one cold night, lit by a huge industrial lamp that cast leering shadows around the cavernous space. Ugo and Evan, staggering drunk, held wooden-handled sledgehammers, and they wheeled and crashed around the stalls, tearing into the ancient wood while Helena, Maria, the three girls and I watched from where we sat on the floor, wrapped in blankets, on a decaying Persian carpet. The women held glasses of wine, and we all laughed and cheered as the partitions were felled. Eva, Heloise and I begged to partake in the destruction, but when we were presented with the sledgehammers we could hardly lift them, and certainly couldn't swing them with any aim. Eva held hers by the end of its handle and twirled in a circle, the hammer swinging out perpendicular to her slight body. 'Whoa, whoa,' Evan shouted as Eva spun towards him.

The general mood was one of irrepressible energy. Ugo, Jerome and Maria slept in the stables while the work was being done, despite the cold. Ugo had his own room inside, but they all seemed to enjoy working until late and then putting down their saws, hammers and paintbrushes, and picking up glasses and cigarettes, drinking and smoking until they fell asleep amongst the debris. They left the big wood sliding door ajar all night, and woke when the sun reached their makeshift beds of blankets and pillows on the dusty Persian rug by mid morning. Only the extending of electrical wiring from the main house to the stables was done by a contractor. When the roof was mended, a skylight added and the floor sealed, Evan, Ugo, Jerome and Maria moved into their new studio. They helped one another cart bits of furniture, easels, stretchers and canvas, paints and brushes, and other paraphernalia into the new studio.

Patrick and Vera were the only ones to have declined Evan and Helena's offer to join the community of strays. Helena blamed Vera, saying that she kept Patrick on a tight leash and cared more about maintaining control over him than about what was best for his career. It was true that Patrick seemed wistful about not moving in. He helped out with the renovations on the stables during the day, when Vera was at rehearsals, but then went home for dinner, despite Helena's insistence that he telephone Vera and tell her to join them. He eyed Helena pleadingly as he backed out the door with a still-cheery departing wave. Evan sighed whenever the matter of Patrick and Vera was raised. He was clearly upset by it, telling Helena in the kitchen when the other artists were out of earshot that he didn't know if he would have gone ahead with the plan if he'd suspected that Patrick might not participate; that they should have discussed it with him first. 'You know it wouldn't have been Patrick's choice,' Helena whispered.

One Saturday morning, a couple of months after Maria and Jerome moved in, Eva and I came downstairs, snatched some bread and butter from the scullery and headed for the back door into the garden.

Helena was in the kitchen, and as we pushed open the screen door she warned Eva, 'Your father's out there and he's in a foul mood. You'd better leave him alone.'

Instead of avoiding him, Eva went straight to the half-moon clearing to find Evan. He was there, slumped on the wooden sun bed, one leg draped over the side. He wore paint-stained work pants and a blue woollen jumper that was too short for him. His white stomach was visible in a line between the pants and the frayed edge of the jumper, and a trail of coarse red hair led down into the low-slung pants. It was a bright morning, and Evan seemed to be dozing in the spring sunshine. A half-full glass of whiskey was resting on his chest. His right hand was cupped over the glass, and his chin had sunken down onto his hand. Eva ran over to him.

He roused himself and gave her a kiss. 'Hello, chook,' he said.

'Hello, Dad. What are you doing?'

He gave her a sad smile. 'Brooding, just brooding.'

'When did you get up?'

'I've not gone to bed yet. I was painting all night. Well, I was trying to paint.' Evan's speech was slow, and I realised that he was drunk. 'Can you keep a secret, chook?' he asked, putting his hairy arm around Eva's waist.

Eva squirmed in his grip. 'What, Dadda?'

'I've lost it, chook. Can't paint anymore. We've got this show coming up …' He trailed off. 'It's all these bloody *youngsters* around that's done it.' For a moment I thought he meant me, but then he went on. 'These Ugos and Jeromes, at the start of things. All excited as if they've *invented* fucking abstraction themselves. I'm old, chook. I've had my day.'

'But, Dad,' said Eva, 'you're not even forty.'

'Ah, forty. How I hate to hear that word. You should know, chook, never to say that word around me.'

Eva stroked his bushy red beard. 'Don't be silly, Dadda.'

Evan grunted in response, letting go of Eva and swinging his legs off the sun bed. He set his glass down, not noticing when it tipped over and spilled onto the grass, and swayed off to piss on the hydrangeas.

I had been standing back from this scene, but as Evan rose I caught the scent of him. The turps and oil paint that stained his hands and clothing, and the sweat of his armpits, not sharp or acrid, but pleasantly musty.

XI

The opening of the debut exhibition by the Melbourne Modern Art Group was held on the ninth of October, 1936. It was a Friday night, and I was in a frenzy of anxiety because no one had said anything to indicate whether or not I was invited. I was too embarrassed to ask Eva; I could not think of a way of asking that would not reveal how much consideration I had been giving the matter. I still regularly stayed at the Trenthams' on Fridays, and I had brought a change of clothes to school with me. There was nothing unusual in this, but I had deliberated over the clothing I was bringing for hours the night before, not wanting it, in its formality, to imply that I assumed I would be attending the opening, yet also not wanting it to be so casual that, were I to be taken along, I would feel inappropriately dressed. My mother asked me on Friday morning whether I was going to Eva's after school, and when I answered, 'I suppose so,' she mortified me by responding:

'Isn't Evan's exhibition opening tonight?'

'Oh, that's right,' I said.

'Well, maybe you should just stay home tonight then. You don't want to get in the way.'

'I won't get in the way.' Panic crept into my voice.

'Well, make sure you check with Helena first. I'll ask her for you if you like.'

'No, don't,' I blurted out.

'Sweetheart, don't just go over there without asking. I know you probably want to be around to see all the

90

preparations, but this is an important night for them. They might prefer to just be together as a family.'

'You don't understand,' I said. 'They don't care about that stuff. They have lots of people around all the time. They won't even notice if I'm there or not. And anyway,' I added, desperately, 'Eva might want some company while her parents are so busy.'

'Alright,' my mother relented. 'You can go for after school, but not for the exhibition. Come home by dinnertime so you're not a nuisance. And make sure you ask permission first.'

I hurried from the house as soon as I could to avoid further discussion.

I was probably more aware of the fact that tonight was the opening than Eva was herself. She didn't mention it at school that day, and at the end of the day she simply asked, 'Are you coming over tonight?' as if it was any other Friday. I felt giddy as we walked arm in arm to the train station, playing our usual game, involving one of us attempting to walk in time with the other, while the other tried to avoid being walked in time with. This led to such a strange, hopping, arrhythmic gait that we always ended up laughing hysterically, pulling on each other for support and lurching all over the pavement. Some of the other girls in our class aimed disdaining glances at us as they passed on their way to the station, but this pleased us.

Eva delighted in being thought immature by certain girls in our class. She pitied them their desire for maturity, the way they shed laughter as if it was tainted with the germs of childhood. The very way they moved changed. They became stiff, sitting with their knees and ankles firmly together and their feet set in a pert tiptoe. They hastened to the washroom as soon as the final class of the day finished, to apply powder before they left the school grounds. Eva scorned these girls, but I recognised in them the blight of self-consciousness. One suppressed snicker from another girl was enough to render these girls mute for the rest of the day. I knew this because

I felt it myself. It was only around Eva that I was able to abandon the stiffness of the other girls, and then only because with Eva there were different expectations. She expected me to be as free and childish as she was, and she was the only girl in our class whose opinion truly mattered to me. Eva seemed a tourist among her schoolmates. Her home, with its many inhabitants, its opportunities for community or solitude, was her native country. Her sisters were her compatriots and fellow tourists in the outside world, and she knew that she could always go home.

When we had walked from the train station to the house that afternoon, along the road that had once been bordered on both sides by orchards and was now being subdivided and built on, the new houses set close to the road as though afraid of being passed unnoticed, we found a pandemonium waiting for us. Heloise was standing beside the front door by herself, crying. When she saw us approaching, she ran off. Eva shrugged at me, and we entered the house and walked through to the kitchen, where there was a mess of champagne glasses and dirty dishes. Maria and a very thin blonde woman I had never seen before were standing behind the counter, sipping champagne and laughing. There was shouting coming from deeper within the house, and Maria rolled her eyes at us. The voice was Evan's. Helena strode into the kitchen, towelling her damp hair with one hand.

'Get ready please, Eva,' she said when she saw her daughter.

'Hello, Mother. It is so very lovely to see you too.' Eva walked past Helena and the other woman, and I followed behind, aiming an ingratiating smile at Helena as I passed.

Helena did not smile back, but gazed through me before turning to Maria and the blonde woman. 'I'm sorry, Georgina. My husband is being a temperamental artist today.'

'No, no, not at all,' the blonde woman replied. 'I don't need anything. Dora just sent me in case I could be helpful. Just pretend I'm not here.'

I followed Eva as she clumped up the stairs, dragging her school satchel behind her.

'Bea!' she shouted as she reached the top.

'I'm in here,' Bea called from her room.

We walked towards her door, and Bea appeared in the frame. She was dressed for the opening already, in a dusky pink dress. It was tight across her chest, with tiny sleeves that accentuated the curve of her shoulders.

'You look beautiful, Bea,' I said.

'Thank you, Lily.'

'Who's that woman in the kitchen?' asked Eva. 'And why is Dad shouting?'

Bea groaned. 'I've no idea. I'm trying to stay away from everyone. They're all in a foul mood, especially Mamma. The lady in the kitchen is from the gallery. Let's get ready and have some champagne, shall we?'

I was feeling increasingly nervous about my presence on this volatile occasion. Helena had only told Eva to get ready, as though she had assumed I was not coming to the opening.

'What should I do?' I managed to ask as Eva opened the door to her room.

'What do you mean?'

'I mean, I didn't really think about the opening. Maybe I should go home. It's an important day for your family.'

'It's not so important. Dad has had lots of openings. Haven't you been to some of them?'

'No, none.'

'Hmm, that's strange. I'm sure I remember you coming to the last one at Gallery First. Anyway, it's not a family occasion, I can assure you. We just get dragged along and left to hang around the gallery until all hours, while Dad gets drunk and Mamma and Dora sell his paintings. Then we have to go to some late dinner and end up getting no sleep and missing school the next day. That's the best part about it. That's why it's annoying that this one's on a Friday.' She smiled at me, and I felt reassured. It seemed ridiculous that I had been so worried. What I had told my mother was true. No one would even notice if I was there or not.

That night was a kind of coming out, or so it felt to me, into the world. It was suffused with a glow the colour of the champagne that was being handed around in shallow, stemmed glasses. The gallery was warmly lit and everything glittered. The parquet floor was so shiny that it seemed to be covered by a film of water, like sand at low tide. The bulbs of the low-hanging lights were multiple rising moons. Glass sparkled and clinked. The room was full of people when we arrived: people who were more interesting, more glamorous, than any group of people I had seen before. There were women in long skirts of flowing fabrics, cinched at the waist. Long strings of pearls hung from their swanlike necks.

Eva, Heloise and I had arrived with Evan and Helena. Bea was following with Patrick and Vera. When Evan walked into the gallery, there was an audible stir. People spun around to see him arrive, and two photographers came forward and began to take pictures. At first Evan seemed to be on the point of lowering his head and ducking away, but Helena took his arm, and they smiled together as the camera flashes burst onto us, leaving a ring of slow-fading white when I closed my eyes. Dora Fisk hurried over and took Evan's other arm, drawing him into the crowd, who began to put out their hands to him. We were left in the doorway, gazing around at the suited men and beautiful women, craning our necks to catch a glimpse of the paintings we had all seen being made – the canvas pulled tight and tacked onto the pine frames, the white gesso applied, seeping into the canvas and drying stiff in the crevices of the woven fabric, the paint brushed or smeared on layer by layer – over the past months in the stables studio at home.

I caught sight of Ugo and Jerome to the left of the bar, smoking. 'There's Ugo.'

'Where?' said Heloise.

'Over there, with Jerome.'

'Let's go over.'

We began eddying towards them between groups of people. As we got close, Ugo saw us and winked. But at that moment a tall woman in a black gown moved in and held out her hand, tucking her programme beneath the opposite arm and saying something we couldn't hear. Ugo and Jerome angled their bodies towards her, forming a closed triangle. We hesitated by a long table where champagne glasses were arranged in rows. Bea entered the gallery with Patrick and Vera, and came over to us. We stood in silence for a while, our backs to the table. Then Ugo appeared next to Heloise, reaching around and tapping her on the opposite shoulder so that she swung around to where no one was standing and then back again. She saw Ugo and beamed. Her smile was transparent. It filled up her whole sweet freckled face, and even her pixie ears made a happy upward movement.

'That woman wants to buy one of Jerome's paintings,' whispered Ugo, gesturing with his shoulder to the tall woman behind him, still in conversation with Jerome.

'*Really?*' said Heloise, mimicking his hushed tone.

'I think he is going to be the star of the show.'

Bea frowned sceptically, pulling in her chin.

'What about you?' asked Heloise, with no trace of disingenuousness.

Ugo shrugged. 'I sold one before the show opened, but nothing tonight so far.'

'What about Dadda?'

'Heloise, shut up,' said Eva.

'Oh, your dad will sell,' said Ugo. He fell silent for a moment and then shrugged again. 'Champagne?' He picked up two glasses from the table, handed one to Bea and one to Heloise. 'You have to share that with Eva and Lily,' he said to Heloise. 'Don't drink it all by yourself.' He grabbed a third glass for himself and took a gulp. 'I'm going to find Maria.' He strode off into the crowd.

We all stared at his broad back as it pushed its way into the room. Then Eva turned to Heloise.

'Give me some champagne.'

'Wait, let me drink some first,' said Heloise, shielding herself with a raised elbow as she drank from the glass. 'Mmmm, it's really bubbly.'

'Enough,' said Eva. 'You'll get drunk.'

'No, I won't.' Heloise took another mouthful and held it in her bulging cheeks before she swallowed. 'Alright, here you are.' She made to pass the glass to Eva, and then at the last second gave it to me instead. 'Guests first,' she said.

Eva glared at her.

I took a quick sip and passed the glass to Eva.

'Give it back now,' said Heloise, trying to wrestle the glass from Eva's hand. Champagne sloshed onto the front of Eva's dress.

'Look what you've done!' said Eva, pushing Heloise roughly.

Heloise stumbled backwards and bumped into the table. The glasses clattered against each other and people turned towards the sound. Helena was visible across the room, and she glowered at us.

'Girls,' said Bea in a pinched voice. She walked away from us, and Heloise pouted, righting herself and smoothing down her skirt.

'Come on, Lily,' said Eva, taking my arm. 'Let's go and look at the paintings.' We left Heloise, alone and sulky by the table.

Some of these paintings I had seen before, in various stages of completion, in the studio. On the stark white gallery wall, though, outlined by wide frames, they assumed a new weight and significance. I saw Evan being interviewed by a journalist while a photographer took pictures. I noticed the intent gazes with which people examined the paintings on the walls, leaning in or back, their hands lightly touching their own faces, waists, hearts, as if to steady themselves against being unmoored from their bodies. I felt the same impulse myself as I approached one of Jerome's paintings. It was like a gash; a wound of colour in the white skin of the gallery wall. On its thick surface were faces that resembled masks, bodies made entirely of angles. The lines crossed and re-crossed, broke and splintered each other. It was a violent image, but perfectly balanced in the way it shattered the square of the canvas into segments. I had not seen this painting before.

'What does the red dot mean?' I asked Eva, who was standing with her arms folded.

'It means sold.'

Just then Jerome walked up to us, glancing at our faces as we examined his painting.

'What do you think?' he asked.

'I like it a lot,' said Eva. 'It's almost as if it's a painting of their thoughts more than their bodies.'

Jerome had an indulgent expression in his sharp eyes. Now he looked directly Eva. 'Yes,' he said, breaking into a smile. 'That's very astute of you.'

Jerome was dressed in a narrow charcoal suit that accentuated his angularity. I thought how handsome he was; not traditionally handsome like Ugo, but almost beautiful, with his austere features, visible cheekbones and neat hair. I thought of Ugo's prediction that Jerome would be the star of the show.

The exhibition was opened, in an echoey hush punctuated by the clink of glasses, by a man Dora Fisk introduced as Justice Herbert Evatt. Eva whispered to me that he was a high court judge, and owned a Picasso and a Modigliani. I looked around the room again, taking in the paintings, the women's clothes, the artists dotted amongst the crowd, and wondered how I had managed to be here. I felt mature beyond my years. I will wake tomorrow, I thought, and this night will be inside me still.

In bed, in the early hours of the morning, I played back my stored images of the night: Ugo handing us champagne;

the dreamy rush that crept through my body as I drank it, leaving me languid and wide open to the colours smeared within those magical frames adorning the walls; the way Jerome had smiled at Eva and me as he approached us; the sense of belonging to the inner circle I felt when the opening dwindled to an end and only the artists, Dora, the girls and me remained among the abandoned champagne glasses and programmes being cleared by the last waiters; the St Kilda apartment of Justice Evatt and his wife, where we went for dinner afterwards, and where Eva asked if she could show me their collection.

As I lay there, buoyed by these scenes, I realised that my mother had not telephoned to ask why I had not been home before dinner. I knew she would assume that I had wheedled my way in, imposing where I should have refused even the most heartfelt offer of invitation. I also knew she would be secretly envious. I shifted in bed, conscious of the importance of the people lying asleep in the same house and, in some fundamental way, of having surpassed my own parents.

XII

The morning after the exhibition, Eva and I woke late. The sunlight was casting a slanting square across my mattress on the floor beside Eva's bed. I was covered by a sheet and a red, ribbon-edged blanket that had not been warm enough during the night. Now, it was oppressively hot. My mouth felt caked, and my legs were clammy. I looked up at Eva, who was still asleep. She had kicked the bedding off in the night and was draped star-wise across her mattress, her face towards the wall, one leg thrust out behind her and the other bent up under her stomach. Her nightdress was bunched around her waist, revealing pink knickers whose looped elastic was coming away at the seams. Her foot was hanging over the edge of the bed, and I studied her ankle as she slept, the way her calf tapered to a sculpted tendon. I stuck my own foot out and kicked hers. She rolled over, tugging her nightdress down and smiling sleepily.

'What's the time?' she asked, sitting up.

'Almost eleven.'

'I'm famished.' She jumped out of bed and held out a hand to me. I let her pull me up, but resisted as we got to the door. 'Come on,' she said. 'Let's have breakfast.'

I crossed my arms over my chest, clothed only in a thin nightdress.

'I think I'll get dressed first.'

'Suit yourself.' She dropped my hand and ran towards the staircase.

The body was just about the only thing I had not changed my attitude to, under the influence of the Trenthams. They were as free around each other as children, apart, more recently, from Bea, who was growing into her own privacy. Evan, on the other hand, seemed to be naked increasingly often. As the days became warmer, he took to bathing outdoors every evening, unwinding the garden hose and filling the outdoor bath. He lit the fire beneath it, stripped down and stood around smoking in the sunlight as the water became tepid. Then he doused the flames and hoisted himself in, opening that day's newspaper above the bath and cursing as he attempted to turn the pages with wet hands. There was an element of voyeurism in me, and I sometimes engineered a trip to the kitchen as Evan was heating his bath, glancing furtively at his body in the sunlight. Evan loved to discuss the size of the organ he had been blessed with, joking that he could only put himself on the line as an artist because he was smugly aware of the superior tool within his trousers. Thinking back on it now, Evan's late-afternoon strutting in the garden coincided with the presence of two more men in the house, and was perhaps an assertion of his status as the alpha male.

As I came downstairs I paused on the bottom landing, listening for noises from the kitchen. I had expected the jubilance of the previous night to be spilling into the next day, a victory breakfast or dissection of the night's events and the reception of the controversial manifesto that had been printed in the exhibition programme. But I heard nothing from the kitchen. Then again, they were probably all still asleep. The festivities would resume in the afternoon. I walked into the kitchen, smelling toast and the hyacinths Dora had sent over the night before. The sun was splashing through the windows across the table. Eva and Bea were the only ones in the room. The way they glanced at me as I entered made me think that there was something the matter. Bea was sitting down, two newspapers spread in front of her, and Eva was standing behind her sister, her elbow on the back of Bea's chair, a piece of toast uneaten in one hand.

'Where is everyone?' I asked.

Neither answered me. Bea tapped Eva's arm to indicate that she wanted to get up. She went to the stove, picking up the kettle and shaking it to gauge how much water was inside. Eva sat down in Bea's empty chair and beckoned me over, and I walked around and took up the position she had occupied a moment before. The paper was open at the inside back pages. *Established artist eclipsed by protégé* was written in block letters above a short article.

'Oh no.'

'Mmm.'

The inaugural exhibition of the Melbourne Modern Art Group opened last night at Gallery First amid much controversy. Gallery First, once reputed for showing predominantly realist art by some of Australia's masters, has recently begun playing host to paintings in the new abstract style being imported to our shores from Europe. At the forefront of this movement is painter Evan Trentham. Regardless of what one thinks of Trentham's work, he has undeniably been a powerful force in the modernisation of Australian art. His work has been popular amongst collectors, including Justice Herbert Evatt, who launched last night's exhibition. The show contains the work of five artists brought together by Trentham under the banner of the Melbourne Modern Art Group. The group's contentious manifesto calls for an end to the conservative politics of the Australian art establishment, naming James MacDonald and others as the prime obstacles in the path of modernisation. These controversies were to be expected, and indeed were part of what attracted the large numbers in attendance at the opening. What came as a surprise, though, was that the star of the

night was not Trentham himself but little-known
painter Jerome Carroll, whose work sold out with the
exception of one piece, while Trentham sold only three
paintings. Justice Evatt told our reporter that he had
purchased work by both Trentham and Carroll at the
opening, and that he believes Carroll is destined to
become an important figure in contemporary painting.
The show runs until the end of October.

'That's not good, is it?' I asked Eva.

'No. *The Argus* is even worse, but in a different way. It just says the art was terrible and degenerate, but this one is …' She broke off, pursing her lips.

'Where are they all?'

'I don't know. Maria was here when I came down, but she didn't know where the others were. I don't know who went out and bought the papers. Oh, look at this too, it's funny.' Eva pulled *The Argus* over so that it covered the offending *Herald* article. 'This is the one that calls Dad a degenerate, but see the photo?' She pointed to a small image beside the text. The caption read: *Evan and Helena Trentham with their three daughters.* The picture had been taken at the gallery entrance as Evan and Helena entered. Eva pointed to the face of one of the girls beside the couple. It was me, standing with Eva and Heloise, instead of Bea, who had arrived after us with Patrick and Vera. I was gazing up at Evan and Helena, the epitome of proud and adoring daughterhood.

Whatever subtle or overt scuffles and jostlings may have resulted from the *Herald* article and Jerome's success on the opening night of the show were pushed aside almost immediately by ensuing events. After breakfast, Bea folded the newspapers and put them on the coffee table, from where they later vanished. Eva, Bea and I spent the afternoon in the library, draped over the couches, half dozing, lazy after the excitement of the previous night. We had not seen Jerome, Maria or Ugo all day, but Evan, Helena and Patrick were sitting outside drinking gin and tonic when the telephone in the hallway rang. I thought it might be my mother. Bea threw off the mohair rug covering her legs and went to answer it. I could not hear what she said, but the sharpness of her voice made it clear that something was wrong.

'Dad,' she shouted. I heard her say something else, and then her footsteps charged down the hallway towards the back of the house. Eva and I got up and stood in the doorway. Then Evan was racing towards the telephone, his long legs moving like shears.

'Dora,' he said into the mouthpiece.

Bea came back up the hall and stood behind Evan. Patrick and Helena appeared further down the passageway.

'Bea,' Eva hissed, beckoning to her sister.

'Bloody philistines,' Evan shouted, kicking the wall beside the phone table.

Bea ducked around her father and came into the library.

'What's happening?' Eva asked.

'The police have gone to the gallery and taken one of Dad's paintings. The one in the window.'

'The police?'

Evan, Helena and Patrick rushed off to the gallery, leaving us alone in the disquiet of the house.

At home that evening, my mother quizzed me about the exhibition.

'The opening sounded interesting, darling. Was it?' We were in the kitchen together. She was making me a hot cocoa, heating the milk in a miniature blue enamel saucepan as I leaned against the sink.

'It was brilliant. You should go and see the show.'

'Maybe I will.'

'Do you know where Gallery First is? Flinders Lane.'

'Oh, right in the city? They must make decent money to be in that location.'

'Well, Jerome's work sold out last night, and Evan's did well too,' I said, blushing slightly at the familiarity of these names on my tongue. I did not mention the police.

'Jerome Carroll, yes? I read that in the paper.' She paused for just a moment. 'The article wasn't very flattering though, I must say.'

'Conservative idiots,' I said.

'I have to admit, it did worry me a little bit,' my mother ventured. 'I mean, I don't have the faintest clue what goes on over there, but the idea of you spending so much time with people labelled degenerates in the newspaper –'

'Ma,' I cut her off. '*They* weren't labelled degenerates, their work was. And that's only because it's different. They're just normal people. Well, they're better than normal people really.'

'By normal people I suppose you mean your father and me?' She sounded hurt, but handed me the cup of cocoa in her motherly fashion.

'Well, in a way, yes,' I said, facing her with a new sense of separateness. 'And I love you both. But I want to be different.'

All evening I was preoccupied by what might be happening at Eva's and restless for the glinting, tumultuous action of her life. I felt it in my legs as I sat working on a puzzle with my father after supper. My mother noticed it and clucked that I was suffering from too much excitement and needed a quiet day tomorrow.

The next day after church, and Sunday dinner, with the house still smelling of pot roast and potatoes, when my mother was napping, her good shoes lined up beside the bed, and my father was twitching in and out of sleep in his armchair, I telephoned Eva.

It was Heloise who answered. I pictured her standing barefoot in the hallway by the library door. The geography of the house was mapped out around her in sound: I could hear the gramophone playing in the library, and shouting from further away.

'Could I speak to Eva, please?'

'I don't know where she is.'

'Oh. You can't call her?'

'I haven't seen her for ages.'

'Hmm. Alright. Will you ask her to phone me back?'

'Alright,' said Heloise, already fumbling the telephone away from her mouth.

'Wait,' I said. 'Heloise?'

'What?'

'Do you know what happened yesterday? With the police?'

'Oh,' said Heloise. 'I don't know. Dadda's very angry. Mr Evatt's going to help him though. He was here yesterday. Oh, there's Eva. Wait. Evaaaa.'

'It's horrible here today,' said Eva when she came on the line. 'Everyone's grumpy and mean. You can probably hear Dad. He's barely stopped shouting since yesterday.'

'What's going to happen?'

'He's probably going to be charged with obscenity. The vice squad have taken the painting.'

'Really? What is the vice squad?'

'I don't really know. The police. But the painting they took was the one Bert and Mary Alice bought, so they're going to help. Bert thinks it will be alright. I don't know. I just want to be away from here. I was about to go to the Dive. You could meet me there.'

'I can't,' I said. '*Mother* thinks I've had too much excitement.'

'Ha.' Eva laughed bitterly.

I hung up and went to my bedroom to rage in private against the vicious, carpeted stillness; against the horse picture on the wall; the passive stacks of schoolbooks on my desk; my father's quiet snores.

XIII

It was during a practice for our final exams that year that the principal's assistant came to the door of the classroom, whispered to Mrs Hazlitt, and then called my name. I went with her to the school office, where Mrs Granger, the principal, asked me to take a seat.

'Lily,' she said. 'I'm afraid there's been an accident. Your father has been injured at work. He's in hospital.'

Mrs Granger's assistant made me a cup of tea, and I sat by her desk under a row of coat hooks, fidgeting with the buckle of my belted school dress until Mrs Barker, our next-door neighbour, came to collect me and take me to the hospital.

My mother was in the corridor of the surgical ward. The ward was brightly lit and lined with a bank of metal-framed chairs. Nurses hurried past, their rubber soles squeaking. My mother was knitting and did not see us until we were close to her. She stood up and clasped her arms around me. Mrs Barker and the nurse stood back while we embraced and cried briefly, and then my mother sniffed and thanked Mrs Barker for bringing me.

My father had been on the floor of the factory where he worked as an engineer, building farming equipment, when a large piece of steel had fallen on him, trapping him under its weight and crushing his thighs. He was in surgery, and there was a danger that he might lose one or both legs.

We sat down on the hard chairs and waited. Beside my mother on the floor was my father's brown leather travelling bag, its hinged top open. I could see his striped pyjamas bundled inside, as well as his shaving brush and Brylcreem. It brought a tightness to my throat to see these worn, familiar items.

My mother began to knit again, a pale yellow jumper she was making for me. We had picked out the pattern together; it was to have a pearl button at the neck and slightly puffed sleeves. Over the following days my mother knitted almost without stopping: while she ate; while she talked to the nurses; while she sat by my father's bed. She fell asleep knitting in the chair beside him, woke up, continued to knit. She was like one of the fates, sullenly, determinedly knitting out the griefs of the world. Somehow my mother's anxiety, and my own, became entangled in the wool of that jumper, caught up in the purl of its weave so that it would always be tainted for me, as if it had absorbed the medicinal stink of the hospital, the image of my father, ashen, with his eyes closed, the thick sheets drawn up under his arms, the knobbly cotton blanket tight across his chest and over the bulky casts encasing both his legs, his toes protruding from the bedclothes so that their colour could be monitored – my mother and I had to fight the urge constantly to pull the blanket over them to keep them warm. I would never wear that jumper.

I arrived at each of my final exams that year with the scent of disinfectant and stale urine in my nose, and with my eyes aching from lack of sleep.

I stayed at Eva's for the first few days of the holidays after my father was brought home. Ever since the dinner at my parents' house years ago, there had been an uncomfortable distance between my mother and Helena. When my mother came to pick me up, to take me home to see my father for the first time since he had left hospital, she poured out the news about his accident to Helena in a tremulous voice, babbling fast as if afraid of being interrupted before imparting all of the essential information: how my father had lain there a full twenty minutes before the ambulance arrived and the metal was removed; how we feared his legs might be lost but miraculously were saved; how he had been bleeding internally and they had only just found out in time; how he would be off work for months, 'hanging around the house,' she said, though Helena failed to play her part in this predetermined women's dialogue about the annoyance of having husbands at home meddling with the delicate domestic mechanisms. The initial fear for my father's life had passed and had been replaced by terror over how they would cover the hospital bills and how long he would be unable to work. My mother was 'beside herself' at the prospect of the school holidays with me at home making a nuisance of myself while she took care of my father. Until then, Helena had been concerned, had shaken her head and frowned at the appropriate moments, but she interrupted my mother now.

'No, it will be lovely for you to have them both at home. I love having Evan and the girls at home. If I had my way we'd all be here all the time and they'd never go to school.'

Eva let out a snort of laughter, and Helena frowned at her.

'What? It's true,' she said with unfeigned hurt.

I was also dreading the coming summer. Inhabiting the Trenthams' huge house and garden was very different from living in each other's pockets in my parents' stifling house with its shoebox paved backyard edged with flower beds.

'Fancy one more?' my mother joked.

'Of course,' replied Helena seriously. 'Lily is no trouble at all. In fact, we'd love to have her stay for a few weeks, or even longer, if that would help you and Sam out, wouldn't we, Eva?'

'Yes!' said Eva, looking at me.

That day I arrived with my blue suitcase, the one my mother had taken on her honeymoon, was different from all the other days I had stayed at Eva's house. My mother walked me up the hallway, following Eva, who had opened the front door and greeted us. To the right, in the library, Maria was lying in the window seat, reading. I held my breath. If my mother had seen any one of the familiar tableau of the Trentham circle she would have spun me around and marched me straight back to the car. These were my secrets, the false bottom of my suitcase where the documents of my true allegiance were hidden. Maria as odalisque on the green chaise, being sketched by Jerome, who was still only learning the human figure. Evan in the late sun by the bath-fire, splashes of sienna at his chin, on his skull, between the kite-bones of his pelvis. Jerome and Ugo smoking reefer over a plate of Ugo's pierogies, swapping the joint for a pickled cucumber. Helena in her kimono at midday, flirting with Ugo at the vegetable patch as he pulled up carrots.

I left my suitcase at the foot of the stairs, and Eva and I made my mother a cup of tea. She sat in the kitchen with her hat and coat still on, glancing around for an adult, for reassurance that she was doing the right thing, leaving her daughter in the house of people who were not blood to her.

Eva chatted gently with her, told her she would take care of me. 'Mamma's gone out to get a duck for supper.'

The duck pacified my mother. I would be fed; fed better than at home. I saw the relief of the duck on her face. These were the days at the end of the Depression when wealth was less common than death, when my mother still extended her apple turnovers with choko.

She put a hand to my cheek briefly, as though wiping a spot of dirt. 'I'd best get back to your father,' she said, bustling herself up from the chair and carrying her teacup to the sink.

'It's lucky you didn't arrive earlier,' Eva said when my mother had left.

'Why?' I asked.

'Because Mum and Dad were having a giant row. He stormed off somewhere and she was ranting and raving and smashing things. Then she went to get the duck. Just before you arrived, really.'

'What were they fighting about?'

'I don't know. Some man.'

'What man?'

'Some man in Sydney. I tried not to listen. You know how they are. They'll probably be fine tonight. Anyway, I want to show you something upstairs.' She raced ahead of me.

When I reached her bedroom she was standing in the doorway with her arms spread.

'Tadaa!'

She had wrangled Ugo and Jerome to move another bed in, from where I did not know, and to move her chest of drawers from the side wall to beneath the window. It was now a tidy little dormitory for two, my own bed made up with a floral pillowcase and red blanket. She had even put a vase of lavender and geraniums by my bedside.

'I've cleared some space in the wardrobe too,' she said, opening the door and revealing a row of empty coat hangers.

That night, when Eva and I came down from our nest, the duck was on the table, brown and hideous and delicious, and there were two empty wine bottles beside the platter of Helena's carrots in cream. Ugo and Maria were carrying the last of the dishes over from the bench as Bea set the table. Evan and Jerome were talking, their chairs pushed back as though the meal was over already. Helena was sullen and removed from the conversation. The duck smelled of purplish meat and overwhelmed the room.

'Oh, you sliced the lettuce,' said Helena. 'I always like to tear it. It reminds me of Paris.'

Ugo rolled his eyes but grinned at her. 'I'm sorry if the lettuce is not sufficiently Parisian. We will have to create the Paris café atmosphere through our conversation, rather than with lettuces.'

Helena pursed her lips.

'So, I hear you're coming to stay for a while, Lily,' said Maria when we were all eating.

'Yes,' said Helena, a carrot on the end of her fork. 'Our newest little stray.'

Eva squeezed my arm, and I bubbled up with pride.

'Oh, while I remember,' said Helena. 'Bert and Mary Alice will be here tomorrow night. We've got to discuss Evan's obscenity case, of course, but they're very keen to see what we've been creating here since the exhibition.'

'I'm afraid I'm out,' said Jerome. 'I've got an assignation tomorrow evening.' He winked at Ugo as he said this, and Ugo laughed and shook his head.

'Is that the girl we met at Petrushka?' asked Maria.

'Mmm,' said Jerome, the constant blush of his cheeks increasing.

'What's an ass-ig-nation?' asked Heloise.

'I presume,' said Helena, her voice transforming as she addressed Jerome, becoming formal as polished cutlery, 'that it won't be too difficult to postpone, and that you will be here for the Evatts' visit. I wouldn't like to show your work without you.'

'Of course not,' said Jerome. 'But Bert just bought one of my paintings. I'm sure he's not going to buy another.'

'What's that word you said?' Heloise asked again.

'Quiet, Heloise,' said Helena. 'That's absurd, Jerome. I've arranged this dinner party for your benefit. I would take it badly if you weren't there.'

'I appreciate that,' said Jerome, cutting meat from bone in prim shreds. 'But you did neglect to tell me. I know I'm living here, but I'm not an exhibit. I've made plans.'

Helena fell silent. Forks coughed nervously against plates.

'I like Mary Alice,' said Heloise.

'Well, she won't like *you* very much if you keep talking at her all the time like you're doing now,' said Helena.

Heloise began to cry. 'I hate you,' she shouted, saliva shooting from her mouth. She shoved her chair back from the table, screeching it across the stone floor, and ran from the room.

'Christ!' said Evan.

'Let's go and sit in the library,' said Helena, once quiet had returned. 'I feel as though we need to restore civilisation.'

I was anxious after the dinner-table tussles, unused to open conflict, which seemed to me almost irrevocable. But incredibly, once we got to the library and brandy was poured, it was as though they had never happened. The artists gathered, pulling the cushions from the couches and flopping down on them. Bea went to her room, but Eva and I lay along the back of the cushionless couch, tired and happy to drift, with no homework to do and the holidays taking all urgency from our limbs.

Helena lit candles on the low coffee table, and Maria opened the windows to the slippery night air. The veils of the inner curtains rose and beckoned towards the dark openings, stirring up the smell of jasmine, and I felt bridal, at the start of a new life; even more so when Jerome picked up a copy of the banned *Lady Chatterley's Lover* and began to read aloud from it. He declared that he could write the erotic scenes better himself, and took up a pen and paper, scribbling away between swigs of brandy, and then read these new scenes aloud, to much hilarity from the others, who threw themselves back against the bare struts of the couches and the cushioned floor in fits.

'Jerome, you are killing me.' Helena choked on a mouthful of laughter.

Evan's laugh wound down like a creaky machine. He wiped his eyes. 'Oh, D.H. I love you dearly, but …'

'The thrusting, the thrusting,' Maria said, laughing. 'All the penetrating and thrusting into everything. The earth; the spring; the seed; the thrusting buttocks.'

Someone knocked the wedding cake of stacked books off the coffee table and onto Evan's leg, and he howled and cursed.

'I'm going to paste those scenes into the book,' said Helena. 'You're right, they were better than the original.'

Eva and I glanced at each other, aware that both of us had been quietly consuming, engorging on the knowledge of these adult games, that we would try out the same adult laughter later in our fresh-dusted dormitory. There was a darkness that fluttered at the edges of my feeling, a tiny trace of rot on the jasmine-scented air, aroused by these rumours of sex that wafted towards us on our chaste couch-back; but I swatted them away.

I looked around at this new family. Jerome was fanning his face with the sheets of paper he had been writing on. He seemed pleased with himself, boyish. Maria was lying back against the couch opposite me, her arms raised and her bangles sitting in a thick band above her elbow. Ugo, beside her, was bending forward to top up the glasses, his face concentrated. Evan and Helena were sitting on the floor in front of the couch that Eva and I were on, so I could not see their faces. But I felt, in that moment, so grateful to them for giving me this exotic life that had somehow, wonderfully, become mine.

Ugo put Billie Holiday's *Summertime* on the gramophone, and the way it slowed to drunkenness and was revived by the winding of a handle blurred into the rhythm of tiredness and alertness on this extended first night in my new home.

I jerked awake at the sound of Maria slapping her ankles.

'Spit on it,' said Evan. 'Stops the bites from itching.'

Maria got up and banged the windows closed, and it was bedtime, with no school tomorrow and my summer as a stray spread out before me, a hot, late-slept, new-wedded morning.

XIV

Until I met the Trenthams, it seemed to me that there were two kinds of people in the world: those like my father's family – practical people, unperturbed by the undercurrents and interpretations of events, with a robust ability to get on and achieve what they set their minds to; and those like my mother, who was the only member of her family I knew. My mother's parents had died before I was born, and although she had a sister with a child around the same age as me, there had been an enormous, unspeakable falling-out between the sisters, and I had never known either my aunt or cousin on my mother's side. The fact of the falling-out, though, suggested to me that my mother's family must operate as she did, attuned to anything that might activate her indignation or impinge upon her sense of moral certainty. She dealt in the implied and unsaid, the ways in which other women glanced at her or her new shoes and what these glances said about the inequalities between one woman and another in terms of their incomes, how they had survived the Depression, the generosity of their husbands, their valuing of beauty over comfort or health or the necessity of buying their children school shoes with seemingly ever-increasing frequency.

But that summer in the Trentham house I could see a different future, one that I felt I might belong in. I felt that I was no longer on the periphery of a life I imagined to exist somewhere out of reach, but that I had broken out of some brittle carapace and was unfurling in the sunlight. Around

Evan and the other artists I was learning the habit of attention, of noticing the world in all its ravishing detail and complexity. The habit of being amazed. They told stories, looking at objects and people until they shook them clean of the dust of everyday and made them myth. On warm evenings we trailed around the garden after Helena, on her wanders with her five o'clock gin and tonic. She pointed out plants to us, teaching us their botanical names. Ugo, Jerome and Maria went to Broken Hill and out into the desert, and came back with sketches dominated by skies, trees, windmills and water tanks; by space and wind. They brought back watercolours drenched in reds and ochres. We all went camping to Timboon. We caught fish, sat around the campfire late into the night. We went night-swimming. The cool prickle of fear and exhilaration in the deep black water.

What I also grew into that summer was the freedom that the Trentham household allowed.

'Robert tried to kiss me on Thursday,' Eva said matter-of-factly one night when we were lying on the roof platform under the clear, star-strewn sky, blowing out thin streams of smoke through pursed lips, which we thought made us look glamorous. Eva received a regular covert supply of cigarettes from Robert.

'What?' I said, scraping my head on the hard wood as I faced her. 'Ouch. How? What happened?'

Eva smiled at my shock.

'Well, I met him at the station and got the cigs. And then he said he wanted an extra payment for *reliable service*.' She shook her head as she remembered the exchange and smiled to herself in a private way. 'I asked him what he wanted, and he said a kiss.'

'What did you say?'

'I said it was him that should be rewarding *me* for loyal custom.'

'Ha. Then what?'

'He said *fair enough*, and said he'd give me an extra pack for a kiss.'

'And?'

Eva remained staring straight up, but reached into her pocket and pulled out a second, unopened packet of cigarettes.

Robert was in love with Eva. I could tell from the way he was with me. I was an object of his interest now, the friend of Eva. I noticed his eyes follow her hand whenever she touched me.

'Lily, do your impression of Mr Buckland's laugh for Robert. I tried to do it for him, but I can't do it like you.'

Her hand on my arm.

We were back at the Dive, sitting on a picnic rug we had brought rolled up in the basket of Eva's bike. Robert had stopped counting the number of his leaps from the cliff. He had grown into an almost-man. There were curly hairs on his chest, and his nose was no longer just a nub. He was still at ease with girls, unlike the other boys from his school, with whom we attended carefully supervised dances. But he seemed to resent his desire for Eva, as if it had cast him into a discomfort he had never felt before.

'You two are very touchy,' he said.

'Of course,' Eva said. 'We adore each other.' She put her arm around my neck and kissed my cheek. 'We're practically sisters.'

'My sisters aren't like that. They're more likely slapping each other than kissing.' Robert picked up a twig and began snapping it into short, even lengths, piling them on the rug like a miniature bonfire.

'When we get married our husbands will have to like each other because we plan to be inseparable forever, don't we, Lily?'

I nodded and glanced at Robert, who was reaching for another twig.

'We're not so touchy in my family,' he said.

I felt sorry for Robert. I lay on my side on the rug. It was only a thin cotton throw, and formed a topography of ridges and furrows where it sat over tufts of grass and clusters of dry gumleaves. Twigs poked into my back. I closed my top eye, surveying the expanse of the rug as though it was a landscape. Eva patted my shoulder.

'Lily, do you have a ribbon?'

'Only the one in my hair.'

'Do you have a handkerchief in your bag?'

'Yes.'

'Is it dirty?'

'No.'

'Can I borrow it? I need to tie up my hair. It's sweltering.'

Eva held up her thick hair like a child waiting for her mother to do up her pinafore, and I passed the folded handkerchief behind her head, pulling in the strands from around her neck, and tied it below her hands.

Robert watching my hands on Eva's face.

Eva and I were living an intimate, entwined existence. She often climbed into my bed in the night, woken by violent nightmares. Frequently in these dreams she was forced to defend herself against foes who appeared in the guise of her own family. She told me of one dream in which she was attacked by an evil replica of her father. She had plunged a knife into his face, and he had crumpled to the floor like an abandoned coat. We called ourselves 'leg sisters' as we slipped back into sleep with our legs tangled together. The nights were warm, and Eva often flung herself in her tumultuous sleeping to the very edge of the single bed to avoid the heat of my body. But she always kept one foot in contact with mine.

It was only in her sleep that this troubled side of Eva emerged. In her waking life she was enviably confident, comfortable in her body in a way I could not imagine. Her ease in the world was obvious. Because of this she was able to be kind to people. There was no need to guard her own position, to convince herself that she was equal to others, because she was certain that she was. I felt somehow privileged to be the only witness to the midnight Eva, the girl who began to emerge as sleep was wafting into the room like an airborne drug.

Time and sunshine began to seem endless. Then, as the start of the new school year approached, I began to dwell on the uncertainty of my future.

At Christmas, I had gone home for a week with my parents. My father was still bedridden and unable to walk, with casts on both legs that itched him terribly and stank from the sweat and dirt that collected in their greying plaster tubes. He had a thin piece of dowel that he poked into the top of the casts to scratch his thighs, and he asked me to poke it in at the bottom to scratch his ankles. The dowel came out with a paste of dead skin on it like the paste I rubbed off the bottoms of my feet when I had soaked in the bath for a long time. He had to use a bedpan, and was angry and pathetic as a caged dog. We had Christmas dinner on the bed, my mother and I perching together on her side, a green and red tablecloth thrown across the blankets and my father's rigid legs.

In the lounge room after dinner, while my father napped, my mother began to sob gently between sips of sherry.

'Lily.' She sniffed. 'I haven't had the heart to tell you, but we're having to give up the house. We'll be moving in with your father's family in Essendon.'

'With Grandma and Grandpa? Why?'

'Because of your father's injury. His compensation only covers half his wage and we can't cope. We're living on charity.' She pulled out her hankie and blew her nose.

'When?' I asked, panicked.

'As soon as we can. And just when we'd scraped through this Depression by the skin of our teeth.'

'What about me?'

'Perhaps you could stay at Eva's a bit longer. Just until your father can work again and we're back on our feet. I've been meaning to ask but haven't had the nerve. Oh, Lily, it's a blessing you're there. Stay as long as they'll have you.'

The sadness of my parents' home was as heavy as a boiled pudding.

Back at the Trenthams' the week after Christmas, I wondered if I should talk to Helena about my situation in their home. But I had never had a proper conversation with her and did not know how to approach her. The thought of moving to my grandparents' in Essendon, perhaps having to start at another school without Eva, was like death to me. Eva and I had attached ourselves so closely that we had cut ourselves off completely from the other girls, who knew they could never prise apart the clenched grip of our friendship. I had no other friends to speak of.

'Bosom buddies, breast friends,' the other girls mocked us. But we were indifferent.

How would I survive without Eva?

'When do you think your parents will want me to move back home?' I asked Eva one day.

'Oh, they don't care,' she replied. 'Stay forever. I *never* want you to go home.'

'My parents are going to stay with my grandma and grandpa for a while,' I confessed. 'Because Dad can't go back to work still. So if I have to go back with them I might have to change schools.'

'What?' Eva shrieked. 'Then of course you're not going.'

'But do you think it will be alright?'

'Of course.' Eva got up from the table, where we were eating breakfast. 'Mamma,' she called.

'Yes,' said Helena, shouldering open the screen door. She had on a straw hat, and held a basket of lemons in one hand.

119

'Lily can stay as long as she likes, can't she? Her parents have gone to stay with her grandparents.'

'Well, not yet,' I said.

'Have they?' said Helena. She seemed embarrassed, and I realised that the reason for the move must be obvious. 'Of course Lily can stay as long as she likes. Honestly, Lily,' she turned to me, 'you're no trouble. I hardly even notice that you're here.'

XV

The household found its way into its own peculiar form of dailiness. There was an architecture to it. Not precise, but an architecture nonetheless, as if everyone was a door or a window pulled from old houses and assembled into a new one. It had a ramshackle functionality.

When the routine of school resumed, the girls and I woke at seven. We walked softly past Evan and Helena's door, left ajar by Evan when he got up to begin work early. Helena was always nested in cushions, her dark hair spread out across the bedding. By then, Evan was usually in the studio. We padded down the staircase, with its carpet strip of faded roses that continued into the upstairs bedrooms. Laughter, the smells of cooking, were already in the kitchen, waking up the pots and pans from their bat-like sleep, dangling by their handles above the bench.

The light was pale, filtered through leaves before it reached the windows. Ugo never switched the lights on, said it was good for his painting to watch objects put on their daytime colours, shed the pewter skin that the dawn slicks across everything like frost. Heloise and Maria sat at the bench, watching Ugo, who was juggling oranges. As each one rose, it hung for a moment in a sunbeam. Maria rested her head on her folded arm.

'Where is the tea lady?' Ugo asked.

'Coming,' said Bea, walking up behind us.

In the first weeks of the school year Ugo and Maria would be sitting, drinking the coffee that Ugo bought from an Italian man on Little Collins Street, while we made our lunches, glancing up at the production line of girls: Heloise at one end buttering the bread; me at the other end pressing down on the sandwiches to keep them together and sliding them into brown paper bags.

'Where is your breakfast?' Maria would shout in mock horror as we banged out the kitchen door. Then one morning we woke to the smell of butter frying in a pan, and there was Ugo with a cooked breakfast for us. Instead of eating in the middle of the morning, as they had previously, Ugo and Maria joined us as we stood around the kitchen mopping up egg yolk with toast or cutting into the 'bread in a coat', as Ugo called French toast. He served it sprinkled with salt, rather than spread with jam, and with a bowl of pickled cucumbers to share. It became an unacknowledged routine.

Bea became shy around Ugo.

'Let me make the tea at least,' she said.

'I don't do it right, do I?' he asked teasingly.

'Well, no, but … that's not what I meant.'

He saw her embarrassment, her eyes that did not leave the sink.

'Thank you, Beatrice. You can be the tea lady. I don't drink it anyway – don't like the smell. Like flower water. Like old ladies.' He gulped coffee, bent his knees in exaggerated pleasure. 'But this … Mmmm.'

She smiled at him.

Ugo linked everyone together, always noticing the person left out of the conversation and drawing them in. He and Maria came to feel like the centre of this tacked-together family. They both shared the European sense of food as affection and did most of the cooking.

Jerome, too, befriended us in his own way. He was good with Heloise, over whom Evan and Helena had thrown up their hands. Heloise was thirteen, but still a child. She held the tears behind her eyes the way a man fingers a knife concealed in his pocket. They were her weapon, carried through from childhood.

She began to refuse to go to school. There was crying every morning as Beatrice tried to drag her out the door. Heloise held on to the leg of the table while Beatrice prised open her fingers, white with clenching. No one knew how it started.

Evan came in, angry and unhelpful, from his painting. 'She can stay home with me today.'

Beatrice glared at him and let go of Heloise. 'Fine.'

Then Helena arrived, wrapping a kimono over her nightdress. 'What's going on here?'

'Heloise won't go to school,' said Beatrice over her shoulder as she jolted the screen door open.

Heloise began to stay home frequently. She seemed happy.

'School is not for everyone,' said Evan. 'I know I hated the place. You're just too much like your father, aren't you.' He cupped her determined little chin in his hand, and she smiled up at him. 'Next you'll be inventing schemes to make the people of the neighbourhood part with their money.'

'But, Dad,' said Bea, 'she can't just stop going to school. How will she learn?'

'It won't be forever,' said Evan. 'And we thought we'd teach her a bit at home, for a little while at least, until she gets sick of it and wants to go back to school.'

Bea gave a huff of false laughter.

'And what are you going to teach her?'

'Enough, Beatrice,' said Helena. 'We don't need to have this conversation with you. We are the parents, remember?'

'Forgive me if I forget that sometimes,' said Bea, getting up from the table and gathering up plates.

Heloise the truant.

'How are you enjoying destroying your future, Heloise?' Bea asked often after school.

'A lot, thank you. Jealous?'

'Not at all. You're the one who'll be jealous when you grow up to be a housewife or a secretary while I travel the world as a diplomat.'

One afternoon we arrived home to find Jerome seated at the kitchen table with Heloise, her maths textbook open between them.

'See, you can do it,' Jerome was saying.

'Only when you explain it to me.'

'No, you're actually good at it. I can see that. You just don't know it. Anyway, school's over, I suppose.'

Jerome got up from the table. He had on loose, well-cut trousers and a white shirt, its top buttons undone, revealing a white singlet underneath. His skin was smooth and perfectly matt, as if he never perspired.

'I was going to ask,' he said, his eye settling briefly on Eva, 'whether any or preferably all of you ladies would be willing to sit for me.'

To pose for Jerome Carroll, rising star. The sisters gave no thought to the request. Their father had made hundreds of sketches and paintings of them as they grew. I had dreamed that one day I might find my way into a painting, like Alice through the looking glass. I imagined it in the same way: a new land. Before being painted and after. Evan had made sketches sometimes of Eva and me as we played, but these were not even studies, merely a way to keep his hand moving. He had boxes of black-bound sketchbooks in the roof above the studio.

'Wear a strappy top if you have one,' Jerome instructed us. 'I want shoulders, bone structure.'

He assembled us, seated on the Persian carpet in the studio. Patrick was in there too, shaping a wax model for a sculpture. We clustered together, jostled four sets of limbs until Jerome was happy. I recalled our outdoor baths together years before. The same shifting attempts to fit bony shoulders and ankles around one another. He began to make sketches.

It was a warm afternoon. We were by a large window, dozy in the late afternoon sun. Dust somersaulted through the air.

'So, another question,' said Jerome. 'Feel free to tell me I'm a pervert, but I would love it if any of you felt inclined to remove your upper garments …'

There was a pause.

'In all seriousness,' he said, 'you know I'm not a pervert. I'm an artist. Unfortunately not with much training in life drawing. I wouldn't ask you individually, but I thought all together perhaps. But not to worry. Maybe I can convince Vera,' he said over his shoulder at Patrick, who let out a grunt of laughter from his place across the room.

'I'd probably rather not,' said Bea. 'I don't pose for Dad anymore.'

'That's fine, absolutely fine.'

'Me too,' I said.

'It's probably a silly idea,' said Jerome.

'I'll do it,' said Eva. She shrugged, her eyes almost challenging.

'I don't mind,' said Heloise.

'Alright, terrific,' said Jerome. 'Or, on second thoughts, do you think we should ask your father first. I obviously didn't give this much thought.' His awkwardness made him trustable.

Heloise and Eva removed their tops.

'Do you want us to go?' asked Bea.

'No, not at all, stay where you are,' said Jerome.

Heloise still had no breasts at all to speak of, only puffy flesh around her nipples. Eva's breasts were also small. Without enough weight to drag them down, they were round, like half oranges. Her nipples were tiny and pink.

We held still as the sun slunk away across the floor. Maria and Ugo came into the studio. Eva instinctively put an arm across her chest, and then dropped it again.

Maria approached Jerome, glancing between us and his rendering of us on paper. 'Very beautiful,' she said, though it was not clear whether she meant us or the drawing. Ugo busied himself with his own paints and canvas, his body angled away from where we sat.

I could feel Eva shift beside me.

'I'm cold,' she said.

'Shall we stop?' asked Jerome. 'Probably too much of an audience anyway.' He glanced at Maria, who shrugged and began to walk away.

'I have seen them sit for their father,' she said.

XVI

When was it that I became a voyeur in their midst? I was the perfect witness, an unsuspected anthropologist disguised within the body of a young girl, surrounded by other young girls who were part of the family. Yet I was a cuckoo in the nest, an imposter who listened and observed, hoarding and collecting information. It was sometime after that morning in art class when our art teacher, Miss Warren, blushed as she discussed contemporary art and said, 'I don't want to embarrass her, but Eva's father has been very important in bringing the modern style to Melbourne.'

That was when history made itself known to me, like the devil to Faust. I saw that I was standing on a page in an art history textbook, saw Evan and the others in the trajectory we had learned in class, from Caravaggio to Kandinsky; from the Port Phillip Painter to a point on some distant timeline. 1936: the first exhibition of the Melbourne Modern Art Group. And I had been there.

Was it that evening that I tore out the used pages from the front of last year's geography exercise book and began to write on the second blank page, leaving the first as a shield over my words? That night I wrote down what the artists had discussed at dinner? Often the talk was that of any other family. Bea was thinking about what to do after finishing school at the end of the year. Ugo's vegetable garden was well established by this time and he pointed out that the potatoes, carrots and peas we were eating were all fresh from the ground. I remember shelling those peas into a battered green colander. The bright green of the peas against the lighter green of the colander pleasing to the eye. Maria talked about the war in Spain and worried about her family. Her brother's wife had just given birth to their first child, a boy.

Then there were the snippets of insight, like minerals glinting on a creek bed. Jerome said he was reading Shelley. He told us the story of the young poet buying lobsters live from restaurants and releasing them into the Thames.

'They probably died within minutes from the pollution,' Evan said.

Jerome talked about Shelley's politics. He was thinking of a series of paintings: Shelley's *Prometheus Unbound* transposed onto an Australian landscape. The conception of the series that would cement his reputation and take him to Europe.

First term had come and gone. I had helped my parents with their move, packing up my old room into boxes that would live in my grandparents' garage. But it was oddly simple not to think about my mother and father, to shake off their sadness with callous, adolescent ease.

I began waking early, going outside to sit on the faded wooden sun bed and write. I kept my writing secret from Eva. She too began to keep her secrets. These were the first between us. Hers were about Robert, who I had not seen again since our afternoon at the Dive. Eva kept the details of their relationship to herself, for what reason I could not guess. I thought she would tell me all about it, her venturing ahead of me into the terrifying, unfamiliar zone of love, or whatever it was between the two of them, more terrifying it seemed to me than leaping from the cliffs of the Dive. She began slipping out at night, sliding up the sash window and climbing out onto the sloping kitchen roof. She must have known I was awake as she eased up the rattling window, but she never spoke of it to me, and I did not ask.

I remember that morning with Jerome in the garden. The soft clarity of six a.m. when the day is going to be hot, as if the sun has not yet thrown off its white sheets. A family of magpies had befriended me, a mother and two juveniles, gangly and insistent with their drawling squawks. I brought them cheese each morning, and each morning coaxed them closer, wanting them to eat from my hand. The young ones were inching towards me each day, while the mother stood back and watched. They eyed the cheese on my outstretched palm, their heads swivelling, eyes twitching between me and the food, leaping backwards if I moved.

I saw him coming towards me through the garden, a book in his hand. He paused and watched the birds. We stayed frozen, smiling at one another. I could see that the magpies were not ready to eat from my hand yet, and I threw the cheese high in the air. The mother magpie swooped upwards, catching the morsel mid fall. Jerome walked nearer, and I shut my notebook. The magpies fled, half hopping, half flying.

'They're terribly ungraceful.'

'I know.' I laughed. 'But they're so quick too. Did you see how she caught the cheese in the air?'

'Mmm. Impressive. Are you trying to tame them?'

'Not tame them, just get them to trust me.'

'That's good. Nothing wild should be tamed. There's nothing more tragic than caged animals.'

'I agree.'

We turned our eyes again to the magpies. The mother dug her beak into the grass. The young ones loitered near her, squawking.

'What are you reading?' I asked.

'Shelley still.'

'We just did *Ozymandias* in English.'

129

Jerome screwed up his face. 'Such a classroom poem. You should read *Ode to the West Wind*, *Mont Blanc*, *Hymn to Intellectual Beauty*. Brilliant. The way he's able to mix the mythic with the political; the ancient with the contemporary. I wish I could paint as he writes.'

'I'd like to read them.'

'I'm reading his letters at the moment.' Jerome raised the red-covered volume in his hand. 'But you're welcome to borrow my copy of the poems. I'm waiting for my mother to bring my books over. I think she's coming this week. I need them badly. As you know, I'm thinking about a series of paintings based on Shelley's *Prometheus*. But you're most welcome to read them.'

'I'd love to.'

He smiled and walked off towards the house.

The car was in the driveway when we got home from school the next day, a black Bentley. A driver was sitting in the front with the window down, smoking. He nodded to us as we passed him, staring.

'Gosh, Jerome must be really rich,' said Bea.

'He told me he was,' said Eva as we neared the front door.

'Really, when?' I asked.

'I don't know. Sometime. He despises it. He says it's obscene, considering what people have been through in this Depression.'

'How rich is he?'

Eva stopped and put her finger to her lips, inclining her head towards the library to the right of the open front door. We heard voices inside. We crowded into the passageway, Eva and Heloise standing in the doorway to the library, and Bea and me at their backs.

'These are my daughters, Margaret,' said Helena. 'Eva, Heloise, and behind them Beatrice, my eldest, and their friend Lily. Girls, this is Mrs Carroll.'

Jerome, his mother and Helena were sitting around a small mahogany table by the window. Jerome was on the window seat, and Helena and Mrs Carroll were on the armchairs that usually sat in front of the bookcase. Jerome's mother seemed younger than I had imagined her. She was not beautiful, but had very clear skin and a high forehead with no visible lines. Her hair was light brown and was set in a wave. She wore a grey fur stole across her shoulders, despite the warmth of the day.

'How do you do?' she said, without smiling.

There was a large silver teapot I had never seen before on the table between them, and three china cups and saucers. Jerome gave us a small wave from his perch on the window seat.

On the floor in the middle of the room were three cardboard boxes. Eva went over and opened the flap of one box. 'Are these your books?'

'Yes. I've got some treasures to show you later,' said Jerome.

'Where's Dad?' asked Heloise.

'Don't poke around in there now, Eva,' said Helena.

Bea began to shepherd us out of the room. 'Let's go. I'll make us some tea.'

Half an hour later Helena called us back from the kitchen.

'Girls. Come and wish Mrs Carroll goodbye.'

They were already through the front door as we walked up the hallway. The driver got out of the car and opened the door for Jerome's mother.

'Goodbye, Mother,' said Jerome, kissing her cheek.

'It's been lovely to see where Jerome's living now,' said Mrs Carroll to Helena, gripping her handbag in front of her with both hands. 'As a mother, you do worry, as you would know. Especially reading the papers.'

'Mother, please.'

'It's only that I worry about you. I wish you would come home.'

'We'll take good care of him,' said Helena.

'I do hope so.'

'Please don't worry, Margaret.' Helena moved towards her.

'Of course I'll worry,' she said, her eyes beginning to well up.

She turned away, past the driver, who had been standing very still with his hand on the door, and ducked into the car. She nodded, and he shut the door and walked to the other side. Jerome stooped to the window. We could not see his face. Then the car started and pulled off into the curved driveway. Jerome shook his head, but remained standing with his back to us.

'Don't worry,' said Helena, putting her hand on his shoulder. 'We'll win her over.'

'What did you think of Jerome's mother?' I asked later when Eva and I were upstairs in our room.

'What a horrible old hag,' she said, unbuttoning her school dress and dropping it to the floor, still wearing her stockings and shoes and her white slip.

'Why? I felt sorry for her.'

'Why? She obviously doesn't understand him at all.'

'No.' I paused. 'But it must be hard for her, especially sitting down to tea with your mother, who's so beautiful and smart. She must feel ugly and boring in comparison.'

Eva frowned.

'I mean, it's obvious that he'd rather be here than with her. That must be hard for her.'

'You're the same, aren't you?'

'I suppose so,' I said, feeling defensive. 'But it's different. My mother doesn't even want me back.'

As I said it, I made the thought present to myself for the first time. Since I'd met the Trenthams, I had always taken all I could of them, never homesick for my own family. Now I realised that, unlike Jerome's mother, my own had relinquished me without a struggle. I had been living with the circle for months by then, and it was almost May. My father's legs had not yet healed properly, and he would require more surgery. My mother was preoccupied by her worries. Although I sometimes stayed at my grandparents' house for a night or two, I was part of the Trentham family now, even more than my own.

'Well, I'm glad she doesn't want you back,' said Eva. She must have seen the melancholy in my face, because she sat down beside me on the bed and put her arm around my shoulder. 'I don't ever want you to go home.'

I managed a smile.

'Come on,' she said. 'Get changed.'

'So you don't mind having so many people living here?' I asked when we were outside in the garden, sitting with our backs against the seed train, our knees drawn up and shoulders pressed together, cigarettes in hand.

'Not really,' Eva replied. 'I like it mostly.'

'Don't you want your mother and father to yourself sometimes?'

'God, no. Sometimes I wish *they* would go away.'

'You should try living with mine. You'd never complain about yours again. Yours are interesting. They have parties and travel and talk about *ideas* and don't care what people think about them.'

'Sounds like you might rather be friends with my parents than me,' Eva teased.

'No. I mean, you're like them too. You don't want to just grow up and get married and be ordinary.'

'No.' She sighed and stubbed out her cigarette.

That evening, while Ugo and Maria cooked, Eva, Heloise and I helped Jerome unpack his books and arrange them on an empty shelf in the library.

'Does Byron go before Baudelaire, Helly?'

'Whoops. No,' Heloise giggled.

Jerome rumpled her curls. He pulled stacks of books from the boxes and passed them to us, and we slotted

133

them into alphabetical order. There were art books, some exhibition programmes, a number of Lawrence novels, books of Australian history and a few hefty law books, and many slim volumes of poetry, from the metaphysicals to Pound and Eliot.

'Ah, here we go,' said Jerome, straightening from the box and holding up a red-bound book. 'The collected poems of Shelley. This is for you, Lily.'

'Thank you.' I placed the book on the floor to take upstairs later.

'Why is it for Lily?' asked Eva.

'I said I'd lend it to her.'

'When?'

'We ran into each other in the garden yesterday morning,' said Jerome. He handed another stack of books to Heloise, who frowned and began to whisper her way through the alphabet.

'I was telling him that we read *Ozymandias* at school,' I explained. 'And he said it was the worst one.'

'Well, maybe not the *worst*,' said Jerome, smiling at Eva, who nodded.

'What should I read then?' she asked him.

'Well,' said Jerome. He reached for the glass of wine sitting on the coffee table. 'Let's see. I think you might be more of a modern girl, am I right?'

'Maybe,' said Eva, looking pleased.

'What about some Eliot? Maybe not *The Wasteland* straight away, but eventually, I think you'd like it.'

'What about me?' Heloise asked.

'Goodness. This is a big responsibility,' said Jerome. 'Here, Eva, here's some more. Hmm. Heloise, I think you might like to start with some Blake. Maybe we can read some tomorrow when you've finished your lessons.'

'Alright, let's,' said Heloise.

Evan appeared in the library door, bringing with him a cloud of turps. He was rubbing his paint-stained hands with a wetted cloth, and the skin of his fingers was a damaged white where he had scrubbed it free of pigment.

'Glad to see you're putting my girls to work, Jerome,' he said. 'But I have been informed that I must fetch you all for dinner.'

We put down our books and filed out of the room.

I hung back and bent to pick up the volume of Shelley's poems. 'Thank you,' I said, waving the book at Jerome.

'You're very welcome.' He smiled and lifted his glass before following Evan out of the room.

XVII

Looking back on them, those were months when a utopian ideal was close to being realised. Despite the derision from conservative members of the art world, it seemed that Evan's idea of sharing the luxury of carefree detachment, distance from the blunt discourse of economies and exchange, had succeeded. We were in our own sweet world, contained within a high fence and a thriving garden.

Then there was the work, which powered the mechanisms of the circle and determined the shape of the days. To read the scathing critiques in the wake of the group exhibition, one would have harboured images of Dionysian excess, the artists draped around the garden in various states of intoxication and undress. They were depicted by the press as middle-class dilettantes, damning and defiling the true course of artistic development from its clear wellsprings in Roberts and McCubbin through the dignified waters of Arthur Streeton.

Before I observed them, I had never thought of what they did as work in the same way as what my father did was work. But it *was* work. Evan's paintings were often six by nine feet, and involved the whole body in their making. They required ladders and long-handled brushes, hours with arms extended. They tired him; made his arms sinuous and hard.

Sometimes I crept into the studio to watch them working. Often they were so focused that they did not notice. I studied Patrick as he took a stick of beeswax and snipped it with a pair of pliers into a saucepan lined with hardened wax like yesterday's porridge. He spun the starfish knob on a gas bottle and lit a burner. He placed the saucepan onto the burner and then began smearing Vaseline into plaster moulds. His finger was thick in the mouth of the jar but deft as it smoothed the cloudy substance into the bowls of plaster. I thought of my mother greasing a cake tin.

He stirred the pot with a metal spatula, scraping the wax from the sides, and a warm honey scent wafted into the room. The wax began to melt down from opaque, rough-cut cylinders the colour of pastry into a glossy golden syrup.

He stirred until no blobs remained and then poured from the lipped saucepan into the moulds. He banged the moulds against the table, and bubbles rose to the top and then smoothed over. He blew onto the wax, his grey hair flopping forward and almost touching the bulging liquid surface. The wax clouded at the edges and began to return to opacity.

One day I came across Helena, seated at the table in the sunroom at the side of the house, painting on a tiny canvas. The painting was lovely. When I admired it, she laughed, pushing her chair back from the table.

'Oh, that's just my puddling,' she said. 'I have no artistic aspirations, even though I did start art school before I married Evan. It's just something I do to relax really.'

'I didn't know you went to art school,' I said.

I had been a presence in the Trenthams' lives for years by this point, and was now an official resident in their home, and yet I had never, as far as I could recall, had a proper conversation with Helena, though I revered her. For her part, Helena seemed to bundle me in with the collective of her daughters. She asked me how I was, how my father and mother were, but I often had the sense that she was not listening to my replies. She was vague, at the best of times, in her interactions with her children, and I must have been to her a lesser version of these girls whose circling around her she often seemed to erase from her awareness.

That day, as Helena talked to me, I felt that she had finally noticed me. I tried my best to respond intelligently, to nod, to voice my affinity with her and to assimilate the history she was recounting, although I found it disconcerting. Thinking back on it now, I am convinced that she was manipulating me in some subtle way, trying to intimidate or shock me, perhaps because she suspected, quite wrongly, that I had become too familiar with her as a maternal figure and had to be made to understand that she was a remarkable woman with an unconventional past. Or perhaps she was unaware of how odd it was to confide such personal information to a girl who was her child's, rather than her own, friend. I assume it was the former; Helena was too intelligent to be unaware of the subtle effects and implications of her exchanges with those around her.

'Yes, I started art school, but not because I was talented in any way,' she began. 'My uncle had grown up with Sarah Morgan, part of the Morgan clan. She married Victor Sorrensen, who taught Evan at the Gallery School, you know?'

I nodded my assent.

'My uncle convinced Victor to let me attend classes,' she continued. 'I despised Sarah growing up. She was a very beautiful, and very cruel woman. I remember being at her house when I was just a girl. About fifteen, I would have been. Sarah took me up to her room to give me some clothes that she didn't want anymore. She dressed me up like I was her doll and then she said to me, "You'll never break hearts, but you look very sweet. Very sweet and compliant. Those are the cards you'll play, I think." I didn't even really understand what she was saying, but I could hear the malice in her words. She was a woman who hated other women, and did whatever she could to shatter their confidence. I think I must have vowed then and there not to be sweet and compliant, if only because she told me that would be my role.' Helena shook her head. She still held her paintbrush in her hand.

'Anyway, that was much earlier,' she went on, smiling. 'When I started classes with Victor, he'd already been teaching Evan and Patrick and their group for a year or so. Evan had just had his first solo show, and everyone was talking about him. I met him a couple of times at openings and things. I thought he was hilarious, and very charming.'

Helena paused. Her expression shifted from fond nostalgia to something more complex. 'Then he ran off with Victor's wife; with Sarah. It was a huge scandal.'

'Really?' I said. 'I didn't know that.'

'Yes, well. It was a big thing at the time.' She put her brush down on the table and tilted her canvas slightly, though her eyes seemed to gaze through rather than at it.

'It was awful, actually. Victor kept on teaching, but he became old overnight. His hair literally turned white. It was a huge scandal in the Melbourne society world too, Sarah's family being who they were.'

'So how did you and Evan get together then?' I asked. Helena glanced at me. She pursed her lips, but I saw a smile twitch at the corner of her mouth.

'I suppose I stole him from Sarah. That's how she saw it anyway. Sarah and Evan ran away to Sorrento. Her family had a beach house there, and my uncle did too. He still saw Sarah when most people refused to, because they'd been children together. I often spent summers there with him, and that's how I got to know Evan. We fell in love, completely. But I must admit it did add to the excitement of it all that I was stealing him away from her.'

I smiled with closed lips, not knowing what to say. 'What did she do?'

'Oh, she just went back to Victor,' said Helena. 'Poor Victor. I don't know why he took her back. For the children, I suppose. Anyway, needless to say I didn't keep going to his classes after that. Evan and I were married almost immediately, and we went off to Europe.'

As she was speaking, I began to see Helena as the girl she

once was. I began to imagine how that time in her past must have been for her. The scandal; the passionate new love; the victory over her rival; the way she told the story after all this time still with a kind of pride at her daring. Helena picked up her brush again, signalling without words that the story was over, and I wandered off.

In a house so full of artwork, I had not noticed Helena's paintings, her miniatures, before or, if I had, I had not known that they were hers, and therefore worthy of special attention. From then on, I began to notice them in barely visible corners of the house. She had put them in places where they were vulnerable to damage: on the window ledge above the kitchen sink; in the laundry next to a jar of powdered soap flakes; against a west-facing window in the sunroom, so that the hot afternoon rays beat against the back of the canvas and the colours bleached to pastel.

They were neglected, mishandled, exposed to the elements. But this did not lessen their impact. They contained the strength of weather within them. I could look at a corner of a cloudy sky in one of her canvases, and it was as if I was peering through a chink in a wall from a distance, with little revealed, but with three steps could put my eye up to the chink and see the whole panorama revealed. Helena's images allowed you to see what was outside their compact frames, almost by the very fact of their occlusion. They invited the viewer to peer through the window of their canvas and watch the scene expand.

A few weeks after my morning meeting with Jerome, Eva and I were sunning ourselves in the garden. It was a late afternoon in autumn, the warmest time of the day in Melbourne, where the movement of the sun from its zenith brings it to a closer angle at four or five o'clock, the light more orange, as though a lid has been placed over things. We were soaking in the last of the warmth, pressed side by side on the sun bed, our heads against its propped-up wooden back. I was reading the book of Shelley poems Jerome had lent me, and Eva was reading an illegal copy of *Ulysses*, smuggled into the country by a friend of Helena's.

'This is so disappointingly not obscene,' said Eva. I looked up from the poem I was struggling to follow. Eva had on a wide straw hat, and there were beads of sweat on her upper lip. She wiped her arm across her face.

'This is so disappointingly not easy to read,' I said, holding up Shelley.

'I can't understand why it's banned,' she continued. 'Frankly it's boring. So far.'

'Maybe you haven't got to the good bits yet.'

'I know, I'm not very far in. But so far the only dirty thing was a description of a man doing a poo. At least I think that's what was happening.'

I put my book down across my sweaty thigh. 'I like Shelley, but I don't know if I really understand it.'

'I mean, really? Is that it? Maybe it is all later, but can I really bear to wade through it?'

'Do you think we'll be able to understand all this one day?'

'I expect so. We're only fifteen after all.'

'Didn't your dad say that art only gets banned because stupid people are angry that they can't understand it?'

'Probably. Sounds like him.'

'Shall I get us some cordial?'

'Yes, please.'

I picked up my book and walked towards the house, feeling the indentations on the backs of my legs from the slats of the sun bed. There were lines in the poems that I had read over and over before I could even make a sentence from their ceaseless flowing on. My eyes seemed to slip too fast over the words before their meaning could make its way in.

In the kitchen I came upon Jerome, with an intent expression and a paring knife.

'What are you doing?' I asked, peering over his shoulder.

'Hmm? Oh, Lily. You probably shouldn't be seeing this.'

Laid out in front of him on the kitchen bench was a bunch of green seed heads on a sheet of newspaper. Beside the paper sat a saucer with two of the heads severed from their stems, shallow lines cut into their ridged, sea-urchin sides. Beads of milk were oozing from the cuts. Jerome had a third in his hand and was in the process of scoring it with the knife.

'My mother's gardener brought these to me,' he said. 'From the hothouse.'

'What are they?'

'Poppies. I was shown how to do this in Europe. The resin has narcotic properties. Not for the faint-hearted, but interesting. It's all in the aid of transcendence. We artists must seek it any way we can. Shelley climbed mountains for it. This is another way.'

I held up the book. 'I've been reading Shelley. Or trying to at least.'

'What do you think?' Jerome put down his knife. He was wearing only pants, a white singlet and braces. His feet were bare. I stared down, self-conscious, noticing the dark hair on his toes.

'I love it,' I said.

'Really? I'm glad. Do you have a favourite yet?'

I did. It was *Hymn to Intellectual Beauty*. But I was embarrassed to say the title aloud, the words seemed so serious and adult. Instead I shook my head.

'Not yet. I like them all. I need to read them again.'

'I think *Hymn to Intellectual Beauty* is my favourite,' said Jerome. 'Or it was at your age.'

I felt instantly remorseful that I had not said the title before. Now if I told him later that it was my favourite, it would appear that I was copying him, that I had been influenced by his opinion and had no discernment of my own. I felt sick with regret at the missed opportunity to show that I had understood. 'That's my favourite too,' I imagined

142

him saying, a new respect in his voice. I imagined myself looking up boldly and smiling, saying something intelligent about the poem's effect on me. Instead I said, 'Yes, I love that one,' and stared down at the floor again.

Eva came up behind me and put her chin on my shoulder. 'What are you doing?'

Jerome sighed. 'I should have done this somewhere else, clearly.'

'Are they poppies?' Eva asked.

'Yes,' said Jerome in a mock-irritated tone. 'Yes, they're poppies.' He shook his head, smiling.

XVIII

In a house, as in a garden, there is a point when over-mingling can occur. At first, when the new plants are dug in, there is too much space between them. They seem artificial, temporary. Then, as they grow, the bed finds a point of balance, the taller trees occupying the upper layers, the sprawling shrubs – the hydrangeas, buddleia, pittosporum – filling out the middle, and the smaller bulbs and ground covers punctuating the under-spaces. Then, without warning, equilibrium is lost. A rampant jasmine covers an adolescent tree; a hydrangea thrives, forcing out a lilly pilly that struggles for light beneath a spreading magnolia. The spaces are subsumed. In the house, there was a period when everyone thrived. Even Heloise had been noticed by Jerome, who was sitting down with her on most days and doing sums and geography, and reading poetry. 'She has real talent,' he said to Helena, over the kitchen bench. She raised an eyebrow ambiguously but didn't comment. Then, slowly, the balance began to slip.

I arrived home from school alone one afternoon. Eva had told me that she had to *do something* and that she would be home later. I still felt uncomfortable when I arrived home on my own, as if I would not be recognised without Eva, although I had been living with the Trenthams for close to nine months by that time. The house felt empty; I wanted to call out, but the quiet forbade disruption.

I took my bag upstairs, changed, and returned to the kitchen without encountering another of the house's many inhabitants. I wandered out to the studio, thinking that the girls might be there with their father. As I rounded the corner of the building I heard a woman's laugh: a shrill, descending interval, like two bells. I walked up to the gap where the big wooden door stood open and searched the dim space. Across the room stood Jerome and Helena. I hesitated in the doorway, unsure of whether to interrupt them.

They were at an angle to me, lit by the silvery sunlight still coming in through the windows. In front of them was one of Jerome's paintings, from his growing *Prometheus* series. I had seen it on the easel, accumulating detail. He was standing back from the painting, angled away from it in a pose of exaggerated, reserved judgement, one hand on his waist. In his other hand he held a glass of red wine. Helena was standing directly in front of the canvas, and I was surprised to see a paintbrush in her hand. As I paused, she bent forward and began to fill in one of the squares that made up the image's foreground – a checkered floor. She covered the square with blue paint, not lifting her brush from the canvas but swirling it back and forth over the square so that the paint was thick and bright at the top but patchy and faint at the bottom. She lifted the brush and stood back, assuming the same spectator pose as Jerome, the tip of the brush handle pushed against her chin. 'That's how you do it,' she said to Jerome.

'I see,' he replied. 'Do another one.'

She laughed again. A paint palette and mixing trowel sat on a table beside her. She dipped the brush onto the palette, bent close to the canvas and filled in another square of blue.

'Evan would never let me collaborate on a work with him,' she said.

'Collaborating – is that what you call this?' said Jerome.

She frowned at him in feigned seriousness. 'Of course. What else would you call it? You can claim all the credit though.'

'You relinquish your right to half the sale price, minus gallery commission?'

'Exactly.'

They were silent for a moment, both gazing at the painting. I knew I should slip away before they noticed me, but I was transfixed.

'You know what,' said Helena. 'I once snuck into Evan's studio and painted a tiny brush stroke in the corner of one of his paintings. It was a long time ago, but I never told him about it. It was quite soon after we were married, and I kept asking him if I could do this kind of thing – paint a little section of one of his paintings. I'm not sure why I even wanted to. It just seemed fun. Illicit. But he never let me. He was so proper about it that it made me angry. Like he thought it would seriously compromise the artwork. One day after we'd had a fight, I crept into his studio and left my little mark on a painting. He never even noticed.' Helena giggled, watching Jerome to gauge his reaction. When he laughed, she smiled at him and laughed properly too.

I edged out of the studio and stood against the wall, the image of the two of them still in my mind, the sense of conspiracy, of mutual flattery between them.

In September, before the school holidays, Evan and Helena decided to go to Sydney for two weeks, leaving us behind in the care of Ugo, Maria and Jerome.

'Are you quite sure you don't mind being saddled with our progeny?' Evan asked.

'Of course,' said Maria. 'It will be fun.'

'Saddled?' said Bea. 'I beg your pardon. I'm quite capable of taking care of myself, thank you.' But even she appeared pleased at the prospect.

On the first night, the artists made this saddling into a game.

'We're the parents now,' said Maria. 'I'll be the mother, and Ugo can be the father.'

'And what am I, one of the children?' asked Jerome.

'Well …' said Maria, tossing him a corkscrew.

'Bea's probably the best parent of the lot of us,' said Ugo, winking at Bea. Ugo had wrangled everyone into the kitchen to cook together. We were to have a wintry-spring picnic in the half-moon clearing, where the coals were already burning in the fire circle.

'With Mamma away, we can even cut the lettuce rather than tearing it,' said Eva.

Jerome laughed. 'You're a terror.'

We sat around the fire with our plates in our laps, and when they were empty we stacked them by the garden bed.

'I'm not doing the dishes tonight,' said Bea. 'Let's leave them out here for the ants to clean.'

For dessert we took pieces of a raisin cake that Maria had made, poked sticks through them and toasted them over the fire, smearing them with butter and trying not to burn our fingers. There was a holiday atmosphere to the night, although we had school as usual the next day. I thought what fun the following fortnight would be, spending time with Ugo, Jerome and Maria without the monopolising presence of Evan and Helena, on whom we all kept a watchful eye, like a ship's captain on the weather.

Maria rolled a joint and passed it to Jerome.

'Could I have some of that?' said Eva, who was sitting beside him on the rug.

'Certainly not,' said Jerome.

'You know I've had it before. Lots of times.'

'Have you?' asked Maria. She sounded sad.

'Remember that first night you came here, Maria, when someone stole the reefer from your purse?' Maria nodded. 'Well, that was me.'

'Really? But you were so little then.'

'So ...' Eva leaned forward on her hand and took the joint from Jerome's fingers. He watched her as she inhaled deeply and lolled her head back to let the smoke out. She inhaled again and passed it to me.

147

'Can I try?' said Heloise.

'No,' said Eva, Bea and Maria together.

'Will you read some Shelley?' I asked Jerome when we were all drowsing in the sweaty smoke.

'I'll do better,' he said. 'I'll recite some.'

I lay back, holding Eva's hand, listening to Jerome recite from *Prometheus Unbound* and feeling the pulse of his closeness and his quiet voice.

'I don't understand this obsession you have with Shelley,' said Maria. 'It's so reactionary. You should be reading Baudelaire. Shall I recite from *Les Fleurs du Mal*?'

'Yes, please,' I said.

'Don't be absurd, Maria,' said Jerome. 'You know I read Baudelaire. And Pound, and Eliot, and the rest. That doesn't mean I can't also love Shelley.'

'It worries me,' said Maria, extending her legs in the air above her prone body.

'And why is that, pray?'

'It alludes to a deeply conservative streak in you.'

'You've got to be joking.' Jerome scoffed, but I could see he was hurt.

'Recite, recite,' said Eva, and Maria laughed and said it was lucky we were there to keep them in line and began to recite in French, so that we could only pick out words here and there and had to content ourselves with the music of her accent.

By the next day, it was already clear that even the fragile shadow of authority cast by Evan and Helena could not be removed without an increase in chaos.

That afternoon, when Eva and I arrived home from school, there was nobody about. We went to the studio, but it was unusually deserted.

'I wonder where they are,' said Eva. 'Oh well, let's get changed.'

As we reached the bottom of the stairs, there was a crash from above.

'Someone's up there.' Eva thumped up the stairs, and I followed.

'What are you doing?' she shrieked from the doorway of our room.

Heloise was crouched on the floor, broken mirror around her like spilled water. Our clothes were strewn over the beds and in piles on the carpet.

'That's my best dress,' said Eva.

Stranger yet, when Heloise stood up, her face was a rash of white spots against pink skin.

'What have you done to your face?' said Eva.

Heloise's eyes told us that this was some secret business that was not meant to be witnessed. 'Go away,' she screamed.

'It's chalk,' I said.

In her hand, Heloise held a stick of chalk. She appeared to have screwed it against her face so hard that the white spots were rimmed with red. There were spots across her shoulders too, and a thick white line down her nose.

'What on earth? You've got chalk all over my dress.' Eva tried to grab Heloise, but she bolted past us and down the stairs.

We heard the screen door bang in the kitchen, and Maria's voice, surprised.

'Heloise?'

Later, Maria engineered a parley in the library. Her hand was on Heloise's shoulder. The chalk had been scrubbed from Heloise's face, and the hair around her forehead was damp. Maria had evidently done the scrubbing; the sleeves of her jumper were wet, and she rolled them up as she seated us on the couch. Eva's best dress was also wet around the collar, and the blue silk was still dusted with white. Eva and I sat beside Heloise, rigid and unyielding.

'Take my dress off, Heloise,' said Eva.

'Just wait, Eva,' said Maria. 'What do you want to say, Heloise?'

'I'm sorry,' said Heloise in the baby voice she still used when necessary.

'Tell your sister what you told me.'

Heloise hung her head.

'Go on. She'll forgive you.'

'I just wanted to be beautiful,' Heloise whispered, barely audible.

'Heloise thinks you and Beatrice are more beautiful than her. She doesn't like her freckles. She was just trying to be like you. Her big sister. Weren't you, Heloise?'

Heloise fingered the piping trim around the arm of the couch. She nodded her head minutely.

'We've had a good talk about it,' said Maria. 'Haven't we? About how you are beautiful too.'

'Are you going to clean up my room?'

'Yes, we're going to do that now,' said Maria. 'But I want you two to make up. You need to be kind to each other. Your little sister needs you.'

'No, I don't,' said Heloise.

'Where are Ugo and Jerome?' Eva asked.

'They went to Petrushka. They won't be home 'til late, I don't think.'

The image of Heloise, her face flushed pink beneath the spangles of chalk, stayed in my mind as Eva and I walked through the garden to the seed train with our cigarettes. I plucked at bushes as we passed, scrunching up their leaves and smelling them, thinking. I felt sad for Heloise. It was the first time I had imagined from her perspective what her difference from her sun-skinned sisters must feel like. But there was something unsettling about the image of her face; something mask-like and almost threatening in a way that I would not have been able to describe but that sat in my stomach like a plum stone.

A few days later, I was in the garden writing in my journal when I saw Bea crying, running from the open door of the studio. She had bare feet and was dressed strangely, in several layers of cascading skirts and drapery. A long piece of turquoise silk fell from her shoulders as she ran, one hand holding up her skirts above the grass, the other pressed flat over her mouth. I had never seen Bea cry before. The realisation stunned me. She had become an older sister to me in the very fact that I had not noticed her for so long now. The shock of seeing her crying, and how it unmoored me, made me wonder how all of this could possibly hold. Should I go after her? It was only because of this recognition of our unnoticed intimacy that I felt I could.

The door of the seed train was open. I approached the carriage and put one foot onto the narrow running board that hung below the door. The carriage sat on thick sleepers, and it was a high step up.

'Bea,' I said into the carriage.

'Go away,' she said.

I hesitated, balanced on the running board, holding on to the dried-out rubber seal around the doorframe. Then I swung myself up and into the carriage.

The light inside was milky; the carriage sat below the three great lemon-scented gums at the back right-hand corner of the garden. Its windows had clouded over from the years of eucalyptus-infused water dripping from the branches above, and from the leaves that fell during rain and slithered down the walls.

Beatrice was sitting just inside the door. I had imagined that she would be in a corner, huddled up; that I could walk up behind her and lay a hand on her shoulder and stand like that. But I was face to face with her, her eyes red and wet, her mouth twisted withsuppressed sound. She was sitting on an upside-down stack of terracotta pots. With her long hair loose and her odd attire of multi-coloured drapery, her lips and cheeks flushed, she made me think of a woman in a John William Waterhouse painting.

'You look beautiful, Bea,' I said.

She half laughed at this, and then let out a loud sob. She clamped a hand across her mouth for a moment, then released it gradually, waiting to see if anything would escape. 'You must be joking,' she said.

'No, I'm not.' I put a hand on her shoulder. She bent in, almost lunged towards me, and pushed her face into my stomach, beginning to cry unrestrained. 'What's happened, Bea?' I asked, distressed.

'I can't tell you. I can't,' she said, her mouth in my cardigan.

'Please tell me,' I said. 'I'm really worried.'

'Nothing's happened, don't worry,' she said. 'I just feel so stupid. So very stupid. I don't think I can go back in there ever again.'

'Where?'

Beatrice pulled back from me. She began to compose herself, wiping her nose with a sleeve of burnt-orange silk.

'I was sitting for Ugo,' she said. 'He's been painting me. I thought ...' She trailed off. 'You can't tell anyone this. Eva would make fun of me.'

'Of course I won't tell.' I waited while she bent her head into her lap, into her open palms. She spoke again without sitting up, her voice muffled.

'I told Ugo I love him.' She groaned.

'Oh, Bea,' I said. I felt her humiliation. I would have felt it myself. But I was also relieved. She will be alright, I thought, my faith in her unshakeable. 'What did he say?'

'He was so kind about it,' she said, sitting up abruptly. 'So horribly *kind*. He said he thought of me as a friend. Or as a little sister. A little sister!' Her voice became shrill on the last word as it constricted into another sob.

XIX

Evan and Helena timed their return for the opening of the 1937 annual exhibition of the Victorian Artists Society, and Jerome and Ugo were to meet them there. Maria had decided to stay home with us, saying that it was her last chance to play mother, though Bea said she doubted it was.

When the front door opened on Evan and Helena, they were in a state of fury. Evan was shouting as he banged their cases through the doorway. The girls hung back, half resentful already in anticipation of a perfunctory greeting.

'Hello, daughters,' said Evan.

'You're right, this *is* personal,' Helena was saying over her shoulder to Jerome or Ugo or Patrick, who had arrived with them. She kissed her daughters and Maria.

'You will not believe what we have just witnessed,' she said to Maria as she removed her coat.

'A direct attack on us and our work, that's what,' said Evan.

Maria had prepared supper and ushered everyone to the kitchen. She put a hand on Heloise's shoulder as we followed Evan and Helena down the hallway.

Bea began to make tea, and Evan swiped up the bottle of scotch from the sideboard.

'So. Mr Menzies, our esteemed attorney-general, opened the show.' He sloshed scotch onto the table as he poured and handed out glasses.

'God only knows why they asked him,' said Helena.

'Is this about the academy we've been hearing rumours of?' Maria asked.

'Precisely,' Evan said. 'He announced that he'll be launching the academy shortly, and basically came right out and said that it was to prevent experimental art.'

Jerome nodded. 'If I remember correctly, he said, and I quote, "Great art speaks a language intelligent people understand, and modernists speak a different language."'

'I wish I'd been there,' said Maria, shaking her head.

'I wish I'd had a rotten vegetable of some kind,' said Patrick.

There was much talk of this academy over the following weeks. In fact, it was all the artists seemed to talk about; they gorged and bloated more each day on their collective indignation.

As a young woman on the periphery of these exotic scenes, I could not always inconspicuously harvest the information I desired. Most of the talk happened after the evening meal, when we girls were expected to make ourselves scarce, and anyway would not want to hang around at the table with the adults when we could go and smoke by the seed train or on the roof platform.

Eva teased me if I showed too much interest in her parents. Sometimes I felt myself to be a dog under the table, scrounging after dropped morsels. I was sly and skulking like a dog has to be. Imagine, then, my sly pleasure when Eva and I were sitting on the cindery rose-patterned carpet by the fire in the library, doing our homework on a Sunday evening, and the artists all trooped in carrying martini glasses, with Bert Evatt amongst them.

They arranged themselves on the couches, Ugo and Maria on the window seat, and raised their glasses. Bert passed a pamphlet to Evan, who glowered over it and handed it to Patrick.

'Maybe we should move,' said Eva. 'But it's so nice and warm here.'

'I know,' I said. 'And we're all comfy and set up.'

'If they get noisy we will.'

I nodded.

'A society which will unite all artists,' Patrick was reading from the pamphlet, 'who are determined both to prevent any dictatorship in art and to nullify the effect of any official recognition acquired by a self-constituted academy.'

'Who produced this pamphlet? George Bell?' Maria asked.

'George, yes, and Victor Sorrensen,' said Bert. 'You'll all be at the meeting next month, I presume.'

Helena was sitting beside him on the couch, and she bridged the sudden silence by handing him a plate of sandwiches.

'Bert,' she said. 'We must be plain with you. There are some … personal issues, shall we say, that complicate matters.'

'Alright,' said Bert. 'I can't say that's particularly plain but I'll take your word for it. Still, I think this has to go beyond the personal, don't you? This academy represents a serious threat.'

'The fact is,' said Evan, leaning forward, 'I haven't been invited to join this society. The others all have, but I've been excluded because of my history with Victor.'

'But that all happened – what? – twenty years ago?'

'Tell Victor that,' Evan said.

'Are you sure it's not just a mistake? Either way, just invite yourself.'

'I won't do that,' said Evan.

'Oh god,' said Eva beside me, stabbing her pencil into the page of her exercise book. 'Is it the radius or the diameter I have to divide by?'

'Where?' I turned the book around to read the question. 'It's the radius, I think.'

'I can't do this. I need a break. Shall I make us a cocoa?'

'Yes, please,' I replied.

'What, none of you?' Bert was saying when Eva had left the room. There was another long pause. I heard glasses being picked up and set down.

'I think,' said Helena, 'that although they are in complete agreement with your sentiment, Bert, these artists have a keen sense of loyalty to Evan, who has, after all, been something of a patron to them. They don't want to be involved where he has been so pointedly excluded.'

I looked up at last and caught a glance between Maria and Ugo, who were opposite me on the window seat. Their expressions made me wonder how much truth there was in Helena's statement of loyalty on their behalf and how much it might be an injunction.

The pamphlet that Bert had brought lay untouched on the kitchen table for some weeks like a letter from an old flame left out in its opened envelope to announce its innocence, a nexus of unspoken negotiations.

Eventually, though, the subject was broached again.

'Evan,' said Jerome at dinner. 'This is awkward for us all, but I feel we need to talk about the meeting tomorrow night.'

'Do we?' said Evan.

'Well, don't we?'

'You're free to do as you like, of course. But I won't be attending, as you know.'

Jerome twisted the stem of his wineglass between thumb and forefinger.

'The thing is, we feel it's an important cause. As Bert Evatt says, it's important enough to put aside differences.'

'Oh, it's *we* now?' said Evan. 'Who exactly are you speaking for, Jerome?'

'I'm not planning to go,' said Patrick.

Ugo and Maria glanced at each other, and Maria spoke.

'Evan, you know we have complete loyalty to you –'

'It's not a matter of putting aside differences anyway,' Evan interrupted. 'The fact is I wasn't invited to join this new society. Victor has deliberately excluded me, so I don't see why I should be the one to be magnanimous about it.'

'Evan, you know I've been attending classes at the Gallery School,' said Jerome. 'So I feel I'm a sort of impartial party, so to speak.'

Evan laughed humourlessly.

Helena put her hand over his on the table. 'Jerome,' she said. 'I can see that you're trying to do the right thing here. But really, don't your allegiances ultimately lie with Evan?'

'I think that's unfair, Helena,' said Maria, gathering up her curly hair into a knot behind her head as she did unconsciously when she was thinking. 'This doesn't need to be about taking sides. We're not siding with Victor against Evan by going.'

'*Well*, you are, actually,' said Helena. 'It think it's a clear message of disloyalty. Victor will take it that way anyway. It's bad enough that you're taking classes at the Gallery School, Jerome.'

Down the children's end of the table, the tension was palpable enough that even Heloise fell silent.

'Oh, look, Helena, maybe we're making more of this than it needs to be. If they feel they should go –'

'No, Evan,' said Helena. 'You're too generous. They owe you their loyalty.'

'Well, I'm sorry, Helena,' said Jerome. 'I'm going to the meeting. You were there at the Artists Society show. I'm surprised you can't see beyond the personal here. This could affect us all in a major way. We could be shut out of galleries and –'

'But that's exactly what's happening to Evan. And you'll be complicit in that.'

Jerome held up his hands in surrender. 'Alright,' he said. 'Alright. I won't go.'

'That was awkward,' I said to Eva in our room after dinner.

'It's ridiculous,' she said. 'My parents are completely ridiculous.'

That night Eva snuck out again, sliding up the window and climbing from her bed onto the corrugated iron roof. It made a loud popping sound as she clambered out. I lay in bed, feeling excluded and alone. In the next room, I heard Heloise get out of bed and open her door. Her footsteps passed our room, and I heard the stairs creak. I pulled back my blankets, wondering if Heloise was following Eva. I opened the door and tiptoed out and down the stairs. From the bottom landing, I could see Heloise in the steel light of the hallway, creeping towards the library. I waited for a light to go on in the library, but it did not. When I reached the doorway I peered around with only one eye, hiding my body from view. Heloise was standing at the front window, gazing out at the white stones of the driveway.

She is watching Eva, I thought. I stared at Heloise's back, her thin nightdress and bony shoulders, her curly hair no longer red but grey in the moonlight, until I became scared that she would turn around and catch me. She stayed very still. I began to shiver and crept back to bed, where the sheets had already lost their warmth. After a while, I heard Heloise pass my door again and shut her own.

I did not find out whether Ugo, Maria and Jerome went to the meeting the following evening. They were not at home for dinner, but no one mentioned their absence.

How did I see the artists of the circle back then? I can only see them now through the lens of the present. I can't recall when things began to shift off their axis in the house. Around this time, my parents began to talk of eventually leaving my grandparents' house and bringing me back to live with them again. My father was recovered, though he would always walk with a cane, and was now able to look for work again. I had been living with the Trenthams for more than nine months. I was not sure how I felt about going back to my parents; I had grown so accustomed to this huge, rowdy family, to being invisible, to being secretly in love with the people I lived with every day. I could not imagine sitting down to dinner each night with my two parents, their gazes on me.

Amid the gathering tensions, within the circle and outside it, I don't think anyone noticed what was happening to Heloise, that she was moving away from us, like someone walking into a cold lake. She decided for herself whether she went to school or not, and I don't know how she spent her days at home.

A few nights after the meeting, Heloise complained of toothache, which grew worse until we could hear her wailing after we had gone to bed, and Helena traipsing in and out of her room.

When we got home from school the following day, Heloise was lying on the couch, her head tied up in a scarf like a Christmas pudding, with hot flannels against her cheeks. There was a bottle of oil of cloves on the coffee table beside her.

All the next night the yellow light poked its tongue beneath our door, elongating our dreams, and Heloise moaned in rising waves. She was taken to the dentist, and it was revealed that she had not cleaned her teeth for close to a year.

'Half the teeth in her head are rotten,' Helena ranted.

'It's going to cost a fortune. They may even have to pull some of them.'

Heloise was wretched, her cheeks red from the hot compresses.

'Were you aware of this, Beatrice?' Helena asked.

'I don't know,' said Bea. 'Not that it had been *that* long. Anyway, why are you asking me?'

'I was under the impression that you cared for your little sister,' said Helena.

'I was under the impression that was your job, being her mother. You don't even make her go to school, so why should I force her to brush her teeth?'

Looking back, her toothache now seems a terrible augur of Heloise's fate, but at the time it passed and was forgotten, the only reminder a gap at the edge of her shy, still frequent smile.

And Eva? I wanted to love her without envy. To say to others, 'She is amazing. So beautiful and kind and clever.' But I could not. I could not say those things without wanting to convey something cruel beneath the words. I wanted to be a girl, like Eva, who did not envy other girls their good fortune, their beauty or intelligence or happiness. But I could not be one of those girls. I could not damp the hot envy that tinged my love for Eva with a desire to see her fail in some small way. To want what she had.

Eva truly was a kind person. I never felt envy from her, but I suspected that this was only because there was nothing about me to envy. Perhaps she sensed this in me. At some point our closeness began to diminish, almost imperceptibly, like the light draining from the air at dusk. She began slipping off after school, saying she was going to the library to study, sneaking out every night. Her eyes were dark-ringed and she had a dreamy, secretive smile that flitted across her face when she thought no one was watching.

I suppose we both had our secrets, though I felt betrayed when I found out later what she had kept from me. I did not see that at some point, unnoticed, we had begun to retreat from the pristine intimacy of our childhood, that we had been walking backwards as we faced each other, objects concealed behind us. In my hand I held a notebook in which I recorded, scrutinised, the people Eva considered her family. Perhaps mine was the greater betrayal.

3
Smoke

XX

I didn't find out until almost a year later how it started. For me – for the rest of us – it started with fire. Waking in the night to the smell of smoke. I still do it sometimes, and lurch from my bed before becoming conscious that it was a dream remnant, a faint hallucination, a lingering of that other, darker world of dream that travels over so that smell can be recalled for a moment as physical experience, the way it cannot in normal waking life. What chemical changes occur in our brains during sleep I do not know, but we must spend whole nights with the smell of the sea or of our mothers' bodies being minutely recreated in the laboratories of our heads.

The image of smoke might seem a gentle one, a slow drifting of awareness. It was not that way. The jolt from sleep to the smell of smoke is violent. The body switches on, becomes beast, the blood pumping audibly through the veins behind the ears. Helena must have woken before I did. She must have retained some seed of wakefulness, a vigilance even in sleep that mothers never lose. I stood in the centre of the dark room for a moment, confirming the scent. Eva sat up in her bed. I walked out into the passageway to see Helena outside her bedroom door. She pulled her silk kimono around her as I came out of my room, and I caught a glimpse of her naked body in the orange glow that lit the wall against the stairs. We began to run down. I heard the thump of Eva jumping from her bed behind us.

Heloise was standing in the library with her back to the door. The curtains were on fire, the flames rushing up the thin voile inner curtains of the third window. The heavier green drapes of the first two had already caught. There was a pile of books burning on the floor in front of her.

'Evan!' Helena screamed as she came to the doorway.

Heloise spun around and saw us. She gave a small lift of her hands, palms upturned, as if in an expression of wonder. Her eyes were wide with fear.

'Did you do this?' asked Helena. Heloise did not move. Helena yanked her by the shoulders away from the flames. Her small body was covered only by a nightdress of the same cotton voile as the inner curtains. 'Get water,' Helena shouted.

I turned to Eva and we looked at each other for a long petrified moment. Helena was pulling a blanket from the couch and throwing it over the burning books.

'Pots,' said Eva. 'Kitchen.'

As we ran, Evan leaped into me from the landing. He knocked me into the wall but didn't stop to see if I was hurt. My head and shoulder were blazing with pain. I put my hand up and noticed how much I was shaking. I heard Eva in the kitchen and ran to her, ignoring the throbbing. She was filling a deep stock pot in the sink. It seemed to take forever.

'Here,' she said, when it was half full. 'Just take it.'

The pot was heavy, and the water sloshed from side to side as I ran. The others were all appearing from their rooms. Ugo and Maria both emerged from Maria's room. The fire was on the bookcases now. Evan snatched the pot from my hands and hurled the water like a clear sheet. Smoke erupted from the books as the water hit them. We all ducked and began to cough.

'The curtains,' said Helena.

'They're easier to put out,' said Evan. 'If the books catch, that's it. More water!'

Eva came in with another pot. Again Evan tossed the water over the bookcases. The air was sucked of oxygen.

There was a rap on the window, and Ugo's face appeared between the burning curtains. He held up a garden hose. Helena crouched and lunged. She grasped the metal ring in the window sash and then yelped and pulled her hand back in pain. Jerome jumped forward, yanking off his singlet. He threw it over the handle and pulled up the sash. A rush of air gusted in and the flames leapt up. Jerome fell back as Ugo tossed the hose in, javelin-like. Water spilled over Jerome's bare chest. It could almost have been comical, slapstick, but instead it was terrifying. Those moments when the adults we have constructed in our minds as invincible are revealed as vulnerable, afraid.

The fire was extinguished.

Ugo turned off the hose, and we stood in a deflated little group on the sodden, ashy carpet, pulling our night clothes around us against the dawn air coming through the open window. No one moved to close it. Heloise had sat down on the damp couch. She was shaking. Red blotches stood out against her pale throat, the blotches that often appeared when she was upset, as if her body felt emotion as a sickness or fever.

'What the fuck were you thinking?' Evan yelled. 'You could have killed us all. Do you understand that?'

Heloise would not look up from her lap.

'Heloise!' Helena walked over and slapped her.

Ugo came in from the garden. His feet were bare and his hair was matted at the back. He went straight to Maria and put his arms around her. I glanced instinctively at Bea, but she was watching Heloise.

Jerome was bent over the charred pile of books on the carpet. He straightened and turned around, his face confused. 'These are my books,' he said, 'all of them.'

Heloise lifted her face. Her expression composed itself into cold, childish pride. She stared past her parents towards Jerome.

'I saw you,' she said.

'You saw me?' Jerome repeated, unsure.

'I saw you, and I saw you.' Heloise directed her hard gaze now onto Eva, who was still holding an empty pot dangling by one handle.

'What are you talking about, you complete lunatic?' Eva shouted at Heloise. She put the pot down on a bookshelf by the door, the shelf where Jerome's books had sat until tonight, and walked over to Heloise.

'I saw you with him.'

'So?' Eva continued to yell. 'That made you want to burn the whole house down? You know what? You're crazy. You need to be locked up.'

The sisters faced one another, the same proud fury on both their faces.

'Hang on, what's going on here?' asked Evan.

'What did you see, Heloise?' Helena turned to Jerome as she spoke. Jerome was clutching a blackened, dripping book in one hand. He was still shirtless, and his sopping pyjama pants clung to his legs. He opened his mouth as if to speak, but then simply let out a breath and closed his eyes. His whole body seemed to slump: his arms fell to his sides and his chin drooped. After a moment, he opened his eyes again and looked beseechingly at Helena. Her face put up its shield as she returned his gaze. I saw the same pride that was in the faces of her daughters.

'Is there something going on between you and my daughter?' she asked.

'I don't know what to say,' said Jerome.

'*Your daughter* is in the room,' said Eva, 'and, yes, there is something going on, and it's none of your business what that is. Especially none of yours, Heloise.'

'It is absolutely our business, Eva,' said Evan. 'You are my child. What are you, fourteen?'

'Fifteen. Almost sixteen.'

'Fifteen,' Evan repeated. 'Well, you are just a child in any case. I had no inkling that this was happening.'

166

'Of course you didn't, Dad. You don't even know how old I am.' Eva walked over to Jerome and put her hand on his arm.

Evan took a step towards them. His face showed his anger, but also how unsettled he was.

Jerome squeezed Eva's hand briefly with his own, and then lifted it gently off his arm. 'Let's all just be calm about this,' he said. 'Let's not blow this out of proportion.'

'She's only fifteen, Jerome,' said Helena, her voice cold.

'Yes, and I'm twenty-four. I'm not some old pervert.'

'No, but you're still a criminal,' said Evan.

'Oh, don't be so pompous, Evan,' said Jerome.

'Get the fuck out of my house!' Evan shouted, thrusting his face towards Jerome's.

Everyone else was standing back from this scene, enthralled and aghast. Heloise was triumphant as she sat on the couch, her act of arson forgotten.

Then, Ugo spoke with surprising authority. 'Let's not let this come to blows,' he said. He put a hand on Jerome's shoulder but didn't touch Evan. 'Go into the kitchen, Jerome.' Jerome obeyed, walking past the others without looking at them. Maria was still in the doorway and she let Jerome pass and then followed him. 'I'll speak to him,' Ugo said, and followed after Maria.

I began to feel intensely uncomfortable, standing by the couch beside Heloise. I left the room as inconspicuously as I could, my feet sinking into the soaked carpet. Cold water squelched between my toes.

Behind me, as I walked towards the kitchen, I heard Eva yell, 'Then I'm going too!'

In the kitchen, Maria and Ugo were leaning against the bench, their arms around one another. Her head was against his chest, and his hand rested in the small of her back. Eva and Jerome were not the only couple to have been smoked out of hiding in the night by the cruel, proficient hunter, Heloise. Jerome was sitting at the far end of the table, his chin cupped in his hands.

I paused in the doorway. The light in the foggy kitchen window was a deep blue. The jagged leaves of geranium pressed against the glass were coral, and we were staring out into deep water from some sunken domestic bathysphere.

Eva pushed past me and went straight to Jerome at the table. I was freezing, standing there on the cold slate tiles, my feet turning from pink to white. The flush and drain of adrenaline had left me empty. I felt hollowed out; too aware of my feet, as though I could experience sensation only in the part furthest from my head and heart. I couldn't hear what Eva and Jerome were saying, but I saw Jerome clasp both of Eva's wrists and saw her pull them away.

Bea came up behind me. She widened her eyes and raised her eyebrows. I widened my eyes too in response. *I know.* Neither of us spoke. She walked past Ugo and Maria and over to the sink. She lit the stove and filled the kettle. The sound of water pouring into the hollow metal body made me flinch with the thought of the futile pots of water we had filled.

The air was still thick with smoke, and with Heloise's crying from the library. Bea reached up to get the teapot from the shelf. I went over to her and picked up the tea tin, with its scratched oriental flower pattern. I opened its hinged lid and dropped two scoopfuls of tea into the pot. The soft rustling of its fall, the fragrance of the leaves, was as comforting as Bea's matter-of-fact movements. We stood in silence, looking neither at Ugo and Maria nor Eva and Jerome, until the kettle began to whistle. The water fizzed in the spout of the kettle as Bea poured it into the pot. I took two cups from the shelf above our heads and sloshed milk into each.

Bea lifted the pot and gestured to me to bring the cups. She opened the kitchen door and went out into the dawn garden. I followed her, glancing at Eva and Jerome. Eva had tears running down her face.

The garden was misty, but less cold than I expected. The grass was wet with dew. The birds were twittering in rising waves and crescendos in the trees.

'I'll get us some jumpers,' said Bea as she set the cups down on the sun bed in the half-moon clearing. Ashes were piled up in the middle of the fire circle. I sat on the sun bed and tucked my feet up. Bea returned with two jumpers and two pairs of slippers. We pulled them on, and I poured the tea. We both wore short nightdresses, and our legs were bare and goosebumped.

'We forgot the strainer,' I said.

'Oh well,' said Bea. 'I'm not going back into the kitchen again.'

'Bea,' I said, thinking of how it must be for her to see Ugo and Maria together.

'Doesn't matter,' she said. 'At least with all this he's probably forgotten about my little scene. I can adjust to this new development with equanimity and poise, and no one will notice.'

I was filled with affection for her. 'Why did Heloise try to burn the house down?' I wondered aloud.

'Jealous maybe, I don't know. She's probably in love with Jerome in her childish way. She doesn't get much attention, poor Heloise, and she latches onto anyone who notices her. I probably felt a bit like burning the house down when you found me in the seed train the other week.' She laughed flatly.

'I had no idea about Eva and Jerome. I think maybe I'm a bit jealous too.' I felt myself blushing as I spoke the words.

'Why did they think it was a good idea to bring these handsome young men into a house full of daughters?'

'Did you know anything about Eva and Jerome?'

'No, I didn't. But I have to admit I'm not that surprised. I actually find Jerome a bit …' She trailed off and then resumed. 'I actually thought he might have been after Mamma.'

'Me too! Or maybe me,' I added, trying to adopt Bea's ironic tone.

I thought of the way Jerome had spoken to me in the garden, right where we were sitting. The way he had encouraged my reading of Shelley and talked to me about his painting. Then I thought of him teaching Heloise at the kitchen table each afternoon. Of him and Helena laughing as she told him how she had made her clandestine mark on Evan's painting. I thought of him asking us to model for him; how Eva had looked at him as she removed her top. Was it happening already back then?

'Neither of us are destined for a career in matchmaking, clearly.' Beatrice paused. 'Ugo's different though. He was probably hiding his relationship with Maria so I wouldn't be any more embarrassed. He's been nice about it.'

'He's lovely,' I said.

'Yes,' said Bea. 'Well.' She drained her teacup and stood up. 'It's almost seven. Shall we get ready for school?'

'School? Let's go back to bed.'

'I've got an exam today.'

We went inside again. No one was in the kitchen. 'You use the upstairs bathroom and I'll use the downstairs one.'

As I emerged from the bathroom, I met Eva coming up the stairs.

'I'll go next if you're finished,' she said. She didn't meet my eye. She looked exhausted. As I was putting my books into my bag, she came back into the bedroom, towel-wrapped.

'Are you coming to school today?' I asked. I noticed a distance in my voice that I hadn't intended but that it seemed I could not control.

'I'm being forced to go,' she said. 'I'll be late though.'

'Alright. I'll see you there.' I left her getting dressed, wondering at my inability to break through the barrier that had sprung up between us, and to question her plainly as our years of friendship should have allowed. I wanted *her* to cross the barrier, since it was her secrecy that had put it there. I wanted her to apologise for keeping this from me.

XXI

All day the pressure built up in me, seeing Eva sitting close by in class. When she paused in her work and stared out the window, I wondered whether she was thinking of Jerome, and what kinds of images she was able to replay in her mind. I had never even seen them touch, or had never thought to notice it. Never seen Eva's long fingers reach to his face. His pale hand on her waist, slipping under a layer or two of garments.

On the train on the way home Eva was in a daze beside me, fraying the edge of her blazer sleeve.

'Why didn't you tell me?' I finally blurted out, having passed station after station without speaking.

Eva shrugged and slumped in her seat. 'I don't know, Lily,' she said. My words, their movement towards her, seemed to release something in her, and all her distance was thrown aside. She rested her head on my shoulder. 'I thought you'd disapprove.'

'No, I wouldn't.'

'I don't want to go back there. Mum and Dad are being so awful. I just want to run away with him.'

'You're not going to, are you?' I sat up, letting her head slide down my shoulder.

'I don't know what will happen. I don't like the way he didn't stand up for me this morning.'

'Don't keep any more secrets from me.'

'Alright.' She took my hand. 'But don't think badly of me either.'

We stayed nervously in our bedroom, doing our homework, not venturing downstairs all evening. The smell of smoke still permeated everything.

Then, before dinner, Helena called up from the foot of the stairs. 'Eva, can you come down here, please?'

'Here we go,' she said, placing her books to one side and sliding her legs out from under the covers. I held my hand out to her, but she had already passed me and was out the door.

By the time Ugo called out that dinner was ready, my stomach was rumbling with apprehension. To my surprise, everyone was at the table. Eva's eyes met mine as I entered the kitchen. They were puffy and red. I raised my eyebrows at her, but she bent her head.

We began the meal in a lull that was almost unbearable. Bea's was the only face I felt I could look at directly. Helena carved the lamb and we helped ourselves, pouring the gravy and passing the jug on with the briefest of exchanged glances. Everyone was seated in their usual places. Helena was between Evan and Jerome. Ugo was on Jerome's other side. Next to him, Maria, and then Heloise, Eva, me, Bea, Vera, Patrick, and Evan at the head of the table, facing Eva at what was implicitly the foot.

I had registered, a long time ago now, this unconventional table arrangement. My parents sat at opposite ends of the table, separate from each other. When they had guests, the couples were seated opposite one another, never side by side. I had always approved of Evan and Helena's difference from my parents in their flouting of table etiquette, as I approved routinely of all their differences from my parents. Of course, if they love each other, I thought, they would prefer to sit next to each other. They can talk more easily, maintain physical contact. But as Evan began to speak, I saw the seating arrangement as odd. It was as if Eva was Evan's small, brow-beaten wife, teary and subdued at the opposite the end of the long table.

'Just so that we are all clear about where things stand,' said Evan, 'I want to let you know that everything is alright.'

Eva was trying not to cry, but tears were springing up again on the red inner rims of her eyes.

'Heloise – as you know, we're still dealing with you. But in terms of the other thing, it's been dealt with.' I wondered what this meant. I had never known Evan to resort to euphemisms. 'Patrick has helped me see that, in the spirit of our arrangement here, I can't just go kicking people out. Issues are bound to arise, living in close quarters like this.' I glanced at Jerome. He appeared as cowed as Eva, and was moving a piece of gristly meat around his plate, making tracks in the gravy that closed again in its wake. 'Eva – and Jerome especially – both know they've done the wrong thing, and it's stopped now.'

Eva pushed back her chair, her face ugly with suppressed crying. She ran from the room.

Evan moved to follow her, but Helena placed her hand on him.

'She'll calm down. Let her be alone for a little while.'

'So she's not even in trouble?' asked Heloise.

'Heloise,' said Helena in a warning tone. 'You are certainly in trouble, so watch yourself.'

Heloise huffed.

'It's important that we're all adults about this; all we can do is see how things go,' said Helena. She turned to Jerome, but her face held no expression. Again, the image of the two of them in the studio flashed into my mind. Jerome nodded shallowly.

Evan picked up his knife and fork, and everyone else took this as a signal to resume eating.

'How was your exam, Bea?' I asked.

'Look, Evan, Helena,' said Jerome, standing up. 'If it's alright with you, I think I should go after her.' He paused while Evan and Helena looked at each other.

'Alright, go and speak to her,' said Helena. 'You're probably the only one who can make her see reason.'

I noticed that she kept glancing towards the door as we continued eating.

When I went upstairs, after helping Bea and Heloise with the washing up, Eva was sitting on her bed. She was freshly bathed, her hair damp and twisted at her shoulder.

'What happened?' I asked.

She began to smile, but tightened her lips to suppress it. 'I've got to practise being angry and unhappy,' she said. 'I suppose angry won't be a problem.' She was speaking to herself, but then she looked at me and smiled openly.

I saw how beautiful she was in that moment. Lit from one side by the bedside lamp, her skin was golden. She was wearing a singlet under a cardigan that had fallen off one shoulder, revealing her collarbone and upper arm. Her face was beginning to be that of a woman. Her cheekbones were becoming more defined, and there was a sensuousness to her mouth. I felt how ridiculous were the fantasies I had harboured about Jerome; of course he would fall in love with Eva.

She's leaving me behind, I thought. I felt tricked. With Eva, I had given no thought to the world of adulthood that awaited us. But she had crossed some secret threshold while I was facing the other way, absorbed still by the childish fantasies she had cultivated for us: our talk of travelling the world together; of having a salon in Paris or on the Riviera, where all the famous writers and artists were; of becoming artists ourselves, marrying exotic European strangers and always living close to one another; of how, when our husbands died, we would move together into a great crumbling mansion and be visited by amazing people from around the world. Now, I saw so clearly that all of that had been a silly game. She had a lover, presumably, while I did not even truly know what this vague and glamorous term entailed. She had become a woman, with no thought to warn me that I should be packing away my own childhood, dismantling it piece by piece like a rotten tree house, and preparing myself for the new world.

I showed none of this to Eva. This is what adulthood is, I thought: this secrecy; this cultivation of separateness. No more of the porous, open intimacy between our souls and minds and bodies. If this is adulthood, then this is what I must be.

'Well?' I asked, sitting down on the end of Eva's bed.

'Well,' Eva replied, again trying to suppress a smile. 'It's alright. He hasn't given me up.'

'So he lied to your parents?' I asked, my nonchalance slipping.

'He had to. You saw them. They would have kicked him out. I suppose that wouldn't have mattered, but he needed to speak to me first. To see what I wanted.'

'So what will you do?'

'We're going to run away together. He's going to get money from his mother and then we'll go.'

'Where?' I said, panicked.

'I don't know. Europe maybe. Dora Fisk's got a buyer for him somewhere. Italy, I think.'

'Does Dora know?'

'No, I don't think so. She's too in love with Dad. Although she does adore that sort of scandal. Anyway, you can't breathe a word of this to anyone. Jerome said not to tell you even, but I had to.' She knelt on the bed and wrapped her arms around me from the side, resting her chin on my shoulder.

I felt sick. I had been so desperate to be Eva's confidante again, and now I wished she hadn't told me. I thought of Evan and Helena and what they would think of me for not telling them.

'Eva, are you sure about this?'

'Yes, Lily, so don't start. Don't prove Jerome right.'

'About what?'

'That you're a goody two shoes. I know you're not, but just don't try to talk me out of it. I love him.'

175

I couldn't sleep that night. For the second day I went to school feeling shattered by tiredness and adrenaline. Each time I stole a glance at Eva she seemed to be smiling to herself. That night at dinner, everyone appeared equally shattered. Evan and Patrick had spent the day pulling up the wet carpet in the library. The urgency had gone, and a tense awkwardness had replaced it. Talk was stilted and false. As we finished our main courses, Ugo began to speak to the group.

'I know this is bad timing, with everything that's been happening, but Maria and I have some news.'

Maria put her hand on Ugo's.

'We're going to have a baby.'

There was an audible shared gasp from the table.

I looked at Bea. She had been caught off guard, and her eyes were unable to hide their emotion.

'Don't worry, this is good news for us. We're happy.' Ugo grinned. 'But the bad news is that we've decided we're going to move out as soon as we can find a place.' He put his arm around Maria. 'We're happy. This is good news,' he said again.

'Well, congratulations!' said Jerome.

Congratulations were echoed by the others. Only Evan and Helena kept silent. Evan stared at his plate, frowning.

'You seem unhappy, Evan,' said Ugo.

'I just wish I'd known this yesterday,' said Evan. 'It might have changed things.'

'Are you sure about this?' Helena asked Maria.

'It's been a hard thing to decide, of course,' said Maria. 'This – what has it been? – year and a half with you all has been amazing. But we're sure.'

'We hope you can be happy for us,' said Ugo. 'We –'

He was cut off mid sentence by Evan, who began to speak, not to Ugo but to a spot at the edge of his plate.

'I can't believe this. I swallowed a very bitter pill yesterday, *letting* Jerome stay, because I thought we all believed in what we're doing here. And now you two tell me you're leaving. The very next day!'

'Letting Jerome stay,' said Eva. 'You think you can decide every fucking thing, don't you?'

'Eva, don't speak to me that way!' barked Evan.

'I know it's bad timing,' said Maria, 'but we didn't want to hide it anymore. I won't be able to hide it soon.' She held her arms out in front of her to make a pregnant belly and puffed out her cheeks to lighten the mood.

But Evan and Helena would not be brought around.

'Why hide it in the first place, that's what I want to know,' Helena said. 'You didn't even let on that you were a couple. Did you think we'd disapprove or something?'

'It's not as simple as that. It sort of just … You know how these things can happen.'

Bea and I exchanged glances. I was relieved to see her roll her eyes, as if her luck was so bad as to have become comic.

'Well,' said Evan, 'it appears that you've decided.' He stood up peevishly from the table and went to the liquor cabinet, returning with a bottle of whiskey. He drained the dregs of his red wine and poured a slosh of whiskey into the wineglass, not bothering to offer the bottle to anyone else.

Ugo's smile had been replaced with an expression of irritation. He took Maria's hand.

Jerome was also frowning. I saw him glance at Eva.

'But have you *really* thought this through?' Helena asked, addressing Maria as though the two of them were alone at the table. 'I just can't help worrying that if you move out you're going to give up your art and become just another housewife. Is that what you want?'

'No, Helena,' said Maria. 'That's not what I want. Of course I want to keep painting. But I also want a family. I thought you'd understand that.'

'Well, I don't really, to be honest,' said Helena. 'You've got a family here. Why you'd want to be like everyone else

177

and live in a little house: mummy and daddy and baby. What about your art?'

'Helena, that's not for you to worry about.' Maria flushed as she spoke. She began to gesticulate with her hands. 'Anyway, who are you to speak? You have three children of your own. Why don't you worry about your own art?'

'Yes, I have children,' replied Helena, her tone changing from concern to coldness. 'That's how I know what it's like. It is very difficult. But I haven't let my children define me.'

'No,' snapped Maria. 'You ignore your children. It's your husband who defines you.'

'How dare you,' said Helena. 'After all we've done for you.'

'Mamma,' Bea yelled. 'Stop it!'

Helena looked at her daughter in shock.

'They're in love. They're having a baby. Leave them alone.'

Helena was silent for a moment. 'You're right. I'm sorry.' She sat very upright by Evan's side. She faced her daughters with a pleading expression. 'I'm sorry,' she said again. It wasn't clear who she was addressing. Her daughters stared back at her without emotion.

At school, the day after Ugo and Maria's announcement, Eva disappeared at recess and did not return to class. Mr Lipp, our English teacher, did not seem to notice. I kept glancing over at Eva's empty desk. I longed for Mr Lipp to ask me where Eva was, to break down and confess; to have her parents called by the school office and warned that they should start searching for their daughter and the man who had spirited her away. Without this intervention of fate, without the opportunity to believe that my hand had been forced, I could do nothing. My loyalty to Eva held a knife to my sense of guilt, my vision of my own actions through the eyes of Evan and Helena, my awareness that I was only part of the circle because I was Eva's friend. Then there were Eva's words: *Don't prove Jerome right.*

Miraculously, after lunch break, in our afternoon history class, there was Eva back at her desk.

'Where were you?' I whispered to her.

But she only shook her head at me.

After school we walked to the train station together.

'What's happening?' I asked. 'I thought you'd gone today. I nearly died.'

'Not yet. We're still working it out. His mother's giving him the money he asked for, but she won't tell his father. We thought we could stay there for a few days, but his mother said his father wouldn't have it. She has to get the money to him in secret.'

'Eva. Don't do this.'

'You don't understand, Lily. You'll know one day, when you're in love.'

'Don't talk to me like that. You're talking to me like I'm a child.'

'I just know you can't understand this.'

Tears welled in my eyes. 'Well, that's your fault.'

'How is that *my* fault?'

'I don't know.'

We did not speak on the train, but Eva put her arm through mine. She stayed with me all afternoon. I thought perhaps she wanted to spend as much time with me as she could before she left. Then I thought maybe she was guarding me, making sure that I wouldn't tell. She was right about me. The longing to tell Helena and Evan, to be relieved of the awful secret, was overwhelming. It took over my body like a somnambulist, and I found myself standing up repeatedly, involuntarily, and then sitting down again.

XXII

And then they were gone.

I did not tell, and they were gone.

'Where are they?' Helena's voice from the hallway was shrill.

I had been lying in bed, pretending to be asleep.

The night before I had lain watching over sheets pulled up to my mouth, as Eva packed a small travelling bag. She kept the bag concealed beneath the foot of her bed, the blanket trailing to the floor like a theatre curtain that she lifted to tuck in shoes, a jumper, a stack of folded dresses. I could not speak to ask her where they were going. It was only two days since she had told me they must wait for the money from Jerome's mother. Instead, I lay in a tense vigilance that receded into a doze and then dragged itself back again in the darkness, in case Eva got up and pulled the bag from beneath the bed.

Then it was morning, and I knew I had failed at my impotent task of keeping watch. Her bed was empty across from me. I slipped from my blankets and glanced beneath it. The bag was gone. I fell back into my own narrow bed and turned to the wall. I stayed there in a kind of catatonic state. It was Saturday morning. I will just lie here, I thought.

I went rigid as bare feet approached the open bedroom door and then receded down the stairs, the footfalls fast and uneven.

'Where are they?' Helena cried out again. 'Eva? Heloise?'

I sat up when I heard the second name, unsure. Helena ran up the stairs again. She stood in the doorway in loose, masculine trousers and a tan jumper.

Bea was behind her. 'Lily,' she said, 'do you know where they've gone?'

'Who?' I asked, rubbing my eyes.

'Jerome and Eva and Heloise.'

'Heloise?'

Looking back from the vantage point of the present, I see how young Jerome, Ugo and Maria were. They were less than half the age I am now. I thought of them as almost divine. But they were infatuated, just as I was, reeled in by the enticing bait of Evan and Helena Trentham. Jerome tried to emulate Evan's chaotic nature, as I tried to emulate Eva's inherited self-confidence. But Jerome was not like Evan. His privileged childhood and education were the opposite of Evan's. And yet Jerome was just as talented an artist as Evan and, as time has shown, just as successful. What I wonder at this distance is how much Jerome's success was helped by his mimesis of Evan's artistic persona. Jerome mythologised himself by joining the circle. He stood in Evan's orbit for long enough to be touched by his reputation, and then he surpassed that reputation in the only way he could have: by toppling him, just as Evan had toppled his teacher before. The myth could not have been more perfect: the wealthy king and queen; the three beautiful daughters; the cunning prince who infiltrates the court and steals away with a princess. Of course, in a fairytale it would have been one daughter only. Not two. But Jerome was a reader of Shelley. One daughter could never have been enough for his version of the myth.

Late in the morning of the abscondment, Helena beckoned me from the door of the kitchen, where I was sitting with Bea. I followed her swishing fabrics down the hallway. We reached the library, where the carpets had been pulled up after the fire, exposing bare boards, and the burnt shreds of curtains had been torn down. The wall between the windows was blistered, and a charred flower with a black centre and grey petals bloomed on the ceiling. The smell of smoke would not be expelled, no matter how many hours the scarred room stood with its windows open. We had not sat in here since that night, and the room was cold, the ashes heaped up in the grate. I wondered why Helena had brought me here.

'Sit down, Lily.' She faced me, all white and trembling like a candle flame.

I could not tell if she was angry or upset. I sat down on the couch where Heloise had been interrogated, for my own interrogation to begin.

Helena remained standing in front of me. 'Did you know, Lily?'

All the cloyed, distended hours of wanting to tell were now meaningless. I could not offer them as evidence or appeasement. Helena would never understand. Not my suffering, nor my silence.

I shook my head, focusing my eyes on my clasped hands.

I could sense Helena's own internal struggle: to be cruel or kind in this begging for news of her child, the bloodletting of this young woman.

'I find that extremely hard to believe.'

I knew that she had chosen, that I would be no friend of Helena's from now on; that I had lost that future in her glorious regard. I shook my head again, still mute.

'But she confides in you. She tells you everything.'

'Not this,' I said. I forced myself to look up at the white flame of her face. I could see that she did not believe me.

'Alright,' she said, shaking her head. 'Alright, if that's how you're going to play this,' and then she strode from the room, leaving me alone on the couch.

Later in the day, Helena walked past me as I sat alone, crying, as I had been since our interview. She paused, and trained her mother's eye on me, magpie sharp.

'You're upset, Lily,' she said. 'Shall I get someone to drive you home?'

Home. Her words a boot pressing with all the weight of the body on my fingers where they clasped onto the ledge of this family I had been part of for close to a year.

In that moment I became homeless. In the same instant I set like blown glass against her, cooling from red hot to transparent, making my heart empty of clues by which she could find Eva. Of course it was Eva with whom my loyalty lay. It had always been Eva. Eva, the only reason I was here; a passport that was now revoked. Why had I ever believed anything different?

Patrick drove me to my grandparents' house in what I felt was a state of disgrace. I cried quietly all the way beside him. He walked me inside and spoke to my parents in the lounge room, presumably explaining the situation to them in what must have been an excruciating conversation, while I lay on the patchwork quilt that covered the bed in the spare room and wept, sleep deprived and overwrought.

I heard the front door shut and I watched out my window as Patrick departed, rubbing his hands over his face as he walked to the car. I heard my mother approaching and I lay face down again. I felt nauseated, shaky, with a terrible sense of distance from my mother, and a strange, sexual shame. She sat down on the end of my bed.

'Patrick told us what happened, Lily.'

I did not move, pressed my face into the quilt.

'Did you know what was going on between Eva and Jerome?'

I shook my head.

'And you …' She faltered. 'You never … He, or any of the other men … Did they ever show an interest in you?'

I shook my head again. I felt her hand smoothing the quilt somewhere near my leg and prayed that she would not touch me.

She sat for a minute and then stood up. 'I'll let you lie there a while. Come out to tea when you're ready.'

I did not go out to tea, but instead fell into a deep sleep, waking briefly in the orange light of late afternoon when my door creaked, and then sleeping again. I did not wake again until morning when I opened my eyes not knowing where I was and then remembered, recognising the familiar jigsaw-puzzle picture of a girl on horseback leaping over a steeple jump that my father and I had done together and had glued down on a board and that my parents had hung in the spare room of my grandparents' house to make me feel at home. I saw that my suitcase had been brought into my room, and I got up, my head throbbing, and changed clothes.

My mother was in the kitchen.

'You slept a long time. You must have needed it.'

'Where is everyone?'

'Gone to church.'

'What time is it?'

'Almost eleven. Are you hungry?'

I nodded, and found myself abruptly in my new life.

After Eva's departure, the days seemed to slim back to starvation. Summer arrived, unsuited to my mood, and I often opened my curtains in the mornings and wished for a grey sky to mirror the featureless pattern of my life ahead. After Christmas we moved out of my grandparents' house and into another neat cottage near my school. My father had lost the job he had clung to so hard after his accident, but had found work as a salesman for another manufacturer of farming machinery. He travelled a lot and often got home late. My mother seemed tetchy and withholding towards him. He kissed her on the cheek she offered him rather than on the lips as he used to do. He seemed worried and tired and nodded off in his armchair after dinner.

'You're probably used to fancier surroundings,' he said, almost shy around me now. 'You must find us a bit quiet.'

I received two letters from Eva. She and Jerome and Heloise were in Sydney, staying in the home of a wealthy buyer of Jerome's in Rose Bay. But these letters were strangely purged of emotion, as though passed by censors. They contained only news, and were not enough to live off.

I went into hibernation. At school I was whispered about. The bolder girls asked me outright:

'What happened to Eva?'

'I heard she ran away with a man.'

'Well, I heard she and her sister ran off with the same man.'

You see, without you I am ordinary, I said to Eva in my head.

XXIII

'I'm going to visit Ugo and Maria and the baby next weekend,' Bea said one Saturday. 'Do you want to join me?'

It had been almost nine months since Eva fled with Jerome and Heloise. This had become our ritual, Bea's and mine. I would meet her after her half-day of nursing college on a Saturday, and we would go to the pictures and then to tea. At some point we talked about them. There was never a day when we didn't want to. We were like bereaved relatives after everyone else has moved on, recalling shared memories, compulsively revisiting the day of the tragedy.

We were sitting in the cafeteria of the hospital. It was cold and smelled of soup and disinfectant.

'Yes, I'd love to,' I said. 'Have you seen the baby yet?'

'No, not yet.'

'I like your clock.' I reached out to the round face hanging from a bar pinned to Bea's chest. 'It makes you really look the part.'

She laughed. 'I am the part. Or at least I will be. It's for checking heart rates.'

I sipped my milky tea from its squat white cup. Nurses bustled past us. Some smiled and nodded at Bea. I couldn't help thinking how much less beautiful she was in the straight uniform, beige stockings and clumpy white shoes. Her hair was pulled into a tight bun and the few wisps escaping, tucked behind her ears, were the only trace of her usual softness. Normally she was changed already by the time I arrived, but she was running late today. She pulled a grey cardigan out of her bag and slipped it on.

'How's school?' she asked. We knew we were warming up, moving towards the question we both wanted to ask as if approaching a horse: front-on, with no deviousness, hand held out, but gradually.

'School's alright,' I said. 'Only one more year after this and then I'm free. What about you?'

'I've just been learning to draw blood.'

'Do you mind it? I think I'd faint.'

'I like it. Will you wait here while I change?'

We did not link arms as we walked out of the hospital. There was none of the girlish physicality of my relationship with Eva. But we clung to each other in other ways. It was not until we were walking to the cinema that she asked.

'Have you heard from Eva?'

I shook my head. 'No. Not since the last letter I showed you. You?'

'Not lately.'

Bea was redoing her hair as we walked along Spring Street. She stopped and put the brim of her felt hat between her teeth, twisting her hair into a bun again, this time looser, with more wisps of hair falling around her face.

'Did you see about Jerome?'

I stopped further along and looked back at her. 'What about him?'

'He's been given the travelling scholarship.'

'What's that?'

'It's a travel fund for artists.'

'What does it mean?'

'That he'll go to Europe, I suppose.'

'And Eva and Heloise?'

'I don't know,' she said, beginning to walk again. 'Mamma looked for Eva's passport and couldn't find it, so maybe she's taken it. Heloise hasn't got one. Mamma said she was going to burn it if she found it. Dad went crazy. He says Victor arranged for Jerome to get the scholarship just to get at him.'

I pictured this scene in the Trentham home. Bea, the only remaining daughter, watching her parents rage through the house, searching her sister's belongings.

The following Sunday, Bea and I met in the city and caught the tram down St Kilda Road. Winter trees on either side, their structure revealed as if by X-ray. We got off at Fitzroy Street, and I followed Bea to the cottage Ugo and Maria were renting in Charles Street. The area was run-down. The low cottages lining the street sagged as if they had been pushed in from both ends, crumpling up against one another. Bea was checking the numbers. An old man wearing a frayed tartan dressing-gown was standing on the footpath. His legs were bare and horribly thin, just the curved bones of the shins with no muscle behind them, the papery white skin marked with scabs and purple veins. Bea avoided his gaze, eyeing the letterbox he was half obscuring.

'Beatrice.' Maria's voice came from behind the gate. She was sitting on the front porch, below street level. Pale winter sunlight fell on her. She held a baby pinned against one breast, and her hair was tied up in a colourful scarf. One side of her red woollen jumper was hitched up to expose her breast, and her floral skirt covered her plump belly. She held a cigarette in her other hand and waved at us. Her face was still as round and smiling as ever, but she looked tired. The old man nodded at us, and kept nodding, smiling, first at us and then at Maria.

'Hi, girls. Hi, Lily,' said Maria. 'Come in.'

'Beg pardon,' said the old man, shuffling away from the gate, still nodding and smiling maniacally.

'Alright, Percy, have a nice day,' said Maria, stubbing out her cigarette on the ground and pushing herself up, holding the baby against her breast with the other arm.

The old man continued to stand just outside the gate. 'You mind what I told you,' he said.

'Yes,' said Maria, 'I'll move the wood to the back.'

'Boys from up the street been pinching me firewood,' Percy said to us.

'That's no good,' said Bea.

Maria tugged the shoulder of Bea's coat and waved goodbye to Percy.

We had to step down again to get into the house. Strong odours of damp and mildew mingled with the familiar scents of oil paints and turpentine and the fried smells of Ugo's cooking.

Maria glanced back as she shut the door. 'Mad as a hatter.'

To the left, an easel was set up in the cramped living room. Washing hung by the fire. Rows of nappies fighting to retain their whiteness. I had a feeling that I had dreamed this before, but different. I had received the idea of Ugo and Maria's life from Helena's cruel predictions and imbued it with romance. A man and a woman in love; their child; their small cottage where they paint and raise a family. There was no romance here, though, only the struggle to survive.

Maria pushed a towel into the gap beneath the front door, holding the baby around its waist with one arm.

'So this is Mathilde.' She inspected the child before facing her to us.

'Hello, Mathilde,' I said.

The child's wrappings slipped from her as Maria held her out, and I saw how small she was. Her hair and eyes were dark like Maria's. The lips were hers too. The chin was Ugo's.

To the rear of the living area I saw the kitchen through an archway. One window was covered over with newspaper. Through the other I glimpsed the back of a red-brick building.

'Can I hold her?' asked Bea.

'Of course. Please.' Maria kissed Mathilde and handed her over. 'I'm going to start cooking some food for Ugo. He's just home from work. Would you like some coffee?' Maria made her way to the kitchen. 'I don't have tea, sorry. I forgot about you English.'

Mathilde began to grizzle, but Bea jiggled her with the confidence befitting a trainee nurse.

A door opened to the right at the end of the short hallway, and Ugo appeared, a towel wrapped around his waist.

'Girls!' He greeted us with a grin. 'I'll just be a minute.' He passed us, smelling of Pears soap and tar.

We paused by the easel. On it was a small canvas board taken up by a woman's face. It was one of Maria's, done in watery tempera, the eyes huge and liquid like a cow's, too big for the face.

'You're painting. That's good,' Bea said as she took the grumbling Mathilde into the kitchen.

I stayed by the painting. The lounge room was tiny. Weak light crept under the sunken eaves and onto the easel. There were shoeboxes of brushes and paints stacked up below the window. The easel sat on a sheet that had collected lines of dust and hair in the creases where it was bunched up against the skirting.

'I was,' said Maria. 'But we've run out of money for materials.'

Opposite the fire, obscured by the clotheshorse, were two mustard-yellow armchairs. I recognised them from the studio. I remembered Ugo and Jerome carrying them across the lawn during those early, exuberant days of building and moving, more than two years ago now. I remembered Jerome stumbling – a pair of skinny shins behind the large chair – falling forward and snapping one of the wooden chair legs on the lawn, his face landing in the seat. Ugo planting the other chair on the lawn and sitting on it. The two of them laughing; Jerome rubbing his nose. I glanced down and saw that the back leg of one chair was propped up by a stack of books. The jagged break had been cut back smooth but not replaced.

Ugo came out of the bedroom in blue pants, thick socks and a brown wool dressing-gown. Through the open bedroom door I could see a bassinette and another clotheshorse draped over with a pair of work pants, the legs stiff and crinkled. On the wall above the bassinette was a painting. By the style, I thought it could have been one of Jerome's.

'Excuse me, ladies,' said Ugo, 'but I'm just going to have breakfast and then I'm off to bed.'

'He's working night shift,' said Maria.

Ugo kissed my cheek and then Bea's. He took the baby from Bea's arms.

'Ugo!' said Maria, when she saw him. 'You look like Percy in that dressing-gown. Imagine what our guests will think we've sunk to.'

'I think they've probably noticed by now,' said Ugo, though without resentment. He sat at the kitchen table, Mathilde on his knee, and reached for a pouch of tobacco. I followed him into the kitchen and sat opposite him at the table. A newspaper was spread over it, and Mathilde was reaching out, pulling it onto the floor. Maria put a plate down in front of Ugo. On it were two fried eggs, a thick slice of bread and a pickled cucumber. She took a tea towel from the back of a chair and wiped out two cups from the draining board.

'Sit, Beatrice,' she said. She took two more cups from a shelf behind her. 'Sorry, there's no milk. We don't drink it. You probably have milk in your coffee, don't you?'

'It doesn't matter,' said Bea.

'There's sugar.' Maria put a fifth cup, missing a handle and filled with sugar, in the middle of the table. The coffee pot began to sputter and the bitter scent cut through the smell of fried eggs. Maria poured the coffee into our cups and sat down. She took Mathilde from Ugo, and I watched him begin to eat. It was comforting, the way he held the plate balanced on the spread fingertips of one hand and cut the eggs using a fork with the other. His familiarity made tears spring up in my eyes.

'Where are you working, Ugo?' asked Bea.

He slurped his coffee before replying. 'Back in construction when I can find it. At the moment it's road works. Night work, which I don't like. Leaves Maria alone with the baby all night.'

I sipped my coffee and grimaced involuntarily. Maria smiled and pushed the sugar towards me. I put a heaped spoon in, and then, when she wasn't looking, another.

'Is that Jerome's painting I saw in the other room?' I asked.

'Yes, he gave it to us before he left,' said Maria.

'But,' Beatrice paused, confused. 'Did you know he was going?'

Maria glanced at Ugo, and he shook his head. I could not read the gesture. Maria hesitated. She squeezed first one, then the other of her breasts, unconscious of the action.

'Hungry, bebé?' she asked. She lifted her jumper and singlet, and Mathilde opened her mouth. 'He told Ugo,' she said. Ugo shrugged and stood up. His plate clattered in the sink. 'But we didn't know he was taking Heloise, did we, Ugo?' She looked around, but he was silent, his back to us, smoke drifting up in a line above his head.

'I'm going to ask Mother to give them some money,' said Bea on the tram back into town.

'Do you think they'd take it?'

'I think so.'

'It's just what your mother said would happen.' I thought of the bitterness with which Maria must recall Helena's words. That she would become just another housewife. That she would stop painting. 'It's worse. They can't even afford to paint if they wanted to.'

'I can't believe they knew,' said Bea almost to herself.

I stared out at the new apartment buildings, in the shape of horseshoes around central courtyards, wondering if she suspected that I had also known of the planned flight.

I didn't tell Bea about the letter. I had come across it on my way back from the outside toilet that Ugo and Maria shared with the neighbouring cottage. It was a wooden shack at the rear of the narrow strip of yard. There was a trough beside it, and a metal bucket full of soaking nappies. When I came inside again, I could see the others through the open front door. They were sitting on the front step in the pale sunshine. I washed my hands at the kitchen sink and rinsed out the coffee cups. Then I noticed a letter, propped against the papered-over window above the sink. Written on the back was the sender's name – *Jerome Carroll* – and the same Rose Bay address as on the two letters I had received from Eva. I glanced around and then picked up the letter, my wet fingers leaving dark oval prints on the pulpy paper of the envelope. I took a sharp breath in and tucked the letter under my arm. I dried my hands on a tea towel, blowing on the envelope and shaking it. But when I replaced it on the windowsill, my wet fingerprints stood out like a dusted crime scene.

'We're out here,' Bea called through the front door.

Panicked, I snatched up the envelope and slipped it into my pocket. It was only later, at home, that I opened it and read Jerome's letter, its disingenuous cheeriness the same as my letters from Eva, only then that I discovered the second letter, the note from Helena to Maria that I did not know was there. In a sweet unconscious gesture – like opening all the bills and putting them into one envelope, throwing the others away – Maria had put the notes from Jerome and Helena, who had been so close and who were now so violently opposed, in together. Helena's elegant handwriting in blue ink against Jerome's tight lettering in black, on hotel paper.

XXIV

And when did I hear the story: the story of Eva and Jerome and Heloise? It was not long after my visit to Ugo and Maria's, the image of them as we waved goodbye still in the cartridge of my mind – a man, a woman and a child sitting in the winter sunshine outside a stone cottage. Ugo in his dressing-gown holding Mathilde on his knee, waving her little fist at us. Maria smoking, shading her eyes with her hand and then, when she lifted her hand to wave, closing her eyes in the sunlight. Such an ordinary picture, with so much to know about it.

After nine months, Evan and Helena at last decided to go to Sydney and bring their daughters home. With the news of Jerome's travelling scholarship, they were afraid that Eva and Heloise would be lost forever, not just to Jerome, but to Europe. They had strayed long enough.

It was September; almost the school holidays. Evan and Helena would leave within a fortnight. All of this I learned from Bea, who had asked me to stay with her in the Trentham house over the holidays while her parents were gone. She would be alone there otherwise. I telegraphed Eva to warn her of her parents' arrival. I did not hesitate over whether to tell her, just as I no longer suffered over not telling Evan and Helena about Eva's plan to flee. My long-cherished reverence towards Helena had transformed into anger.

Eva called from the station on Saturday morning. She knew from my telegram that I was staying at her parents' house, but I was startled to hear her voice.

'Lily?' she said, her voice quiet on the other end of the line.

'Eva? Where are you?'

'Is anyone else there?'

'No, just me. Bea's at the hospital. Where are you?'

'Stay there, I'm coming.' She hung up.

I ran to the front door and opened it. The garden was misty, and I could not see up the driveway. I stood in the doorway, staring into the shifting fog, until my eyes began to see a figure emerging over and over again. When Eva did come into view, she was unmistakable. She wore a scarlet coat. The image of her hurrying down the driveway, her coat the colour of blood, has stayed with me amongst that small archive of images we keep like postcards from our own lives.

When she reached the house, she did not embrace me. She glanced behind her as though being followed. Her body spoke its wish not to be touched.

'No one's here?' she asked again.

She looked different. Since we were eight years old I had never gone so long without seeing her. She was very thin. It was visible in her face and her wrists below the sleeves of the coat. I brought her to the library, where a fire was burning.

'New carpet,' she said. The night of the fire flashed between us.

'Bea will be home this afternoon,' I said. 'But not for hours. I'm meant to meet her in town later.'

Eva sat down, still holding her travelling bag. 'I haven't slept,' she said. 'I came straight here.'

'From Sydney?'

She nodded and got up again, setting her bag on the floor and going over to the fire. 'Will you make me some tea?'

'Of course.' I went to the kitchen, put the kettle on and stood by the stove. I realised I was scared to go back to the library where Eva was; scared by the manic movement of

195

her eyes and by my lack of a sure response to her other than physical touch. The kettle began to boil, and I watched the steam curl from its spout.

I poured the water into the pot and set it on a tray with two cups and a china jug of milk.

'Tea's up,' I said as I came back to the library.

Eva was asleep on the couch, her head resting on its arm and her feet tucked up under her. Her brown shoes were sitting side by side on the floor. Her coat was still on. Setting the tray on the coffee table, I eased Eva's stockinged feet down along the couch. She stirred and shifted until she was vaguely horizontal, and I propped a cushion behind her head. Her breathing returned to the long inhalation and short, audible exhalation of deep slumber. I remembered listening to her sleeping breath when she used to climb into my bed after a nightmare. I tucked a blanket over her and telephoned the hospital, leaving a message for Bea to say that I would not be meeting her later. Then I sat down on an armchair and poured myself tea, watching Eva sleep as though she was my child. After half an hour she jerked awake, flailing under the blanket. She sat up.

'Sorry. I fell asleep. Did you make tea?'

'It's gone cold.'

She looked worried. 'How long have I been asleep? We should go.'

'Go where?'

She stood up. 'I really felt like that tea. Do you think it will be completely cold?'

'I can just make more,' I said. 'Where do you want to go?'

She began to put her shoes back on. 'Don't worry about tea. We can get some later. I don't want to stay here. Let's go to a hotel.'

I frowned, confused.

'I've got money,' she said, as if this explained it.

'Why? It's only me and Bea here. Don't you want to see Bea?'

'I just don't want to be here. No, I don't want to see Bea yet.'

'I'll have to tell her. She won't know where I've gone. And we won't be able to get a hotel room anyway, will we? We're too young.'

'We have to,' she said. 'I can't stay here. I just have to go now.' She began to cry.

'Alright,' I said. 'I'll think of something. We can phone Bea later.'

'Thank you, Lily. I'm sorry.'

I was shocked by how fragile she seemed. I resolved to be gentle with her. It was school holidays, and I had nowhere to be. Nothing was more important than this.

It was not until two nights later that she began to talk, and even then it was in small pieces, the way a sick man begins to eat again. Until then, I observed her. Two or three times I was shaken by a gesture, a mannerism, that she had absorbed from Jerome. His presence was palpable. To me, he was still terrible and impressive. *She has come from him. All this time she has been with him.* I could not imagine her life for the past nine months. I felt irrevocably separate from her.

We went to an expensive hotel on Spring Street in the city. I had telephoned Maria before we left the house, and she agreed to meet us in town and to put the room in her name. Her lack of surprise made me suspect that she knew already of Eva's return. On the first night Eva ordered tea and ham sandwiches for us in the room. She had a lot of cash with her. Our room was pleasantly sparse: a large wooden bed with a cream damask cover; a stiff, pale-blue upholstered lounge with carved arms; a small writing desk and chair. The ceilings were high, and the winter afternoon sun came through the tall windows at a low angle, spreading the floor with a buttery light.

In the night, I woke to find Eva curled against me. But in daylight she was still sealed off as if under glass. Most of the next day she slept. I drew back the curtains a little to let in some light. But the day was a dull grey. I wandered the tiled vestibule of the hotel, among potted palms, not wanting to be too far from her. I telephoned Bea again.

'How is she? Will she really not see me?'

'She seems exhausted. I'm sure she'll see you, I think she just didn't want to be at home.'

Bea came and met me in the lobby, and I took her up to the room. It was almost two o'clock, and Eva was still asleep, one arm bent above her head on the pillow.

Without hesitation, Bea climbed onto the bed and put her arms around Eva. 'I've missed you.'

Eva woke and saw her sister.

'Bea,' she said, tears filling her eyes. She burrowed into Bea's embrace.

I glimpsed the shame and humiliation on her face, and I understood that, for Eva, seeing Bea was like facing a loving mother after having disappointed her, struck out alone and returned empty-handed. But Bea knew how to handle Eva, and I saw too, in that moment, what family is for. There was none of the distance that I had kept because I felt it was what she wanted. Bea simply swept across it with a sister's disregard for privacy. She squeezed Eva and kissed her forehead while Eva cried.

All three of us shared the bed that night.

'Leg sisters again,' said Eva, giving me a meagre smile.

'I have to ask about Heloise,' said Beatrice. 'She is my sister too.'

'She's still there,' replied Eva.

'With him? Is she alright?'

'I don't know,' said Eva, barely audible. 'She went very strange.'

I stayed quiet, letting Beatrice press her sister.

'What do you mean?' she asked, when Eva had been quiet for a time.

'You know,' Eva said, 'that we were both … That he was with both of us.'

'I didn't,' said Bea. 'Or I didn't want to think about it. My little sisters.'

'I didn't know at first. I thought he was bringing her just because she found out and she said she'd tell if we didn't take her too. I thought he felt sorry for her.'

'You don't have to talk about it,' said Bea, smoothing Eva's forehead.

'She pursued him,' Eva continued. 'It was as if she hated me.'

'You can't entirely blame Heloise,' said Bea. 'She's just a child. Jerome was the only adult there. He's got to take a bit of the blame, don't you think?'

'Yes,' said Eva in the darkness.

I felt her roll onto her back, lying very straight in the middle of the bed between us. She was quiet for a long time, and then she began to speak again. 'Even though she destroyed my life, I'm really worried about her. She kept threatening to burn the house down and things.'

Bea inhaled deeply.

Words began to drain out of Eva over the following days.

'Early on, when we were in the hotel still, he got invited to this party by some artists there, and he took me and left Heloise in the hotel. We'd only been there a few weeks, but when he introduced me, people knew somehow. I heard someone say, "Where's the other one?" It was awful …

'You have no idea how horrible it was. We were all living together. Jerome had a buyer who let us use his house. He was away in England. I didn't want Heloise there, and Jerome acted like he didn't really either. Like we had to keep her for some reason, but he wanted to just be with me. It took me so long to work it out …

'Jerome was painting in the day, and then he was trying to teach us history and geography and things, because we weren't in school. And then …

'He had this way of making me feel stupid if I got upset.

199

He said all these things about Mum and Dad: that they thought they were so bohemian but really they were bourgeois and conservative …'

These were the stories she could speak aloud.

'Do you think Heloise will be alright there by herself?' Bea asked her.

'She'll be happy now that I'm gone. She's got what she wanted.' Eva's voice, hard as glass.

'Mum and Dad will find her,' said Bea, half to herself.

4

Retrospective

XXV

'Mmm, it smells amazing in here,' I say, walking into the kitchen.

Tim has been to the Victoria Market at lunchtime to buy a leg of lamb and new potatoes. He has a Neil Young record playing and a glass of red wine on the counter.

'Is Lucinda home?' I ask.

'No. She was working at the café 'til close, but she should be back by now.'

Lucinda has been staying with us for more than a fortnight now, since her break-up. It has been nice to have her home, but tiring too. In the privacy of her sadness, she cannot stand any pity, any tone of concern. It makes her mean. I try to give her distance, but her restlessness draws my eye constantly like shadows moving outside a window.

I pour myself a glass of wine and open the oven door a crack. Steam rolls out at me. The lamb is nestled round with potatoes, beginning to crisp on top. Cloves of garlic and sprigs of rosemary poke from juicy cuts in its surface.

Tim pulls a baguette from a paper bag, wraps it in foil and slides it into the oven.

'Shall we sit for a minute?'

We take our wine into the living room and flop onto the couch.

'How was your day?' Tim asks, kissing my cheek.

'Okay. I was a bit scattered. Had a meeting with a grad

student just before and I barely listened to what she was saying.'

'Is it Luce?'

'What?'

'Is that why you're scattered? Are you worrying about her?'

'Oh. No, I don't think so.' I reach for my wine. 'Maybe partly. I think it's the exhibition tomorrow.'

Tim squeezes my leg.

'Bea will be there, won't she?'

'Yes.' I sigh. 'I had lunch with her today. It got a bit tense actually.'

'What do you mean?'

'We were talking about the past. About our childhoods. She got upset with me.'

I feel the emotion rising in my chest and I close my eyes.

'Upset? Why?'

I take a gulp of wine and don't answer him.

'Are you alright, love?'

'Oh god. Should I even be going to this opening?' I put down the glass and rub my face. 'Do you mind if we don't talk about it?'

'Of course. Are you sure you don't want me to go with you? Tomorrow night?'

'No, I don't think I do.' I shake my head. 'But thank you …'

Tim looks at his watch. 'Where's Lucinda? The meat'll be done by now.'

Half an hour later, Lucinda is still not home. Tim is becoming annoyed.

'Could she be with Eli, do you think?'

'I hope not. I'll call the flat and see.'

I pick up the phone. It rings for a long time, and I am about to hang up.

'Hello?' Eli answers.

'Hi, Eli. It's Lily.' I haven't spoken to Eli since Lucinda moved out.

'Hi, Lily. You after Luce?' He sounds less bashful than he should.

'Is she there?'

'Yup. I'll get her. Lu, it's your mum.'

I hear Lucinda's voice in the background, very high pitched, although I can't make out what she is saying, and then Eli saying, 'Well, what do you want me to say?' There is music playing. Something with a loud bassline. There is a pause, and then Eli speaks again.

'Um, Lily, can she call you back in a bit?'

'Does she know she's expected home for dinner? We're waiting for her.'

'They're waiting for you for dinner,' Eli says away from the phone. I hear stomping and then Lucinda's voice.

'Mum.' I can tell by her voice that she has been crying. 'We're in the middle of something. I can't talk to you right now.'

'Tim's made the roast lamb you asked for.'

'Mum. Did you hear what I said?'

'Are you coming home later?'

'I don't know. I'm hanging up now.'

Tim and I eat our lamb in front of the TV, dropping crumbs of overcooked bread between the couch cushions.

'Argh, I thought we were past all this,' I say.

'Never. Malcolm's son just moved back home at thirty-four after his business collapsed.'

'Oh god!'

We smile at each other.

After dinner, I go to my study. Sitting at my desk, I am surrounded by reminders of the past. The invitation is propped to one side, with the note from Eva. Since it arrived, I have read it over and over, like someone lovesick or bereaved. My old journals are on the other side of the desk, beside a framed photograph of Lucinda as a three-year-old. She is sitting cross-legged on the veranda of the holiday house her father and I had taken her to in Apollo Bay. It was a last attempt to fight the inevitable end of our relationship. It is a beautiful photo of Lucinda – her expression caught between seriousness and a smile, her dark eyes perfectly in focus – but it is also etched with sadness, and I wonder why I am compelled to collect and to examine the often painful traces of the past, like a madman counting over and over the same dozen objects in a wooden box; objects others would have long discarded.

It is not just since Eva's letter that I have been circling back on my years with the Trenthams. It was two years ago now, not long after news of Heloise's death, that I got those books of the past down from the dusty top of my wardrobe, in the cardboard box that once housed a plastic Christmas tree. I struggled to lug it over the lip of the wardrobe, not wanting to ask Tim or Lucinda for help.

Stacked together, those journals formed strata, each layer a change not only in the facts of the past, but in me, in how I interpret and recall. On the bottom were the diaries from my year in the Trentham house, written in time-blanched school exercise books whose innocuous covers once provided my disguise.

Then there were the hard-bound journals of my failed years at art school, the authority of their black linen covers and the weight of their unlined pages that I thought would imbue my life with significance.

On top of them the plain spiral notebooks I preferred in London in the late 1950s, the pages pocked by the irate tears I shed over my separation from Stewart, Lucinda's father, the discovery that I was pregnant, my retreat back to Melbourne.

Over the past year, I have considered beginning a memoir about my time with the Trenthams and their circle. I pull a journal from the pile and open it. It is from 1938, the year after Eva left. I browse the pages, my mood contaminated instantly, even now, by the sour, sickening grief and its necessary adolescent remedies: anger, blame, self-indulgence. At seventeen I was a cruel and artless diarist.

I close it again, appalled at the condescending faux-analysis that cloaks my lasting hurt. What is striking is the prominence of Helena. Helena as replacement mother, as rival, as phantom.

I get up from my desk and press my face against the cold window. Outside, the moon sits, enormous, low down in the sky and clouds scud past it like banks of foam in a fast-moving stream. I fall into a trance-like moon-gazing. In this gentle state I allow myself to approach the possibility that even my current understanding of the past may be as self-deluded as all the other versions.

At each stage in this repeated task of revisitation, I see myself as having matured into clarity, able to see things – my past self included – with detached insight and unflinching honesty. But in the light of my conversation with Bea today, I cannot help but feel that this archive offers little but the evidence of my illusion.

Bea was there already when I arrived for lunch, a glass of wine in front of her. She hadn't seen me yet. As I made my way between the tables towards her, I noticed how tired she looked. There was grey showing at the roots of her hair, and the scarf draped around her shoulders was sitting crooked. She stood and kissed my cheek.

'So, the opening's tomorrow night,' I said, when the waiter had delivered our plates and we were eating.

'You're definitely coming?'

'I think so.'

'It seems like a strange way for Eva to go about reconnecting with you.'

I nodded and sipped my wine. 'To be honest, I think I'm terrified of seeing her. And your parents too.'

'Why my parents?'

'Well, Helena really. I haven't seen her since she basically kicked me out of your house. She was so angry with me. I know it's a million years ago now but …'

'Was she?' Bea said, frowning. 'Why was she angry with you?'

'Because I wouldn't admit that I knew Eva was planning to run away.'

'But you didn't, did you?'

'Well, yes, but I never admitted it to her.' I had drunk my wine too fast, and I was feeling fuzzy.

Bea glared, and I saw that her eyes were filling with hurt and anger.

'I thought you *didn't* know.'

'Bea …'

The waiter eddied towards us. He tilted his head at my empty wineglass, and I nodded. He turned to Bea, but she waved him away.

She stared down at her plate, fiddling with her discarded quiche crust.

'Bea,' I said again, genuinely confused.

'I can't believe you knew,' she said. 'After all this time.'

'I thought you realised. I just assumed …'

'Well, I didn't,' she snapped back. 'I actually believed you. I was the only one stupid enough it seems.'

The waiter reappeared and discreetly deposited my wineglass on the table.

'I'll have a cappuccino, please,' Bea said.

He nodded and departed without a word. His silence seemed to infect us, and the years of familiarity clouded over.

'Bea … I don't understand.'

Bea shook her head, her hair moving around her plump face. 'Clearly not.'

I reached out a hand and touched her forearm. 'Bea, I'm so sorry. I thought you knew. I had no idea it would upset you. I …'

208

She breathed in, blinking up at the ceiling for a few moments.

'It's just … It's still hard to think about. And to know you could have stopped it happening.'

I had often imagined, in the intervening years, how things might have been if I had told Evan and Helena and prevented Eva and Heloise's escape. But in that instant, seeing Bea's face as she struggled to compose it, I knew with crushing clarity that I had made the wrong choice.

'It's just Heloise, that's all.'

'I know.' I looked down.

'I know you were just a child,' Bea said after a while. She took my hand and squeezed it. I looked up at her gratefully. We sighed and wiped our eyes with our napkins, and she offered me a sad smile.

As the café's glass door jangled shut we embraced, allies still against the cruelty of the past. Yet as I watched Bea walk to her car, wiping her eyes again and pulling her sunglasses from her handbag, I felt regret settling undigested in my guts.

I am woken later by the phone ringing in the hallway. I feel old as I stumble from under the quilt.

'Mum,' Lucinda says, her voice wet. 'Can you come and get me? I know it's late.'

'Of course, honey. Of course. Are you at the flat?'

'Yes.' She sniffs thickly.

'Okay. Just sit tight. I'll be there in twenty minutes.'

When we get home, I change back into my nightie and pull on a pair of Tim's thick hiking socks. I hear the kettle whistle in the kitchen, and I go out to see Lucinda digging the lid off a tin of Milo.

'Want one?' she asks.

'Why not.'

Her eyes are swollen from crying. She pours hot water and milk into the mugs and hands one to me. I follow her back to the lounge room, and we sit quietly for a while.

'Mum?' she says.

'Mmm.'

'How long did it take you to get over Dad?'

'Oh god, I don't know. Years and years. But we'd been together for a long long time. On and off.'

'When did you know it was really over?'

'I guess I knew a long time before it actually was over. But then at the same time I didn't know until it had been over for ages. Really until he married Elaine.'

'But that was years later. I was, like, four or five by then.'

'I know.' I scan Lucinda's face, the dark grey eyes she got from her father, the way they angle up at the outer edge. I feel ashamed that I cannot offer a model of strength.

'We just couldn't make it work,' I say, thinking that it is such a trite expression. What I want to say is that Stewart could not commit, just like Eli. He did not want to become an adult or lead a life that appeared to him conventional in any way. Yet some desire not to be a mother who derides her child's father makes me offer this cliché instead.

'I mean, we had a very strong attraction,' I add in an attempt to speak more plainly. 'He was a pretty interesting person, despite being a terrible boyfriend.'

'That's exactly how I feel about Eli,' she says, her face full of recognition.

When I first met Eli, a photographer and musician, with the golden skin and lacquered black hair of his Japanese grandparents, I had seen the tyranny of history repeating.

'These artistic men are very appealing in a lot of ways,' I say.

'And yet so, so shit in others.' Lucinda tenses her hands around her mug, shaking it in frustration. 'I feel like all the things I love about Eli and all the things I hate all go together. I can't imagine being with someone who's not independent and complicated and interesting. I mean, how did you go from Dad to Tim?'

'Tim's interesting,' I say, defensive. 'He's just not complicated in that destructive way.'

'I know, Mum.' She shakes her head. 'You know I love Tim. It's just, now I'm in this situation myself and, well, you know. Dad was an artist and you had this chaotic, exciting life, and then you got together with an economist.'

'It wasn't exciting, let me tell you,' I say. I am irritated by Lucinda's condescending tone, and I remove my arm from her shoulder, thinking at the same time that I must not react in this way.

'I know, Mum. Don't be offended. He's just really different from Dad. He's very stable and no-drama.'

'You're right,' I say. 'I didn't want drama. I'd had twenty years of drama. More. But it did take me a long time. Maybe you just haven't reached your threshold yet.'

'Maybe,' she says.

We drink our Milo. I pat her leg and stand up. 'You should try to get to sleep.'

'Mum,' she says. 'Don't be annoyed. I'm just trying to work it all out.'

'I'm not. It's just, what is it? Three in the morning?'

'More like four.'

'Four? Well, it's definitely not the best time to be thinking about this stuff.'

In bed, I lie on my back beside Tim, clutching the doona to my chest. I am angry with myself. I failed to speak from that compartment in myself, as that persona who represents motherhood, the one who knows my daughter will always in some way look down on me; will not know my dark places and my desires, my ambivalences, even towards her; will think herself wiser, braver, more modern, her inner life more intriguing, her challenges more compelling. I have cherished the self who knows this and accepts it. It is without vanity, able to resist the urge to be understood.

Tonight Lucinda pierced that fleshly, maternal armour,

211

because the desire to lead an unconventional life is in her too, that reverence towards the daring, the creative, the extraordinary. I am also embarrassed that my very irritation revealed those ghosts to my daughter, revealed that part of me is still drawn to the romance of the fully lived life. It is true that I chose conventionality, at last, though it took me a very long time. After my lunch with Bea today, I am reminded of why. Still, there is some vestige in me, the chink my daughter exposed, some foolish reluctance to accept that I have chosen an ordinary life.

XXVI

It is obvious, as I approach the gallery, that Evan is an established commodity; obvious from twenty metres, from the people milling around the doorway with their invitation cards. There will be no articles in the paper tomorrow decrying him as a degenerate. I cross the road to the gallery and look around. I catch sight of a woman I am sure is Maria, near the entrance, smoking. It has been so long, but I'm sure it is her.

I stand still, drawing my coat around me, my feet amongst the leaves. I see Bea walk up and embrace Maria. With Bea is her husband, Paul, and one of their daughters, also with her husband and child, little Mardi. Bea's son-in-law lifts Mardi and pretends he is going to throw her into one of the long pools flanking the gallery entrance. She shrieks and laughs. They all turn and walk into the gallery. I am left standing in the twilight.

Inside, amidst the noise and the light, the waiters in suits carrying trays of champagne at head height, the first face I recognise is Ugo's. He is a handsome man in his seventies. Still broad-shouldered without a trace of a stoop. His pale hair is almost gone; just the wisps of a newborn. His eyes are dim behind thick glasses.

'Lily, my goodness,' he says when I introduce myself. He introduces me to Mathilde, now a tall woman in her early forties, and her brother Drazik, Ugo and Maria's second child.

Maria comes over, with her third husband. She speaks to Ugo and to her husband, standing side by side, in the same flirtatious tone, as though all their history is yet to come. She is small, shrunken and glamorous; she laughs loudly. Ugo, his hands in the pockets of his trousers, rocks back and forth on his feet, smiling, listening to Maria. For some, the years spent with another person – the fights, the lovers, the separations – are all knowledge of that person, all shades of intimacy and history. For others, the anger over one cruelty never evaporates, forms a stone round which their body seals shut.

And then, there is Eva, seen again with the clarity of distance. She is across the lit space. Her image flickers as people walk past her, but she sees me and her smile slips between the bodies and the trays of champagne that are like hands passing across her face. We walk towards one another; there is a strange romance to it. I kiss her cheek, and she squeezes me very tightly for a moment.

'Lily.'

'Eva.'

She is still beautiful, but up close she is gaunt, deeply lined, like someone who has led a hard life. I know that she has. Her hair has not greyed, or is coloured to her natural deep brown. She seems confident, in black ankle boots and a light camel-coloured coat with mid-length sleeves that reveal her thin wrists.

'It's good to see you,' she says.

'You too.'

'I'm sorry it's been so long.'

She studies my face, holding both my hands in hers. How fast, after all this time, I remember what I loved about her.

'How long are you here for?'

She tilts her head, as if trying to decide. 'You know Dad's not well?'

'Yes, I heard.'

214

'It's very sad. Mum and Bea look after him. We'll keep him at home as long as possible. I'm thinking I may stay a couple of months; give them a break.'

'We should catch up properly then, if you're going to be here a while.'

'I'd love that. I'd say let's have dinner after this, but I need to drive Mum and Dad home.'

Bea has walked up behind Eva. 'I'll drive them home,' she says. 'You two go and have dinner.'

'I'll talk to Mum,' says Eva. 'Are you free?'

I nod.

'It's okay,' says Bea. 'I'll go and tell Mum.'

I notice that Bea has not greeted me. Even within her generosity there is a stiffness. I had thought things were alright where we left them yesterday. Now, I wonder if I am imagining that she has withdrawn from me on some deep level. She kisses Eva's cheek and goes to speak to her mother.

'Tell me about yourself,' says Eva, her expression enquiring, polite. After all this time, I think, is this going to be just an evening of small talk and exchanged pleasantries? Will the past lie like a body in a casket while we ask each other about our health and discuss the weather in Melbourne and New York?

'I'm not sure how much you know from Bea,' I say. 'I have a daughter, Lucinda. I'm married, though not to her father.' Eva nods. 'I lecture in art history. You know, there's not much to tell, really. Things are fairly uneventful these days. Although Lucinda has just separated from her boyfriend and moved home for a bit.'

'Sounds nice,' Eva says.

Am I right in thinking I hear a wistfulness in her voice?

'And you?' I ask.

'Oh, me.' She sighs. 'Well, there have been some dark times, as I'm sure you know. But things are pretty good now.'

I think of what Bea has told me of Eva's life: her *lost years*, when she became an alcoholic; how she broke into the family home on two occasions and stole paintings to sell; how she moved to Sydney where she vanished again for years. It was not until she found out about Heloise's hospitalisation that she made contact with her parents again. She had been hospitalised briefly herself at some point, and then moved to America, where she met her second husband, a wealthy art dealer.

Eva plucks two glasses of champagne from the tray of a passing waiter. She hands me one, and we clink them together, glancing into one another's eyes. Hers are tired, but her expression is affectionate.

'Come and say hello to Mum and Dad,' she says. She links her arm through mine as though we are still schoolgirls. I go with her across the room to find Evan and Helena.

In my mind, Evan is still the archetype of virility. He is the wild body: the storm of red beard; the naked male form; the exhibitionism; the shitting in the garden. Energy to the point of mania.

He is in a wheelchair beside his wife. His beard is neat and creamy white. His eyes remain unfocused as the current generation of the art-world elite approach him deferentially, condescendingly.

'They should have had this retrospective ten years ago,' Eva says to me. 'It makes me angry that Dad can't enjoy it anymore.'

Helena is standing with a protective hand on Evan's shoulder. She is dressed as I always remember her, in loose, natural fabrics and neutral tones. She has a long string of pearls that she fingers with the other hand. She must be close to eighty, but she looks much younger. She is thin, and her face, though lined, is powdered so that it appears merely soft.

'Lily?' she says when Eva takes me over. 'How are you?'

'Hello, Helena. How are you?' I take her outstretched hand. She seems overwhelmed; her eyes are distracted, straying towards the stream of people advancing on Evan, bending down and congratulating him.

216

A microphone is tapped and squeals briefly. The director of the gallery ascends to a podium and thanks us all for coming. He introduces Jack Finley, who wrote the essay in the exhibition programme, as well as the first major monograph on Evan's work.

'Evan Trentham,' Finley starts, 'began to paint in what would later be labelled as an abstract or modernist style not, like so many others who succeeded him, because it was the fashion, but because he was a genuine innovator.'

Jack Finley discusses the developments in Evan's technique and subject matter, his audacity in the face of convention and criticism, his obscenity trial, his international reputation. He praises what Evan and Helena have done to support the art community and younger, emerging artists.

'If we could pinpoint a moment in Australian art history, post-settlement, when a clear sense of an authentic Australian identity emerges, not a mere transposing of European values onto Australian subject matter, it would be with Evan Trentham's early painting *Sky Boy*. I don't think it would be an exaggeration to say that, at that moment, everything changed.'

I find myself half consciously looking around for Patrick, for the kind, smiling eyes I will never see again. I remember those short weeks we spent together. The chance meeting at a gallery. I had been there with new friends, among them Stewart, the man who would be Lucinda's father. I was already besotted with Stewart. He was another person with whom I felt that instant certainty, that my heart had picked him from all the others, each with their own heartbreaking particularity.

That evening, I remember, I was tired from the effort of being around new people. The sight of Patrick's familiar smile had been such a relief. He was there alone, and asked if I wanted a drink.

'I'll see you later,' I said to the group I was with, enjoying the surprise on Stewart's face.

We had walked to Carlton and had dinner together. We spoke about the past. The circle. I had never had Patrick's perspective on events.

'It was bound to happen in a way. The girls were pretty neglected, really. I love Evan and Helena, don't get me wrong, but they are not who I'd choose to have as my parents. And Jerome was just a kid like the rest of you.'

I was taken in that night by Patrick's warmth and by his interest in me. I had begun art classes myself, but was coming to terms with the fact that I had no talent, and was considering starting a degree in art history. I was living with my parents and was miserable. Patrick suddenly seemed like the kindest person I had ever met, and in gratitude I leaned over and kissed him, pleased by his shock and then his reciprocation.

I had not asked about Vera, but when Patrick shyly asked me back to his flat for another drink I gathered that they must have separated. He was living in an apartment above a bookshop on Johnston Street. There was artwork on every wall of the tiny space and a cat on the worn brown leather couch. Coals glowed in the fireplace, and Patrick stoked them and put a couple of logs on top. He poured us whiskey while I stood with my back to the fire.

'So,' I said as he handed me my glass. 'Are you a bachelor again?'

'As you can see. It's complicated.'

'Let's not talk about it then.'

'Alright by me.' He rested an arm along the mantelpiece above my head and bent in to me as I moved towards his tall body.

It was a brief affair. It anchored me at a time when I felt unmoored between my old life and a possibility so wide that it could not be taken in without stepping back. Patrick gave me the confidence to approach Stewart, who I discussed openly with him. He was part lover, part guide, warm and funny and passionate.

Thinking of Patrick, standing here with Eva as the opening speeches are made, I am glad to have come to the exhibition alone, without Tim or Lucinda. This sentiment is too close to the bone of the past. My memories of Patrick are shared with no one now that he is dead. As we were coming to a gentle end, he reconciled with Vera, and I began seeing Stewart. Our last night together was tinged with a pre-emptive nostalgia. We were already like old flames reuniting once more, years after the urgency of their former love has calmed.

I kept in contact with Patrick, and visited him in hospital before he died. Vera was with him, but he took my hand and held it to his lips. Vera eyed him quizzically, but he had floated into the half-daze that he entered often in the final days. Only to me was this kiss a parting written in braille.

'How's the gallery going?' I ask Eva, after the show is officially launched.

'Okay,' she says. 'I've finally found someone I trust to manage it, which is such a relief. It means I can stay here for a bit longer and come back more often. I'm actually missing quite an important show there, but I couldn't miss Dad's retrospective.'

'Of course not. It must be exciting to be working with new artists all the time.'

Eva hesitates, waves to someone across the room. 'You know, to be honest, I feel tired of it all. Maybe it's that I'm getting older, but when I look at Dad's work tonight … And all the others we grew up with. Jerome's …' She pauses over the name, as though it is still difficult to say after all this time. 'I just feel like most of the young artists I work with are so cynical. They'd laugh at the earnest conversations Dad and Patrick and the others used to have.'

'That will always be the case though, won't it? Generational change.'

'Probably. And probably rightly so. I mean, I don't even

share that earnestness – I don't think even *our* generation does. But I also haven't got to quite that level of cynicism.'

'That's not my experience of young people here, at all,' I say. 'I teach a lot of earnest young students. I've actually thought how they're more like your dad and Patrick than our generation was. They're so idealistic.'

'Perhaps it's different in the university.'

'Or here in Australia maybe?'

'Mmm. Maybe.'

I do not try to get close to Evan or Helena again during the opening. Evan seems entirely absent, and Helena is repeating the same pleasantries over and over on her husband's behalf. Instead, I look at the paintings. Some I remember from my childhood: the large, crowded canvases with their strange mixture of medieval horrors and Australian iconography. They still have the power to shock, just as Bosch does, and I see the strength of Evan's artistic vision as it is laid out in this retrospective. There are pieces on loan from the collection of the Evatts, from Dora Fisk's family, from Vera – who is Patrick's beneficiary – as well as from many collectors I do not know.

The exhibition is arranged chronologically. Near the beginning is the painting that had been in Evan and Helena's bedroom, of a beautiful, naked Helena with Evan face down between her legs. I glance over at them, pinned to the far wall of the gallery by the ever-approaching sea of people wishing to pay their respects. Despite the damage they did to those around them, I can say with certainty that Evan and Helena have loved one another.

XXVII

'Years ago, when dad first started getting sick, he tried to destroy his own work.'

Eva and I are at dinner together after the opening. We have eaten our mains and are finishing a bottle of wine, sharing a piece of pear tart for dessert. We have progressed through the easy details of our work and our own generally good health, the work and health of our husbands, Eva's gallery in Soho.

'That must have been so traumatic for your mother,' I say.

'You saw him tonight. He's completely docile now. Apparently it was part of the progression of the disease. It was awful, though. He had to be locked away from his own paintings.'

In my mind I see Evan, raging, crashing around the studio, his disease a quiet enemy within his own brain, unsheathing its knife. Helena had been unable to calm him. She had called Patrick, who had to punch Evan, awkward and unpractised in such violence, especially towards his oldest friend. His hand had been fractured, and Evan had cried. The fury at his strong body turning against him.

'Does he know people still?' I ask.

'Mostly. He knows Mum. And Bea most of the time, because she's spent so much time with him as he's declined. He didn't recognise me at first, but I know he knows me on some level. He remembers the past. He'll bring up little jokes we used to have when I was a child.' Eva takes a forkful of tart, avoiding the cream. 'Mum said he's been asking about Heloise. She'll tell him, and then he forgets again. It's awful.'

'Oh god, that's terrible.'

Eva puts her fork into the tart crust and pushes it down. It clashes against the plate as the crust splits apart. It is a gesture I take to convey her reluctance to talk about Heloise, so I am surprised when she continues.

'You know Heloise wasn't in contact with us at all before she died.'

'Bea said.'

'She had it in her head that Mum and Dad were to blame for everything. I mean' – she laughs – 'I often feel the same to be honest, but without the delusions of persecution.' Eva divides the last of the wine between our glasses. 'I've wondered recently if there's any relationship between what happened to Heloise and what's happening to Dad now. We all thought it was the stress of the situation that brought it on – with Jerome, and being stuck in London during the war. But maybe there's some hereditary faulty brain thing that's manifested itself in different ways and at different ages.'

'Didn't your parents try to bring her back here at some point?'

'Years ago. But because Jerome married her when they first went over to London he had power of attorney.'

'Do you hear anything of him these days?'

'Just what I hear in the art press. Obviously he's doing well. You know the gallery here bought almost the whole *Prometheus* series seven or eight years ago. It was one of the largest acquisitions of Australian art, ever. He did look after Heloise, financially I mean, even after he remarried.'

I take a few deep breaths.

'It's all so sad.' I finish the last of my wine.

'Well, yes,' says Eva. I am thinking of Heloise, and wonder if Eva is too.

'What happened to us, Eva? Why couldn't we stay in touch?'

222

She lays her fork carefully on the empty dessert plate.

'I don't know, Lily. I just couldn't.'

'I understand.'

'But I did miss you. Terribly. For a long time.'

When I get home, after midnight, the house is glowing. I sit in the car for a moment. I am wistful, not ready to return to my husband and daughter. I realise I have unconsciously been hoping the house would be dark at my arrival, just the hall light illuminating the panels of blue glass beside the front door. I would creep past the silent rooms and go to my study. I would ease myself back to the present; perhaps make some notes in my journal about the night; try to identify this feeling through solitude's clarifying lens.

What I feel is the sense of futility that emerges when the past is laid side by side with the present, like two photographs taken many years apart, when it becomes clear that there is no more time. The sadness is for Evan, for the way energy, potency, cannot last. It is for Heloise, for the way her fragile self could not withstand its particular hardships and cut itself loose, discarding family like ballast. It is for Patrick, for his death, for the fact that his kindness was not rewarded with success, long life, the old age I pictured for him, orbited by grandchildren like bright moons. It is for Eva too and, yes, even for Helena. I feel something beginning to shift in me, and I am not sure I want it to; it is a re-evaluation, a tiny release of the grip I have held on anger and am struggling to maintain against the frail spectres I saw tonight.

I open the car door reluctantly, and the chill night air elbows in. It is a breezy night. I consider shutting the door again and going for a drive, somewhere out to the edge of the city where there are no street lights and my headlights show me only the entrance to a tunnel of moving trees, bark and leaves flying across the windscreen, the pull of each gust of wind on the body of the car as it hurtles through darkness.

The house smells of the warmth of cooking still in the air. Garlic and butter and herbs.

'Hi, Mum,' Lucinda calls from the lounge room.

'Hi, Lily,' another voice follows it. Hannah.

I go to the lounge room where my daughter and her best friend are sitting. Lucinda is on one end of the couch, her knees drawn up, a tumbler of wine held in both hands.

'We have proper wineglasses, you know,' I say from the doorway.

'I know.' Lucinda shrugs.

Hannah is on the armchair pulled up against the couch at an angle so that the two of them appear conspiratorial, their heads leaning in together. Hannah waves to me, and I go over and kiss them both.

'It's so lovely to have you back, Hannah. Like old times.'

'I know, isn't it,' she says.

This girl has been almost a second daughter to me. I welcomed her into our family; it softened the guilt I felt for having an only child in the face of my long resentment of my own siblingless state. From her first sleepover, when she cried with homesickness at nine p.m. and her father had to drive over and take her home, to the family holidays she accompanied us on, Hannah has been a regular presence in our lives. I sometimes run into her in the corridors at Melbourne University, where she is doing a Masters in women's studies. She is like a pixie, with her heart-shaped face and wispy cropped hair.

'Where's Tim?' I ask.

'He retreated to the bedroom,' says Lucinda.

'I think our excessive feminine emotionality was too much for him,' says Hannah.

'All our laughing and crying and laughing again,' says Lucinda. She seems happier than I've seen her since she and Eli split up.

I kiss both their heads and go to find Tim. He is sitting on the bed, still clothed, his legs crossed at the ankle on top of the covers. A cello is playing on the radio, and one of the crime novels he likes to read is open on his lap. There is an unfinished glass of watery scotch on the bedside table. He smiles up at me, and I come back to the present, to his familiar face, the smooth skin of his cheeks, his tired, loving gaze. This good man who has raised my daughter as his own from the age of six.

'How was it?' he asks.

'It was fine.' I drop my bag and coat and climb onto the bed beside him. I rest my head on his shoulder and put my finger into the soft hollow between his neck and collarbone, just above the edge of his jumper.

He turns his face into mine and presses his lips against my eyelid. He is warm and quiet, not pushing me to tell more.

'I had dinner with Eva afterwards.'

'What was that like?' He closes his book and sets it by his knee.

'It was good to see her. She's here for a while, helping look after Evan. It was a shock to see him. He's just a ghost.'

There is a shriek of laughter from the lounge room, and we smile at each other.

'They said they'd driven you away with their excessive displays of emotion.'

'No.' He laughs. 'I was just giving them some space. Luce seems a bit better. It's good for her having Hannah around. She was actually joking about Eli.'

Tim offers me his scotch, and I sip it, but the ice cubes have melted and it tastes stale and fridgy.

'So, Eva asked me for lunch next Sunday at her parents' house. She's going to confirm with Helena and let me know.'

XXVIII

The next morning I wake early beside Tim, his arm draped across me. I lie there thinking about the retrospective; the dinner with Eva. Eventually, I slide out from the warmth of the bed.

Soon I am in the garden, where the leaf tips are shedding their drops of dew. I remember the box of tulip bulbs waiting in the back of the fridge. I meant to plant them the weekend before, the first weekend of May, but had gone away with Lucinda instead to our cottage at Fish Creek.

I retrieve the bulbs and then go to the shed, inhaling the smells of straw and pine mulch. I take a trowel and my yellow gardening gloves and return to the moisture of the garden. The cold bulbs are dozing between their layers of newspaper in a shoebox. The paper is dry and crackles when I peel it back.

I kneel on the grass at the edge of the bed behind the house and begin to dig the earth with my trowel, smelling the rich, almost bodily scent that rises from below the surface. There are worms that wave their blunt ends when exposed to the air. I make shallow holes at irregular intervals; there are forty bulbs, so this takes some time. As I dig, my thoughts circle back, of course, to Eva.

The days in that hotel room are a shadow still on the edge of my perception. A certain time of year, a certain slant of cold light, and I feel the memory-flicker of hopelessness that was born there and that licked at my heels for years after.

When she began to talk, in the strange no-space of that room, I thought that Eva must improve. Bea went to the hospital during the day, and Eva and I were alone. She slept late, lying straight in the centre of the bed, not spreading out to fill the space left by the absence of Bea's and my bodies. Bea went home to collect clothes for us all. Instead of returning to her parents' house at the end of each day, she now came to the hotel room. I imagined the empty Trentham home. Its cold, cavernous kitchen. The library windows unlit, curtains open all night. The moonlight falling on the books.

We ordered room-service sandwiches. One afternoon we had high tea in the hotel dining room. Some nights I woke to see Eva sitting in a chair by the window, her limbs tucked up, the curtains parted. One night Bea and I got up too, and we all sat on the carpet at the foot of the bed. Eva lay her head on Bea's shoulder but didn't speak.

'Shall we call room service and ask for hot cocoa?' said Bea, her voice excited, as though speaking to a child.

Eva smiled her new, tiny smile. 'I don't think I feel like cocoa.'

During the days, Eva and I walked through the city.

Since her return, she indulged her whims the way a dying woman might.

'I feel like ice-cream,' she would say.

'But it's cold.'

'I don't care.'

We sat in Parliament Gardens with our ice-creams. I shivered in the breeze.

'We saw Ugo and Maria not long ago,' I told her. 'And the baby.'

Eva nodded, licking around the edge of the cone.

'You know what Jerome told me,' she said after a long while.

'What?'

227

'That he and Ugo and Maria only moved in with us for the money.'

'No.'

'I don't know, Lily. He said a lot of awful things. I did too at first. I was so angry with Mum and Dad. But …' She trailed off, staring into space with her ice-cream held in front of her mouth.

Each day I felt that Eva was slipping further towards despair, as though sinking into some dreadful swamp into which Jerome had taken and then abandoned her. It had been five days, existing in this liminal zone. That afternoon she ran a bath. She shut the door, and I could hear her splash a little and then go quiet. I sat on the edge of the bed and then lay back, my arms spread, feet still on the floor. It was a relief to be alone for a moment. Around Eva I was constantly vigilant, trying to read her mood and respond in a way that would not upset her and would allow her to talk if she wanted to, trying to make the silence comfortable if she did not want to talk.

As the afternoon slunk past, my mind cooled to fear. Images of Eva stretched out in red water, her face growing paler. I scanned around the bathroom in my mind, searching for sharp objects, wondering if I would have noticed if Eva had concealed something in her hand. I pictured a shard of broken mirror lying on the white floor tiles, its edge licked with blood. But I would hear the mirror break, of course.

I crept to the bathroom door, tilted my ear towards its forbidding plane. No sound was audible: no movement of her long limbs in the water; no running of the taps or slosh and drip as she stood to reach for a towel. Every in-drawn breath risked masking some small sound. How my failure to warn Evan and Helena of Eva's departure will shrink in comparison to this moment's passive inaction.

I lunged at the door handle, expecting resistance. It gave, and the door swung wide open. Eva turned towards me in fright. There were trails of unwiped tears along her cheeks.

'What are you doing?' she snapped.

'I'm sorry, I got scared.'

'Of what?' she asked. And then, 'Oh.'

She was so thin, lying in the water, only her face and knees above the surface, her long hair spread around her. Her skin was pale, and her hipbones jutted, faintly bovine.

'You've been in here so long. You must be freezing.'

'I am. I hadn't noticed.' She sat up, pulling her knees against her breasts. Then she began to sob, the noise jagged, shocking in its lack of restraint, careening around the small tiled room.

'Eva.' I stood helpless, wishing Bea was there.

'What am I going to do, Lily?' she cried.

'What do you mean?'

'I can't go back to Mum and Dad's. I can't go back to him. I can't stay here. I've got nothing.'

'Why can't you go home?'

'I can't,' she said, her voice a half-shout. 'How could you even ask me that?' Her teeth began to chatter between sobs.

I pulled a towel from its rail and held it out. I led her to the bed, and she lay down, staring vacantly at the ceiling.

When Bea opened the door that evening, Eva was asleep. I held my finger to my lips and motioned her into the corridor. I told her about the day, and the fear I had felt when Eva was in the bath.

'I telegraphed Mum and Dad today,' Bea said. 'I wasn't going to tell you.'

Relief washed over my body.

The following days were a sargasso of anticipation and sick foreboding. Eva spent more of each day in bed. She would only eat sandwiches – chicken or ham – and drink tea. She slept late and then sat around the room in her underwear, her limbs floppy. Every day she took a long bath. Every day I was afraid. Never less so than the day before. Her empty expression chilled me. I tried to interest her in leaving the hotel, for excursions to the Botanic Gardens, or the pictures, but she only stared at me, her face bland as milk, and said, 'Don't worry about me, Lily.'

I was filled simultaneously with longing for Evan and Helena to arrive and terror of Eva's reaction when she found out we had told them where she was.

'Come back to school,' I said to Eva. 'You could live at my house. It will be exotic in its boredom.'

Again that weary smile, like that of a sick child.

It was only Evan who came for his daughter. Helena had stayed in Sydney, tracking down Heloise, fearing there would be violence if it was Evan who found her and Jerome. Bea arrived, bringing her father into the room while Eva was in the bath.

'Where is she?' he asked, surveying the room.

I gestured to the bathroom. His hair was a mess, uncombed at the front and flat at the back from the train seat. He walked to the window, twitched the curtain aside, turned back to the room. He didn't greet me, but sat on the edge of the bed, crossed his long legs and asked how I thought Eva was.

'Bad,' I said quietly.

He just nodded, eyeing the clothes draped over the arm of the sofa, the underwear we washed in the hand basin at night and dried along the edge of the desk, pegged down with the Bible and with a set of hotel cups and saucers.

'Should I tell her you're here, or should we wait until she comes out?' Bea asked.

'She stays in there for hours,' I said.

Evan stood up, panic in his eyes. 'How do you know she's not …'

'She's done this every day,' I said, unable to meet his gaze.

'Tell her I'm here,' he said to Bea.

Bea nodded but did not move. She glanced at me, took a deep breath, and walked to the bathroom door.

'Eva, darling.' She knocked. There was no response. 'Eva,' she said louder. 'Dad's here.'

There was a sound of water sloshing onto the tiles as Eva moved violently in the bath.

Evan walked over and pressed his beard against the glossy surface of the door. 'Eva, come out. I'm worried about you. I just want to see you.'

Eva did not respond, but after a minute the water began to chug and gurgle as it drained down the plughole.

'She's coming out,' said Evan, retreating from the door.

We waited. Then the door shot inwards, and Eva hurried out, fully dressed, her face red and her hair wet. Evan put out his hand, but she pushed past him and went to the far side of the bed. We watched without moving, unsure, as she bent down and pulled out her travelling bag. She began stuffing clothes into it, punching one dress on top of another. Her hair dripped into the bag.

'What are you doing?' asked Bea.

Eva didn't look up, but bent and plucked her underwear from beneath the Bible and one of the saucers.

'Fuck you, Bea. And you too, Lily. How dare you tell him I was here.'

Evan stepped towards his daughter and tried to clasp her wrist, but she pulled back, dropping the bag, and stood with her hands held up, palms out, in what resembled surrender, but was in fact the same refusal to be approached or touched that she had had when she first returned home.

'Leave me alone,' she said to her father, looking at him for the first time.

I could see him struggling to decide how to respond: to be forceful or soft. She snatched up the bag again and went to the bathroom, and he did not move. There was a clatter of glass on the marble benchtop and she emerged again, closing the bag as she walked across the room to the door. Evan leaped towards her, grasping her shoulder. Eva spun and swung the leather bag at him, hitting him hard in the chest. He stumbled back, falling onto his elbow on the bed. Eva opened the door and strode out, slamming it behind her.

'Go after her,' Evan yelled to Bea.

She set off with a strange little hop, and then ran to the door in pursuit of her sister.

I was left in the room with Evan. He walked to the door, but did not try to follow. I had been standing as though nailed to the carpet. Evan walked back and sat on the corner of the bed.

'We have to get her back,' he said. I nodded, mute. 'Maybe I'll go after them. Do you think I should?'

'I don't know.'

Why was Evan asking me for advice? He stood up.

'Wait,' I said. 'Maybe leave them. Bea's best with her.'

'Alright.' He slumped down again. He closed his eyes and pinched the bridge of his nose. 'Have you been staying here with her?'

'Yes. Bea and I.'

'Thank you.'

After a while, Bea came back to the room. 'I lost her,' she said, sobbing. 'I don't know how. She just disappeared.'

And so Eva was gone again. Only now, she was truly lost to me.

The only time I saw her again was almost three years later. She did not contact me, and her family had not heard from her either. It was wartime, and Bea had gone up north to work in an army hospital. Jerome was in England with Heloise. I was enrolled in art classes at the Gallery School. I was finally beginning to feel that I might find a way towards a future of my own, after all. Then, one day, Eva showed up in class. She saw me across the room and immediately looked away. At the end of the class, I hurried over to her as she packed up her things.

'Go away, Lily,' she said.

'Eva, please. I miss you.'

'I said go away. Leave me alone, Lily. Please.'

After that she did not reappear in class. I asked around

232

and found out that the girlfriend of a friend of Stewart's knew who she was. I learned that she had married Robert, and that they were living in Prahran. Six months later I heard that she had left him and disappeared again.

That day at the art school I had wanted so badly to speak to her, to tell her of the hole, the gaping crevasse, that I had fallen into after her second departure. How we had left the hotel in a terrible silence: Evan and Bea back to their big empty house; and me back to my parents, who thought that I had spent the two weeks of the school holidays uneventfully with Bea. How the school holidays had ended and I had resumed the drudgery and loneliness of my final terms of high school. How I was still ostracised by my classmates, tainted by the unspeakable scandal: the running off of not one but two girls – one fifteen and the other not quite fourteen – with the same man! How I had returned home each day to the cream carpets and matching armchairs, the paved yard and closed windows of my home and drawn a bath, staying in it for hours until the water was cold, in some perverse pantomime in memory of Eva. How I had found the razor blade, in its grey cardboard slip, inside my father's shaving case and pressed it each day a little harder against my wrist, sinking its sterile tooth a little closer to the blood. I could not think of the future. The life I had imagined for myself seemed to mock me now, and I thought of the anger that Evan and Helena and Eva felt towards me and how it would shut me out forever. It was my mother who had found me in my bath of red, in the very image I had conjured of Eva in the hotel bathroom, my hair fanning out in the water, and had grimly hauled me out onto the fluffy pink bathmat.

And I had wanted to tell Eva, perhaps defiantly, what had saved me. How, the year after she had fled from Jerome and then again from Beatrice and me, the Herald Exhibition of French and British Contemporary Art came to Melbourne. War was breaking out in Europe, and I was preparing for my final exams, and the flat horizon of the future. I had not written in my journal for months. Instead, I tried to shut the past away in the shed of my mind, like stacked paintings never looked at. That Saturday afternoon in October I went alone to the town hall. Inside, the space was crowded with people. There were more, by far, than at any of Evan's exhibitions. But there was a familiarity in the faces and bodies, the same intent focus, the forward postures and the hands touched lightly to lips or placed over hearts. There were paintings by Cézanne, Picasso, Modigliani, Van Gogh, Matisse, Dalí. I recognised Gauguin's *The Moon and the Earth* that Ugo had shown us a reproduction of on his first day in the Trentham house. It was so much more beautiful, the texture of the paint visible, the colours painful in their intensity.

That afternoon changed something. I had thought that without Eva, without the circle, my future could contain no art or beauty, no trace of the extraordinary. Then I looked around me and knew that none of what I saw was connected to Evan and Helena Trentham and their strays. I would make my own way, without key or contact, towards a future in which art was at the centre.

More than thirty years later, the scars still sleep on my wrists. Once or twice at dinner after the opening, I felt Eva's eyes travel over them. I see them now as I dig my hands into the cold soil, pushing in the last of the dry, husked bulbs. The soil, the living things I have planted over those thirty years, in gardens as small as a pot on a warehouse windowsill and as large as the two acres around the cottage at Fish Creek. Strangely, the love of plants – the urge to know their names and how to cultivate them – was something I took from Helena in the Eden surrounding the Trentham home. It may have been, in the end, as important to me as art.

XXIX

I am standing on the kerb beside the Trenthams' high front
gate. I come bearing a spiced apple cake, its still-warm tin
tied up in a blue and white tea towel, as my contribution
to lunch. The decades have made vast changes in the
neighbourhood. No longer is the house held in the spacious
arms of paddocks. The houses around it are not even new.
They have established gardens with full-grown trees. There
is lichen patterning their terracotta roof tiles. I notice at once
that the stand of lemon-scented gums no longer towers over
everything. I take hold of the cast-iron ring that opens the
gate and swing it wide. Behind it is the garden, obscuring
the house. The garden that still forms the setting for my
dreams: its airy sunlit spaces and the hidden heart of the
sacred bamboo.

Eva opens the door, already smiling, so that I know she
has begun to smile as she walked down the hallway towards
the sound of the bell.

'It's such a nice day, I thought we could eat outside,' she
says over her shoulder as I follow her to the kitchen.

I glance into rooms. The library by the front door is much
as I remember it after the repairs were done – the burned
and flooded carpet and the drapes replaced, the blistered
section between the windows and the far bookshelves
stripped, and the walls repainted.

Helena wipes her hands on the tea towel she is holding
and approaches me. 'It's lovely to have you back, Lily,' she

says as though it has only been a matter of weeks. 'Lunch is almost ready and Evan is waiting in the garden, so just excuse me for a moment while I dress the salad and then we can all catch up properly.'

Eva is rummaging through drawers in the dresser to my left. 'Do you have a tablecloth, Mum?' she asks.

'The good ones are in the linen press, but there's a couple over in the bottom drawer beside the sink.'

I present my cake and help Eva lay the table in the old half-moon clearing where, instead of a fire circle, there is a set of heavy wooden chairs and a table with a hole in the centre for a shade umbrella. Evan is sitting at the table, the sun on his face. The paper is spread out in front of him, but he is not reading. Eva whisks it off and flings down a green and white tablecloth.

'Hello, Evan,' I say, kissing his cheek. He smiles, but without recognition. His eyes are watery and his skin is thin. As I lean towards him, I see the dryness of his scalp between his sparse hair. He smells freshly washed. We sit down to mushroom soup, garnished with cress, a loaf of crusty bread on a wooden board beside a wheel of Camembert cheese, and a salad with the last of Helena's cherry tomatoes, as she tells me.

'What happened to the trees, to the citriodoras?' I ask her.

'Yes, I know, it's sad, isn't it.' She sighs, gazing up to where they used to be.

'We subdivided about five years ago. The garden got too much for us. We only go back about half as far as you'd remember now. They cut them down just last year but they haven't built yet.'

'I'd love to have a wander round the garden after lunch if that's okay,' I say.

'Of course,' Helena replies, looking pleased. 'We heard you on the radio a while ago, Lily.'

'Did you hear that?' I laugh. 'My five minutes of fame.'

'More than that,' says Helena. 'I believe you're something

of an expert on … I'm so sorry, but I've forgotten what it was you were talking about.'

'I was talking about Elizabeth Gould, but I work mainly on early Australian women artists.'

'Yes, that's right. Forgive me. Patchwork quilts and things, wasn't it?'

I detect a trace of amusement in her voice, but wonder if I am imagining it.

'And you've got a book coming out, don't you?' she continues.

'Yes.'

'Have you read Jack Finley's book on Dad?' Eva asks.

'I have. I thought it was good. Did you?'

'We did,' says Helena, passing me the bread and cheese. 'Evan thought it was better than Jan Nuttall's, didn't you, love?' She kisses Evan's cheek. He is eating his soup without any evident attention to the conversation. I feel that the man sitting with us is not Evan. It must be uncanny for Helena, to be left with this uninhabited body. 'That's why we made sure Jack wrote the essay for the programme,' Helena continues.

'What did you think of it, Eva?' I ask.

'I thought it was pretty good, especially on the work itself. A bit hyperbolic. As he was in his opening speech the other night.'

There is a lull as we pass the salad between us, and Helena sits back in her chair, enjoying the unseasonal sunshine.

'I've actually been thinking of writing something myself, about that time,' I say, wishing already that I had not mentioned it.

'Really?' says Eva. Her tone is worried. 'What sort of thing?' She deposits salad onto her side plate and a cherry tomato rolls onto the tablecloth. Helena is watching Evan, but she returns her attention to me and puts down her spoon as though to signal that she is listening.

'Well, I suppose it would be a sort of memoir. About my

time living with you. About Australian modernism too. But from a more personal point of view.'

'A memoir, that's a departure for you, isn't it?' says Helena. 'You haven't published anything personal before, have you?'

'No, I haven't.' There is a distinct pause. Helena's expression is inscrutable.

'So, about us?' asks Eva. She glances at me sharply, as if trying to catch me out.

There is a coldness to her voice, and I think that she has perhaps become more like Helena than she was in the past. Like Helena, she was always skilful at influencing the behaviour of others with the nuances of her approval, and I see that her disapproval may have also developed into a significant tool in the years since I have seen her.

'Yes, I suppose so. In part, yes,' I say, flustered.

Helena is staring past me, as though lost in thought.

'Most of that muck's already out in public anyway,' Helena says, coming back to us. 'I didn't read it, but I believe the book about Jerome a few years ago went into his relationship with Heloise. I think they even tried to contact her. They certainly tried to contact us, didn't they, but we told them, in the nicest possible way, to fuck off.' Helena smiles at us. 'Actually,' she reconsiders, 'that was when Evan was still on speaking terms with the world, so I take it back – it wasn't in the nicest possible way at all.'

We all laugh and look over at Evan. Eva's and Helena's eyes both moisten as they watch him lift a piece of bread up to his mouth, his hand shaking.

'I suppose what I don't understand is why you'd want to bring it all up again when it's all known, and so far in the past,' says Helena.

'It's a good point,' Eva says. She leans back in her seat with her hands clasped above her head, but there is something false in the casualness of her pose.

'You're right,' I say. 'And it might be that I decide not to pursue it at all.'

'I'm just interested in your motivation,' says Helena. 'Perhaps you feel the need for some kind of confession or atonement. I'd be wary of that as a motive for publishing something like that.'

I feel my face grow hot. 'I don't think so,' I say, noting the defensive tone in my voice. 'It's just a fertile subject.'

Helena smiles, a little too astutely.

'Why do you feel I would need to confess anyway, Helena?' I continue, aware that I should hold my tongue. 'I find *that* interesting.'

'You know why, Lily. For your part in what happened.'

'I was a child, Helena. I don't think that's fair.'

'Oh, you were very knowing. I saw that about you back then. Always very *interested* in what was going on. You cast your dice like the rest of us.'

'Mum,' Eva cuts in. 'You can't really blame Lily for anything after all this time, surely.'

Helena shrugs. 'You always maintained that you didn't know Eva and Heloise were planning to run away …' She trails off. Eva frowns at her. 'Anyway,' she says, patting Evan's hand. 'You don't need my permission. And I'm too old to really worry about it. Whatever you write is not going to hurt us. I'll be very interested to read it. If I'm still alive by then, of course.'

'Helena, you didn't even go after them for almost a year! You could have stopped it yourself.'

I can't tell whether it is anger or remorse on her face.

'Let's just leave it,' I say. 'It's obviously still a painful subject for all of us.' I think of my interaction with Bea during the week.

Evan begins to murmur, and our attention is gratefully diverted.

'Helena?' he says.

She takes his hand. 'I'm right here.'

I offer to fetch my cake, glad of a path out of this discussion.

'Excellent idea,' says Helena. 'You'd like some cake, wouldn't you, Evan?'

After lunch, Eva and I walk around the garden. It is much smaller than it was, but also more established. The sacred bamboo is tall and so thick that there would be no room now for small girls to tunnel into its green-lit centre.

'This garden was such an oasis for us, wasn't it?' I say.

'Mmm.' Eva has her hands buried in the pockets of her coat. She stops in front of a Japanese maple, trimmed with red leaves, and plucks one off, holding it on her palm and studying it for a moment, before letting it flutter to the ground. She pulls a pack of cigarettes and a lighter from her pocket and shelters the flame. I notice the sinews of her hands.

'Remember the first time we got stoned, behind the seed train?'

She laughs, but does not join in my reminiscences. She picks a fleck of tobacco from her tongue.

'Look, Lily,' she says. 'I know Mum said all that stuff from the past is out in the open already, but for me ...' She pauses, taking a long drag on her cigarette. 'I think I might feel quite angry if you wrote that memoir.'

I start to speak, about to reassure her that of course I will not continue with it if she doesn't want me to, but I stop myself. Instead, I simply study her, seeing the Eva of my childhood. Even now, the urge to please her is overwhelming; to reassure her that I will not do anything she does not want me to. I think of all the time that has passed without any contact; I try to tell myself that I don't really know this person anymore, that I owe her nothing. But it is Eva. It is her, standing here with me again in the garden. In the end I simply smile at her and raise my shoulders in a sort of helplessness. She looks back at me and smiles too, but sadly. She drops her cigarette butt on the ground and crushes it with the toe of her boot.

'You seem to have had a good life, Lily. You seem

happy. Maybe remembering that time can be something nice, for you. But for me … I just prefer not to think about it.' I nod, my eyes on the butt lying in the dirt. 'Shall we go back in?' she says.

When I get home, the house is empty. I make myself a black coffee and go to my study. I sit for a long while looking out the window at the garden. The same small patch that my position forces me to gaze at perennially. I have planted this section with the knowledge that it will be framed by my window, and have included something for each season. There is a delicate clumping bamboo that stays green all year round; the winter irises are coming into flower now. In spring, hyacinths will pop up.

What Helena says is true, I think to myself. The events of the Trenthams and their strays have long since been recorded in the pages of art history. And yet, those books are about Evan and Jerome. I did not say it to Helena, but I read the biography of Jerome Carroll when it came out, a decade ago now. It did mention his relationship with Heloise and Eva. Perhaps a page or two was devoted to the scandal, the disintegration of the circle, the ensuing tragedy of Heloise's breakdown. The story was then taken up as an interpretive lens through which to analyse the work from Jerome's middle period. Themes of guilt and atonement were heavily emphasised; motifs of triangles and doubled women; mirrors. Always, as in the two monographs devoted to Evan's life and work, the artist himself was at the centre, with Helena, Eva, Heloise at the distant peripheries. They were cast as 'events' that accounted for the prevalence of particular themes, detailed in the same manner as the influence of the war on Jerome. Heloise's life a footnote explaining Jerome's brilliant work.

XXX

What set me back on this trail of blood that leads from my past, perverse as any night-time cemetery walker or gatherer of bones, was the phone call from Bea two years ago. When she called that sunny morning, when Tim brought the portable phone out to me in the garden, I was cutting rhubarb to stew. I anticipated an invitation to lunch or coffee. Instead, Bea's motherly voice had a veil across it, which tore a little as she said my name.

'Lily.'

'Bea, are you alright?'

'Lily, Heloise died yesterday.'

'Oh god.'

The image I saw was of Heloise the child. Small and pale and smiling, her strong little chin tilted up, her eyes so painfully free of any potential for harm. *What happened to her?*

I asked Bea the same question, but meant something different.

'Heart attack. She was very unhealthy.'

'Oh, Bea, I'm so sorry.' I put my hand up to my mouth, forgetting that I was wearing gardening gloves. 'Will you go over there, or will the funeral be here?'

'We're not sure yet. Dad can't travel. I might go over and bring her ashes back. Put them in the garden where she used to be happy. Where we all knew her.' She began to cry.

After the phone call, I sat down on the damp grass and sobbed with a vicious, grit-teethed intensity. I had not seen Heloise for many years, and even when I had seen her last it had not really been her. But the sadness of what her life had been, the sadness of that sweet, strange child and what time had done to her was too much injustice.

As the days and weeks passed, I thought about Heloise. It was at that point that I got down my journals from all those years ago, when we were girls together, to remember her and how she had been then: sitting in the outdoor bath; eating apples from the fruit barn; brushing her sisters' hair on Friday nights by the fire. That was how I came to revisit the past – because of Heloise, who had been lost to its heartlessness. I wanted to be part of the family again then, when Heloise died, like an estranged sister brought back by tragedy. I knew it would be terrible to see them all in their grief, that it could make them turn against me all over again. But I craved even the cruelty of family in that austere sadness I could not share with my own husband or daughter.

Bea went to London, where she met Eva. Eva came back with her, and the family had their small ceremony for Heloise, scattering her dust in the garden. I willed Eva to call me then, but she did not.

I had been teaching art history at a small, unprestigious college in London for four months already before I decided to visit Heloise. It was 1954. I had finally made my own flight: from Australia; from my relationship with Stewart. His infidelities; his unpredictability; the fact that we were thirty-two years old and still living in a run-down house with four other struggling artists. Only to have him follow me to London, declaring his remorse and his inability to live without me in his charming, resolve-shaking way.

I had come to London with the haunting presence of Heloise in my mind. I saw her as a fourteen-year-old girl: her pale, freckled face with its passing shadows of openness and complexity. She was a tiny wraith in my mind, knowing as I did what had happened to her in the intervening years. But in my preoccupation with moving countries, with Stewart's arrival, and with my new job, the child Heloise moved back behind the shroud that usually covered her in my consciousness.

Then I finally visited the Tate, and saw Jerome's paintings of the red-haired girl – in the first holding a burning torch, and in the second on fire herself – and I resolved to visit Heloise on my next day off. I walked from the gallery into the weak English sunshine with a sadness so palpable that I could not eat for hours afterwards.

The hospital was out of London in an imposing four-storey brick building with lighter brick patternwork around the windows and in an arch above the entrance. The reception area was dimly lit and silent. There were exposed pipes, painted the same yellow-cream as the walls, behind the counter.

I walked up to the receptionist. She removed her glasses as I approached and smiled.

'I called earlier,' I said. 'I'm here to visit Heloise Trentham.'

'Do you mean Heloise Carroll?'

'Yes, sorry,' I said, repeating the same apology I had made over the phone that morning, and feeling the same jolt when I remembered that Jerome had married Heloise when she was just sixteen years old.

'They've been notified on the ward that she's expecting a visitor. If you'd like to wait over there, I'll call someone to take you up.'

I thanked her and took a seat on a wooden bench that may have once been a church pew. There was a white formica table in front of the bench, strewn with tattered magazines.

After a few minutes, a young nurse approached me. She had a pretty face, but wore dowdy wire-rimmed glasses that did not suit her.

'You're here to see Heloise, I believe? Her voice was soft but very proper.

'Yes I am.' I stood up and replaced my magazine on the pile.

'I can hear that you have the same accent as she does.' Her smile and her tone of voice were those of someone accustomed to speaking to the infirm and uncomprehending. She led the way towards the elevator. Once the doors had closed on us, she spoke again.

'I'm not sure how much you know of Heloise's condition …' She paused expectantly as if she had asked a question.

'I just know that she's been hospitalised for a long time now.'

'Yes, that's true. She does go up and down. We are equipped to house both critical and non-critical patients here, but I should let you know that Heloise has recently had an acute episode. She's currently in the critical-care ward. If you'd visited a month ago you would have been able to visit her in the gardens. But not today, I'm afraid.' The doors of the lift opened and the nurse ushered me out and then hesitated before a wooden door with a glass panel to our left. 'She may seem quite … disordered. Just so you're aware of what to expect.'

'Thank you,' I said.

She pushed open the wooden door and led me into a small visiting room. It was pleasant but plain. I remembered Bea telling me that Heloise was in a very expensive treatment facility; that Jerome and her parents both contributed to her care. Though this one was not dilapidated or depressing, I could not help wondering what the less costly facilities must be like.

The visiting room was airless. There was a built-in radiator on the wall by the door. The carpet was brown, and the two couches were cream with a pattern of large burgundy roses. A single daffodil in a cut glass vase sat on a coffee table between the couches.

Opposite the door was a window, and as I waited I looked out onto the garden. The front of the building had been flanked on both sides by a high brick wall, but I could see now that the grounds of the hospital were large. There were spreading trees and a rose-covered, arched trellis. What made the garden appear institutional was the proliferation of green-painted wooden benches everywhere. They were positioned at the base of every tree, along the edges of the garden beds, and even in the middle of the open stretches of lawn. There were only two people in my line of view. One was a young man dressed in a loose brown suit. He was strolling across the lawn, smoking a cigarette, and could have been in any park. The other was a middle-aged woman, her hair cut so short that she appeared bald from a distance. I wondered with a start whether Heloise's hair would also be cut off.

I felt a draught of cooler air as the door opened behind me, and the nurse ushered Heloise into the room. What struck me immediately was her size. She was fat; so fat that the pale blue t-shirt she wore was caught up in the rolls of her stomach. Her face was almost unrecognisable; it merged with her neck, leaving no evidence of a chin. Her cheeks were wide, and her eyes dim. For a long moment I was stunned to the point of immobility, and only my sense of propriety shook me out of my catatonia.

'Hi, Heloise,' I said. 'I don't know if you remember me. It's Lily.'

'I know,' Heloise replied.

The nurse directed her to one of the couches and asked if we would like a cup of tea.

'That would be lovely,' I said.

'Heloise?'

Heloise nodded. 'And a biscuit,' she said.

The nurse smiled and left the room.

I sat down opposite Heloise on the edge of the couch. 'How are you?' I asked.

'Tolerable. Do you have a cigarette?' Her voice was strangely flat, without intonation.

'Are we allowed to smoke in here?' I asked.

Heloise laughed a deep, humourless laugh. 'You haven't changed,' she said.

Despite having prepared myself for any response from Heloise, from unrecognition to violence, I felt irritated and somewhat hurt by this remark. I reached into my handbag and pulled out a pack of cigarettes and a lighter. I held them out, and she took the pack and lit a cigarette, leaning back with her knees spread wide and her heels together. I studied her subtly as she lit up and drew in deeply. Her hair, far from being shorn off, was long and thick with frizzy curls. It was the kind of rich flaming red that is rare to see, almost artificial in its intensity. She smelled strongly of smoke and sweat. The fat of her upper arms hung from the sleeves of her t-shirt and wobbled when she lifted the cigarette. She did not hand the packet back, but tucked it in the band of her elastic-waisted pants.

'They told me you were coming,' she said.

'I hope that's okay with you.'

'Don't be so polite.'

'Alright.' I paused, unsure how to continue. 'What's it like living here?'

'Did my parents send you?'

'God, no,' I said. 'No. I haven't seen them for years.'

She frowned as though searching my face for evidence of deception.

The nurse opened the door again, backing in with a tray in her hands.

'You know you're not meant to smoke in here, Heloise,' she said.

'Sorry,' I said. 'That was my fault.'

Heloise laughed the same deep, smoky chuckle again but didn't put out her cigarette. The nurse let it go and placed two cups and a plate of plain biscuits between us.

247

As soon as the nurse had withdrawn again, Heloise took two biscuits. I began to pour the tea.

'I wouldn't drink that.'

'Why not?' I asked, and then regretted it.

'They put something in it. To stop you from lying. Then they'll ask you things.'

I nodded, worried now that I would anger her if I ignored her warning and continued to pour my tea. I set the pot down.

'Have you been doing any drawing or painting?'

She brightened for the first time. 'I have a bit. Not for a while, since I've been sick again.'

'I'd like to see them.'

'What?' she asked.

'Your drawings.'

'Can I ask you a favour?'

'Of course.'

She pushed her hair back from her face and took another cigarette from the pack. While she was distracted I poured milk into my half-filled teacup and took a sip. She didn't seem to notice. She leaned back on the couch and blew smoke towards the ceiling. There was something sensual about her – a lack of inhibition in the movements of her body. I noticed that she licked her lips repeatedly, and that they were dry and cracked.

'I need you to help me get a passport,' she said.

'How? I mean, I'm not sure I'd have any way of doing that. Where do you want to go?'

'Africa. I've tried applying to the embassy but Mum and Dad have been in their ear. They want to stop me leaving the country.'

I began to feel that I was becoming entangled in the confusion of Heloise's beliefs about the world. Surely Evan and Helena had no involvement in preventing Heloise from getting a passport, if she had in fact tried to obtain one. I saw how easily I could slip into the filigree of her paranoias. I decided it was best to avoid the subject of her parents.

'Why Africa?'

'I've got work to do there,' she said. 'But I can't tell you about it. Especially now that you've drunk the tea.'

I sigh as I think of Heloise. She is, as Beatrice said, the one who was lost. After that first visit I called the hospital again, but was told that Heloise had been very severe in the days after I left.

'Any reminder of the past, particularly her parents, sets her off,' the nurse said. 'We feel – Heloise too – that it would be best if you didn't visit again. She has made a decision, for her own health, not to be in contact with her family, and I think you are too closely associated with them for her to be able to cope with seeing you. I'm sorry.'

Looking back, I wonder if there was always a trace of madness in Evan Trentham. A sliver of what would crack apart his daughter. There are people who skate close to madness all their lives like a hole in thin ice. They are eccentric or unpredictable, but it is clear that they have never submerged in that chilling zone below the surface. Evan's work played around themes of the demonic, of Faustian bargains and terrible recompense. But Evan and Helena were clever people and knew that the adoption of the eccentric artist persona helped Evan's career; that people wanted to buy a piece of the artist, not just an aesthetic object, when they purchased an Evan Trentham painting. Like the collection of the body parts of saints, they hoped that some touch of the godly, or in this case perhaps the ungodly, would transfer through possession of the prized item. In some way, Evan and Helena did make a bargain, engage in a trade that involved lives, loves, spectacular fortunes and falls from grace. But it was their own daughters, more than Evan, Helena, or the other members of the circle, who paid the debt that was owing.

I rub my eyes, feeling tired after my interaction with Eva and Helena this afternoon. I try to recall that it must be Helena for whom Heloise's loss is perhaps the hardest; that there are reasons for her bitterness. But I am flushed, still, with anger against her. That she has not, after so many years, reflected on her own responsibility for what happened to her daughters. Then I wonder if the idea of a memoir represents, to her, not a confession but an indictment. I realise that I am in a position to expose that very responsibility. I have made Helena vulnerable for the first time in my life. If she uses metaphors of confession and atonement, I think, it is because these are the terms at the forefront of her mind when she recalls the past. For me, compulsion is a better term.

The journal I was leafing through the night before the opening is still on the top of the pile on the desk. I open it to the back page and take out the note from Helena to Maria, written so long ago, after Eva and Heloise had fled, and Ugo and Maria moved out, and acquired by me through such devious means. I unfold it once again, the action like picking at a wound:

Dear Maria,

Today I found one of your drawings. Just a small one. You see, I had been skulking around where your easel and desk were set up in the studio. There are still some books of yours and Ugo's here that I keep meaning to send you. It is a lovely drawing, and it makes me happy, though also sad, to look at it. It is of you, I think, with your big beautiful eyes. I wonder if I might keep it. I know that you are struggling with money now that the baby is here, and I am including a cheque for the drawing, if you are willing to sell it.

I miss you terribly. I think I cannot quite get over my sadness that the family I thought I had finally found – the real family of my heart and soul – has all disappeared. To have you here, as the sister I had always wished for – someone to confide in and fight

with and grow so comfortable with, as my girls are
with each other – was such happiness to me.
　　Your string of garlic is still hanging in the kitchen.
　　I have not been well – the doctor says it is anaemia,
so I have been eating more red meat, which I detest,
as you know.
　　I hope you have been able to paint when you are
not too busy with Mathilde. You must bring her over
some day to play in the garden. I think of you often,
and am always sending you my love. I hope you are
not cross with me still.
　　Your sister in spirit,
　　Helena

Reading the note again reminds me that there has always been another side to Helena, as there are always other sides to those we think we know well. The Helena it reveals is unguarded, poignant. Reading it, my anger cannot sustain itself. I remember that Helena longed for paradise, and was instead shut out. In many ways the circle was Helena's project, not Evan's. Her utopian vision; her attempt to make herself a family beyond the narrow lines of biology; her failure. Perhaps it is because I recognise the only child in Helena that I cannot despise her. She wanted to surround herself with people, to create a circle, to be adored and needed and never disliked by anyone. Although her own children would seem the best salve for her lack of blood ties, Helena craved siblings rather than dependent offspring, people with whom she could approach the wordless understanding, the secret codes and violent closeness shared by sisters. I believe she envied her daughters their relationships with one another, just as I did. And so she brought three girls into the world and let them roam it without telling them to fill the pockets of their pinafores with bread and to leave a trail of crumbs that would lead them, in a crisis, home.

In the wake of today, I see that, though my anger has prevented me from realising it before, it is Helena who took me in, Helena who represents for me, more even than my own mother, the mother figure that I have fought against my whole life. Perhaps, in that, she did succeed in redefining what it means to belong, to be family.

As I fold the letter once more, its creases becoming thinner each time, I hear the front door open.

'Hi, Mum,' Lucinda calls. 'It's just me and Hannah.'

I slip the letter back into its place and close my journal. The day is still warm, and I think how nice it would be to sit in the garden with my daughter and her friend. I would sit beside them and pretend to read while secretly eavesdropping as they talk, in the idiosyncratic shared code of female friendship. As they discuss their heartbreaks and frustrations, their fascinating ideas and close-held desires; as they encourage one another and make plans for the future.

Acknowledgements

While *The Strays* was inspired by stories of the Melbourne art world in the 1930s and 1940s, and contains references to certain historical events and people, it is a work of fiction and none of the main characters are based on real people.

This novel started its life as one half of a Creative Writing PhD, and I'm sure it would have stalled somewhere along the way without the support, generosity and encouragement of my supervisor, Professor Kevin Brophy, and without the financial support of an Australian Postgraduate Award and a Henry James Williams Scholarship from the University of Melbourne. Many thanks to my co-supervisors, Dr Elizabeth MacFarlane and Dr Amanda Johnson, and to the other members of the Creative Writing faculty.

I am also extremely grateful for fellowships from Writers Victoria and Varuna, which provided chunks of time devoted to writing, in beautiful settings, and for the opportunities provided by the University of Melbourne Penguin Manuscript Prize and the Victorian Premier's Literary Award for an Unpublished Manuscript, for which *The Strays* was shortlisted in 2013.

Huge thanks to Affirm Press, particularly Aviva Tuffield, Martin Hughes and Keiran Rogers, for taking me on and making me feel so welcome. Special thanks to Aviva, who has been a joy to work with – enthusiastic, insightful, exacting and untiring. Thank you to my agent, Clare Forster of Curtis Brown, for making it all happen.

I have been extremely privileged to come into contact with so many wise and inspiring writers over the course of writing this novel, many of whom have shared their knowledge and experience with incredible generosity. Thank you in particular to Michael Gawenda, Helen Garner, Kalinda Ashton, Tony Birch, Antoni Jach, Helen Elliott and Claire Thomas.

I feel very lucky to be part of a supportive and exciting community of writers, who I have met through the Creative Writing program at the University of Melbourne, as well as through *Antithesis*, workshops, residencies, masterclasses, festivals, journals and around the traps. There are too many to name, but I thank you all – you are the fun part! Special thanks to the Masterclass gang for all their valuable insight and encouragement.

Thank you to my dear family – Mum and Alan, Dad and Sandra, Andrew and Nat, Annie and Elwyn – for your love and support. And to my amazing friends, especially Ali, Joh, Sarah and Jack – all incredible women.

Last but most, thank you to Hootan for supporting and nurturing me in every possible way, and for making me laugh at the end of almost every day.

This book is for Claire G., my first and oldest friend, for my *ant* Annie, who taught me to love art, and for Mum, who taught me to love books and language, and many other things besides.

Come visit us at
www.legendpress.co.uk

Follow us
@legend_press